THE BELL FORGING CYCLE, BOOK II

Old Broken Road

K. M. Alexander

Old Broken Road

Print Edition ISBN: 978-0-9896022-4-2
eBook Edition ISBN: 978-0-9896022-3-5

Published by K. M.Alexander
Seattle, WA

First Edition: October 2014

This is a work of fiction. Names, characters, places and incidents either are products of the author's imagination or are used fictitiously. Any resemblance to actual persons, living or dead, business establishments, events, or locales is entirely coincidental.

Copyright © 2014 by K. M. Alexander, All Rights Reserved
K. M. Alexander asserts the moral right to be identified as the author of this work.

No part of this publication may be reproduced, stored in a retrieval system, or transmitted, in any form or by any means without prior written permission of the publisher, nor be otherwise circulated in any form of binding or cover other than that with which it is published and without a similar condition being imposed on the subsequent purchaser.

Cover Design by: K. M. Alexander
Cover Lettering by: Jon Contino at www.joncontino.com

Did you enjoy this book? I love to hear from my readers. Please email me at: hello@kmalexander.com.

WWW.OLDBROKENROAD.COM
WWW.KMALEXANDER.COM

1.3.1

For my parents,
Kim and Debbie Alexander

Life is a hideous thing, and from the background behind what we know of it peer daemoniacal hints of truth which make it sometimes a thousandfold more hideous.

—H. P. Lovecraft, *Facts Concerning the Late Arthur Jermyn and His Family*

OLD
BROKEN
ROAD

PROLOGUE

Titanic moans reverberated across the night sky like the death rattle of a dying god. The clouds themselves seemed to shiver and cower with each echo. A breeze had picked up, carrying with it the dead leaves and the dust of long-dead centuries, like a vanguard of the horrors to follow.

The merchant wanted to shudder but instead tried to ignore the impossible noise. Her feet carried her down the hill into the high grass, away from the laager, crunching fallen leaves as she walked. Away. She just needed to get away, get away and clear her head. She wouldn't run, she wouldn't allow herself to go mad like Wilkins. The old wain driver had been half off his rocker, anyway. She was lucid. She was clear of thought. She knew she had to finish this, for her family, for her father.

More echoes of that terrible sound quaked through her and she winced them away. Grateful that it was at least warm. A chill would have only made it worse. She hated the cold, and was glad that this autumn's unseasonable warmth had kept it at bay.

She looked up. Jostling clouds loomed above her, their bellies full with the promise of rain. Her father had always called her a summer child and now she understood why. She already felt miserable and it was warm; she couldn't imagine trudging across the rolling hills of the upper Territories in early winter.

By the Firsts, father, she thought. Why you chose a Lovatine caravan company, I will never understand.

She had argued with him about his decision, but he had been adamant. People said that they were some of the best, and he only hired the best.

Dwelling on the old argument, she marched through chest-high brown cheatgrass and looked for a spot to squat and relieve herself. In places, the grass extended above her head, forcing her to brush away abandoned cobwebs.

From somewhere in the distance she could hear the sound. The sound that had followed them westward from Meyer's Falls, the persistent howl their unwelcome companion.

It was chilling. Half moaning, half howling. Rusty laughter. Sound made of machine engines and fleshy voices. Louder and more disturbing than the brays of wild wolves in the mountains back home.

She set her jaw and kept moving away from camp, far from that fool of a caravan master. She needed to pee but she needed the distance, too. This whole journey, this whole ordeal, had become some mad errand. She had wanted the Big Ninety. Wanted the familiar open road. Fate had deemed that impossible.

The road priest hadn't helped, either. His words of doom, the way his hands shook, those frightened yellow eyes peering out from the shadow of his hood. Those damn eyes. She couldn't forget the dread that poured out of them.

Her father was no Reunified, she wasn't raised in the Church—despite her mother's protests—but they had taught her to respect the road priests. They were men of the cloth, servants who labored for the traveler, to the benefit of both the caravaneers and the ranchers.

His warnings rattled in her head. Some town to the east. The bodies. The dead. A whole forest of them. What had he called the place? What was the word he used? Something old. Something poetic.

Perdition.

She stumbled over a stump, falling in a stand of coarse grass. The ground punched her in the stomach, knocking the wind out of her. Groaning a curse, she rolled onto her back and stared at the sky.

The moon's muddy-green glow emanated from behind a curtain of clouds. Wet drops pelted her face. More early autumn rains. More mud. It'd slow them down. Slow the whole caravan down.

They had contracts in the city. Merchants in hungry Lovat wanted her produce, but that window was closing. Merchants were fickle. If she was late, they'd find their apples elsewhere. The time spent idling away in watering holes in Syringa had placed her livelihood—her family's ranch—in a precarious position.

Rot.

Rot was going to become a danger. The fruit would turn, you couldn't stop that. Some of the apples had already started turning, their flesh losing the crispness desired by merchants. It would only get worse, especially with this rain. Rain soaked into everything, and rain brought rot.

Losing the harvest would be devastating. Her father would be disappointed, even ashamed. She remembered the look on his face when her older brother Clint lost his arm to a stampede along the northern line. He had overcorrected and fallen from his saddle, dropping beneath the hooves of the stock. Broken ribs, shattered knee and arm. He had lost that arm. Still, he was lucky.

After, father had trundled into Clint's bedroom, frowned down at his bandaged and broken first-born. There was concern in his eyes, but buried under it was something else, something sadder.

Disappointment.

His eldest had let him down. Let the family down. Father wouldn't forget. He never forgot. He hated disappointment.

What had he told her, those long months ago? She remembered him seated in his throne-like leather chair in the living room, feet propped up before the big stone fireplace. A tumbler of whiskey in his huge hand reflected the oranges and reds from the fire.

"You're the family's only hope."

The words had tumbled out, slurred. Half praise, half frustration. She could see the truth in his glassy eyes. He had set her older brother aside—labeled him a cripple, abandoned any hope in him—and now turned to her as his heir apparent. His voice had been gruff and emotionless as he had spoken. His mustache sagged further as he took another sip.

"I'll need you to take the harvest to the city. With the loss on the north line, it's all we'll have for the season. You need to make sure we break even this year. The family is counting on you." He had paused, his eyes flicking up to meet hers. "I'm counting on you."

He had been drunk, but he was serious. She wanted to make him proud; prove she was the right choice. That she could run the ranch if need be, instead of her arrogant brother. She would take the harvest to Lovat and sell it for twice their typical return. That would prove her worth to him.

At the time, her head had lolled automatically in a nod as she accepted, not realizing what the delivery would entail. Not realizing who it would entail. Bell Caravans. Led by the cocksure caravan master with the dusty eyes and the sardonic grin. He wasn't her only problem. There was the lanky maero partner with the crooked jaw, the fiery Reunified priestess, and the overbearing chuck that refused to call her by her proper name.

If she had known these were the people her father would be hiring, she wouldn't have agreed to accompany the delivery. She'd have turned it down, let his disappointment shift on to her as she stood aside and watched him send Clint, the one-armed disappointment. She'd have watched as he turned and waved his childlike wave, his stupid half-smile expressing more arrogance than intelligence.

That's how you lost your arm, Clint, she thought. Your arrogance. Arrogance you encouraged, father.

As she lay in the grass, she wondered what her old man's reaction would be if her thoughts could reach him. She sighed, realizing that he'd tell her to get her ass up and get his harvest to Lovat.

She rose, pushing herself off the ground, feeling the ache in her legs and backside. Her shirt and jeans were damp from the moisture held by the cheatgrass. She tried to brush the dirt and mud off her pants, her face, but didn't think she achieved much more than smearing it about—damn the night.

The sound rose to a howl now. Filling the sky like thunder with its wavering groan that curdled her stomach and sent gooseflesh running down her back. She fought back a shiver and tried to ignore it. It was terrifying in its duality, both natural and unnatural. It scared her. Though she wouldn't mention that to the caravan, not even to the cousins who had accompanied her.

On the heels of the sound came nightmares. Horrible pictures that flashed unwanted in her skull as she slept. Hooded figures. Menacing faces. Shattered ruins. Above it all, the dimming sun, cooling as its fires were extinguished. Nightmares more vivid that anything she had ever experienced. She was sleeping less and less, but it barely mattered. Awake, she faced the sound; asleep, she faced the nightmares. She could not decide which was worse.

She had considered talking about it with her cousins. Chance had a good head on his shoulders, was family-oriented and focused; he might even have good advice. Range, on the other hand, was young, too young by her count to even be out on the roads. He wouldn't understand. Would probably quake in his boots.

Laughter bubbled up from her guts. Some part of her suspected that she was going mad. She found herself spending most of her time under the cover of a tarpaulin or in the back of her prairiewain, trying to block out the sound, but desperate to stay awake.

She had started to realize she wasn't the only one. Others were awake as well, sitting in the dark, hands over their ears as the sound roared on. It had exhausted the whole caravan, sapping strength from body and mind. She could see it in the caravan master's dust-colored eyes, could see the lines forming beneath them. He was growing weary.

If the sound came during the day, he would often pause at the head of the caravan, cast a bleak expression at the dimanian priestess; or stop and stare at the clouds, as if they spoke secrets only he could hear, ignoring the column that rolled past him.

With a lungful of fresh air, she kept trudging despite the failing light. Casting a glance over her shoulder, she could still see the circled laager of cargowains on the crown of a hill that formed the caravan's camp. A fire burned at its center, as it burned every night, carrying with it the scent of the chuck's cooking and marking the crest of the hill to fellow travelers.

Or serving as a beacon to bandits, she thought darkly.

The chuck's words were a bitter memory. "I told you we shouldn't have continued this way, Maggie. The sound should've been our first clue something was wrong. This road ain't fit for travel. I thought it'd be fine at first, but I was wrong. I said as much. But you couldn't be dissuaded. You knew better than a company of seasoned caravaneers."

She hated her. Hated her moon face and her cackling laugh. She had made a call, and she stood by it. With the Big Ninety closed, and the Low Road impossible, they had little choice. Syringa wouldn't buy her produce and she had only a handful of weeks to fulfill her contracts in Lovat.

The road priest's plaintive message rose again in her head as she walked. "The road ahead is not meant to be traveled by living souls. It is a wicked place. Condemned. God is not here. He has long abandoned this road.

"God has long abandoned us."

As the words haunted her, the sound jumped an octave, making her wince. She had been so sure, but the priest had spilled doubt on her decision. She couldn't imagine the look in her father's eyes if she returned home empty-handed. It'd be better to never return home.

She turned, putting herself in a wide orbit around the encampment, keeping the bonfire at her right. The rain was only spitting and she still had to pee. She needed to collect herself, gather her wits. A clear head is clear action. She needed to feel the boil in her blood lessen.

Damn that chuck, damn her and her—

CRACK.

She jumped at the noise. Somewhere behind her? A snapping branch? A clacking rock? It was close—close and loud.

The sky had fallen silent. She could hear the heavy slap slap of droplets against tall cheatgrass stalks, the early warnings of a downpour.

She turned, spinning, looking for the source and growing nervous. The chuck had spoken of bandits. Had their luck run out? She expected to see a wild dog, or one of those shuffling shamblers who were fearful to look upon but as docile as one of her father's sheep. Instead...

Nothing.

Only stalks of wet cheatgrass, lit by the occasional fleck from the bonfire on the hill.

She waited.

There—something else. A sound she could only describe as a wet slurp. She spun, hand going to the sidearm on her hip. The silver barrel reflected meager light as she pulled it from its holster.

The darkness seemed thicker now. As if the rain affected it the way it did the muggy air.

"Who's there?" she demanded. "Range? That you?"

No answer.

"I'm armed. Show yourself!"

The response shook her.

Part moan.

Part laughter.

Close.

A quiet echo of the sound that had crashed through the sky, but no less horrible. Her skin went taut with gooseflesh.

"I will shoot you," she said, her voice cold and impassive.

No response.

She looked toward the caravan's laager, but saw only a deep gray mist. Like the hill had disappeared altogether.

The merchant spun, her heart hammering, the images from her nightmares flashing through her mind.

Nothing. No sky. No vistas. Nothing but gray-black oblivion where the horizon once was.

A gaunt shadow appeared, shaped like a slim man. Narrow hips. Wide shoulders. It emerged from the gloom, moving towards her. One of the caravan? She opened her mouth to challenge the figure, but the words stuck in her throat. She struggled to comprehend what she was seeing. She could shout for help, but somehow she knew no one would hear her. The gloom would strangle the sound just as it had the light. Gradually the shape began to shift. His head and arms fell into himself, and he slapped forward, collapsing into a mass of... of... something. A hideous, gibbering, glopping mess of dark flesh. A crawling nightmare.

She backpedaled, her throat tight with screams.

The thing slopped towards her like a thick, crawling tar. Arms formed only to be reabsorbed as they dragged the horror along the ground. Faces with yellow eyes would appear, only to disappear back into the mass.

She fired her gun, the light blinding her as the slugs exploded out of the end of the barrel.

No effect. Its fleshy mass absorbed the bullet.

The thing continued its slow creep towards her. Mumbling that sound from multiple gaping mouths. Moaning metal, gabbling laughter.

Recoiling in horror, she turned and began to sprint, not caring which direction.

The thing picked up its pace, slopping forward with increased momentum. Pacing her, and ever so slowly gaining ground.

"Help!" she screamed, stretching the word out.

Her gun was no use. She stumbled, pressing onward, the thing right at her heels. It was intent on her, and somehow she knew that she couldn't fight it.

It was the nightmares and the sound made flesh. It was everything she'd witnessed. The road priest was right. The chuck— damn her—was right. The Broken Road was a damn mistake.

The merchant slowed, turned and faced the approaching thing. It flowed towards her, faces, limbs, wide lidless eyes, and gaping mouths emerging from the roiling mass. It chattered the sound that was part laughter and part moan as it rushed at her.

She felt sick, but forced it back down. She would not vomit in this moment. She refused.

It launched itself at her, its ragged misshapen edges catching what little light existed in this void. It slapped against her, at once enveloping, touching her all over. She shuddered and screamed again.

The mass wasn't damp or wet, it just was. A dark thing, a gash in reality. It sucked the warmth from the muggy air around her, it felt around, inside her, probing her. She felt its presence reach into her nose, around her eyes, penetrate her ears, violating her.

She felt her screams, but could not hear them. Felt her body convulse as the creature enveloped its fleshy form around her.

Soon it would be over. She knew it in her bones.

She felt cold.

She hated the cold.

ONE

The air here is so thick with dust that it forms mountains in your lungs. It grinds itself into your pores, gets in your hair, irritates your eyes, and crunches between your teeth. Every bite during a meal feels like you're chewing sand, every drink tinged with the flavor of earth.

Dust haunts you like a bad memory, following you around like a shadow. Walls do little. It finds its way in, blowing through cracks, rushing around door jams, and slipping underneath window frames in belching bursts.

Welcome to Syringa. The edge of the high plains.

I sat with my partner in a crowded no-name tavern down a no-name alley off a no-name street in this maze of a city. Autumn had been delayed. No one had informed the summer its time had gone, and its oppressive heat lingered. We had come to escape the sun and talk about the promotion of our scout Hannah Clay to full partner.

I took a sip from my drink—a hard cider popular among the locals—hoping to wash the taste of dirt from my mouth.

It didn't help much.

Above me, an electric fan droned its endless hum as it churned in its orbit, mixing the sweltering air into a murky haze. The grimy light from the gas lamps that lit the tavern struggled to penetrate the dust-filled air, reminding me how far I was from Lovat. Hell, I wasn't in civilization.

In a crowded corner, a kresh pianist plinked away at an old jazz number. The rhythm was off and his piano needed a good tuning. It filled the place with a lonely sound, and felt odd juxtaposed with the crowd gathered in the muggy tavern.

I watched a pair of roaders—a fellow human and a four-horned dimanian—take shot after shot of clear grain alcohol while leaning against the long bar that ran the length of the space. Their laughter grew with each swig and their knees had begun to wobble. They were doing their best to perpetuate the stereotype that all of us roaders are loud, obnoxious, carousing types.

The joint was crowded with us. Roaders. Caravaneers. Trail people. Whatever you want to call us. Trapped in the thin space that is Syringa. A scratch of life between the beginning of the eastern mountains and the end of the high plains.

It was a place of business: contracts were signed, hands were shaken, and goods were traded and transported. A place to refuel: grab a bed, find a bite to eat, get in a fight, maybe conceive an illegitimate child or two before the next series of mountain passes or the next set of miles beneath one's boots. Caravaneers, roaders, traders, travelers, merchants, and road priests—we all made Syringa a port of call.

While other cities restricted caravansaras to outside city

limits, Syringa was itself a caravansara. A massive one, her towers as much a part of the trade as the rickety stalls that lined her streets. The city had been large once, stretching out across the valley floor between two sets of rolling foothills. But as the high plains encroached, the city had pulled in, leaving bones of abandoned buildings scattered around its periphery like the scattered seeds of the farmers that work the endless miles of fields to Syringa's east.

It was dense. It crawled with life. Humans with dark skin and suspicious gazes. Horned dimanians. Giant maero that towered over the crowds. Bufo'anur with their thick gray skin, wide muscular shoulders, and bulbous eyes. Sundry stores, liveries, restaurants, hotels, pitchfork dens, brothels, and taverns squeezed the tangled threads of the streets.

Merchants would set up temporary stalls before continuing on their journeys, farmers from valleys to the south and west would bring in goods for delivery. Lovat's hunger was insatiable, and Syringa kept it fed. Produce mainly: potatoes, carrots, onions, and apples—always apples coming in by the wainload. Ponderous cargowains rolled across the Big Ninety carrying the food westward.

Syringa had become small. She was not a city of levels like Lovat, nor was she wedged deep into canyons and fissures like Hellgate. There was no Sunk, no Crust, and as far as I knew, no tunnels wormed their way beneath the city's foundations.

A few stubby towers rose from its narrow streets, maybe twenty stories at their highest. Nothing like the vast towers of Lovat. They huddled around a ditch in the earth that Syringans claimed was once a roaring river. Now eleven years into a drought, it was a polluted brown trickle that was more trash than water.

The two roaders at the bar took another shot, laughing and hacking as the liquor burned the dirt from their throats. A thin, dusky man in dark robes standing nearby crinkled his hooked nose in disgust before edging away.

I looked at them with not a little envy. There are worse ways to pass time, and liquor helps a man forget.

But let's be clear. There's a lot of talk about roaders. Yes, some of us fit the stereotype. But the road doesn't make a man an alcoholic. It's not the road life that makes a man turn to the drink. It's the waiting that does.

The endless tedium between jobs. Weeks just waiting. Memories flicker from the past with little to temper them. Mistakes. Lost loves. Sometimes worse, depending on who you are.

Boredom is like erosion: eventually even the strongest of stones get worn down. One fills the stretches between jobs numbing oneself.

I took another drink and swallowed the bitter cider. I glowered at the news report flickering on a monochrome hanging from the ceiling and took another sip of the vile hard cider, wishing for something stronger, something colder.

Images of recent events flashed in the harshness of black and white, promising more waiting.

A dauger reporter wearing a titanium mask stood among static that could have been a dust storm, a blizzard, or a bad signal. She shouted at the camera so she could be heard. Her hands tried to shield the eyes behind her mask as she delivered her report from somewhere in the west. Syringa News Service's reporter at large, Maia Titan, on scene at the Grovedare Span.

Carter's cross, it wasn't good.

"Good evening, Robert," she said, her voice barely audible over the dull roar of the tavern.

"Quiet!" shouted a voice.

The crowd ignored it.

"I SAID QUIET!" came the voice again. The bartender. The king of this tiny kingdom.

The crowd lowered to a murmur so that the caravan masters, myself included, could hear the report.

"I'm standing here on the eastern bank of the Rediviva not far from the Syringan camp. As you can see, temporary fortifications have been erected on this side of the Grovedare Span. This has essentially blocked all traffic along the Big Ninety. I repeat: all traffic along the Big Ninety is currently blocked."

The crowd groaned. I sighed.

The span is the major crossing on the Big Ninety—the principal route between Syringa and Lovat. It stretches across the Rediviva, the massive river that cuts the territory in half and separates the Territories into two distinct and very different nations. Lovat, the towering city, nestled in an archipelago of emerald hills along the rain-soaked coast; Syringa on the edge of the high plains, brown, bone dry, and choking from dust.

"Moments ago, I spoke with General Flora Bobal, the Syringan general in charge of operations," the reporter continued. "She stated that Lovat's mayor demands a formal apology from the Syringan Council for the military offensive. The general said the Syringan council have no plans to back down from a rightful defense of their lands within the territory, and Lovat needs to recognize the rights of other sovereign nations."

As she spoke those last words, a pair of gun placements along the shore behind her lit up, causing her to wince and move for cover. Across the river, Lovat responded in kind.

"By the Firsts!" someone said. Someone threw a crumpled napkin at the screen.

I couldn't agree more.

In the time it had taken me to hobble from Lovat to where I currently sat, the Syringan Council had decided, seemingly at random, that Lovat posed a threat and had marched the city's militia towards the Grovedare Span. Naturally, Lovat, seeing the Syringa militia marching towards them, sent their own constabulary out, putting the territory's two great powers into a deadlock.

There they stood, staring at one another over a rickety old bridge above the widest river in the Territories, blocking the way of every roader and caravan in the territory.

Carter's cross, I hate politics.

The standoff was now in its second week. Neither side was interested in capitulating. It left a whole bunch of roaders like myself and my company off the Big Ninety, staring at monochrome news reports in dingy taverns in the world's most boring city.

No, the road doesn't make a man an alcoholic. It's the waiting that does.

The bartender turned down the volume as the news anchor—safe somewhere in his Syringan studio—repeated what the reporter had said. Eventually the news update ended and an amateur jai alai game resumed. The crowd in the tavern turned back to their drinks.

"Great. Just great."

I looked across the table to Wensem dal Ibble, my partner in the company that bears my name—Bell Caravans.

Wensem is maero, a seven-fingered, exceedingly tall, lanky, and pale race that are tougher than a box of nails and harder to kill than roaches. He's good people, my best friend, and we've been running Bell Caravans for about seven years now. He even named his kid after me.

The light from the monochrome reflected in his small blue-gray eyes as he watched the delivery of the bad news. No change. The opposing forces were digging in like weevils. Peace talks had broken down. A cease-fire wouldn't be declared anytime soon. I didn't like what that meant. It could make this military action last several more weeks, maybe months.

My employer would not be pleased.

Wensem looked at me with a frustrated expression. He had a year-old son at home, and he was itching to get back to him.

"Think it could be months?" He rubbed his thin face with a pale seven-fingered hand and sighed heavily. Somewhere in the tavern, the piano player also gave up. Discussing Hannah's promotion would have to wait.

I nodded. "Looks like."

"Kit ain't going to like months."

"No one will," I said. Kitasha wen Gresna, or Kit as she was fondly called, was Wensem's wife and mother of their son, little

Waldo dal Wensem. Unfortunate name, really, but Wensem had insisted.

He frowned. "What do we do?"

I shrugged. "Not much we can do until Hannah comes back with the report. But whatever she finds, I bet our options are limited. Shaler keeps threatening to take us before the city's caravan authority for breach of contract."

"They'd have to understand."

"If we were home, maybe. Here in Syringa, though?"

Wensem swore. The Caravan Authority was the legal system set up to protect caravan companies and the merchants who worked with them. Here in Syringa, the Authority took a percentage of any fines they enforced on behalf of a wounded party. They also didn't like Lovatines.

"If the southern route is blocked—" I began.

"Then we pay out the ass," Wensem broke in.

I breathed out a lungful of dusty air.

"It's a full refund plus fifty percent, Wal. We can't afford that. Not right now, at any rate. Even if we sold the wain."

"I know," I said. "Believe me, I know."

"You know what Taft will suggest," Wensem said.

I raised my hand, cutting him off.

"Fine. Fine. Just saying." He held up his hand innocently, "Just a suggestion."

"And a terrible one at that."

"So that leaves…"

"Bridgetown?" asked a familiar voice. We looked up to the two figures approaching. They couldn't be any more different.

Taft, our human chuck, and beside her, the graceful dimanian priestess Samantha Dubois. I watched Samantha slip into the empty seat beside me as Taft leaned on the table.

I smiled at them. "Ladies. Hannah back?"

"She is," Taft began. "And it ain't good news."

I braced myself.

"The route is open to Bridgetown, but there's trouble north of there."

"Carter's cross," Wensem sighed. "What now?"

"Seems ol' Conrad O'Conner and his Purity movement goons took advantage of the weakened police force in Lovat and moved on Destiny in the lull. They have the whole route from the south blocked off, won't let anyone into or out of Lovat from Bridgetown. It's a bit of a powder keg.

"Rumors are flying left and right. There's stories going around that they murdered a family of cephels who tried to slip past. Supposedly they're hanging above the trail like trophies, as a warning."

"By the Firsts…" I swore, and caught Samantha crossing herself. My stomach sank. A family? Recent memories threatened to overwhelm me, but I beat them back.

"What do they hope to accomplish?" I asked.

Samantha shrugged, "Hannah doesn't know. No one seems to. They aren't asking for anything."

"Why Lovat tolerates this insanity, I have no idea," began Wensem. "I vote. We all vote. Maero, dimanian, cephels, hell even umbra and kresh. It's one thing to allow free speech, but to let them operate out in the open, murder innocent people, and string them up as a message to us non-humans?" He shook his head. "The mayor's gone soft."

Taft smirked bitterly, her thin lips parting her wide, fleshy face and making her cheeks round as apples. She was Syringan. Her smile showed rows of tobacco-stained teeth. "Lovat's a big place, and Central doesn't have the officers to patrol the city properly. Them Purity types are bound to slip past. They look like anyone else. O'Conner's brilliant strategy. You can't just start stringing up every human because everyone fits the profile"

"The Reunified Church tried that with the Hasturians two centuries ago. You know where that got us," Samantha added.

"Right," said Taft. "Let's not talk about the war again."

"So what do we do now?" Samantha sighed. "It doesn't look like the Big Ninety will be open for some time, and if the south is blocked…"

I smiled weakly, and Samantha made one of those annoyed faces that carries hints of playfulness. Dimanians look mostly human, but with ossified spurs growing from various parts of their bodies—usually where bone is close to the skin. Samantha has two small nubs sprouting from her chin, and small horns at both temples that amplify her cheekbones and delicate features.

"Most routes lead to Grovedare," I said. "Unfortunately, the river's too fast for serious ferrying. The only other major crossing was a few days north at Applehome."

"Was? What happened at Applehome?" Samantha asked.

She had taken to the roader life. We joked that if the whole professor thing fell through, she'd make a fine road priestess. She's sharp as a tack and more than a priestess, really. She is one of the leading authorities on ancient religions and cults within the Reunified Church. I had never been a religious sort, but Samantha's earnestness had piqued my interest. When she found out Wensem and I were guiding a herd of travelers back east, she asked to come along. She had an appointment with a bishop in Syringa, and she accompanied a group of clergy on their way to deliver supplies to a monastery near the city.

I had agreed to let her come, much to Wensem's amusement. He still wouldn't let me hear the end of it.

"Bridge collapsed," Wensem said. "Whole thing just pancaked in after heavy rains." He slapped his hands together. "Applehome was only there because of caravan travel. When the bridge went out, most folks just up and left. Not much there now but the river and the skeletons of buildings."

"And squatters," said Taft.

"And bandits," I added.

Samantha nodded, the murky light illuminating the left side of her oval face. Her curly dark hair, cut simply and ending at her shoulder, framed her face. Big dark eyes. Dusky skin. A narrow nose atop full lips. Light lines teased from the corner of her mouth revealing hints of a harder side.

"So that leaves us…where?" Samantha chewed the end of her pinky.

I raised my glass of hard cider. "We keep waiting."

Wensem shook his head ponderously. "Shaler will be furious."

"She doesn't have much of a choice," I said calmly.

Taft hefted herself into the empty seat and called for the bartender. When he came over, she ordered a whiskey and a beer, indicating she wanted both the same size. The bartender blinked and then nodded, leaving to fetch her order.

Taft hadn't been with us very long—maybe two months. Wensem and I hired her based on the recommendations of a few old friends, and to impress the travelers we guided eastward. She had proven herself to be quite the storyteller, and not half bad as a chuck. I was grateful to get some decent meals on the road, not just the endless supply of hardtack and beans our last chuck had passed off as trail food.

Taft was human, with tan skin and short brown hair. She was as big as a barn and twice as heavy. A pair of huge breasts the size of prize pumpkins were carried atop a stomach as big as a cargowain. When she walked she strutted, each step kicking up clouds of dust like a bull. She drank harder and heavier than any of us, which instantly endeared her to my crew. With a quick wit and a jovial personality, she had become a fixture at laager.

She leaned in conspiratorially, her voice barely audible over the noise. "There is another solution."

Wensem and I looked at each other. Our eyes met; we both knew what the chuck was about to suggest. Samantha looked at us blankly, then turned to Taft. "What are you talking about?" she asked.

Taft just grinned a wide smile and leaned back.

"Wal, what is she talking about?"

Wensem began to shake his head.

"No, no, no," I said. "You know the stories. We all know the stories. Even if you don't believe all the garbage about cannibals and ghosts, it doesn't matter. Roaders are superstitious. No crew is going to gladly march down that trail."

"What trail?" Samantha asked, frustrated. Behind her, the crowd cheered as a jai alai team on the monochrome finished the game.

"I'm just throwing it out as an option," Taft said innocently, leaning back in her chair and taking a swig.

"When's the last time you've even heard of a company go down that road?" I said. "They'd mutiny. They'd leave. It's not up for discussion. Don't suggest it to the crew or the client. Carter's cross, Shaler does not need to hear about this."

"I haven't suggested anything," Taft said, raising both hands defensively.

"Suggest what?" demanded Samantha.

Taft grinned at me sardonically, motioning with a hand as if to say, "Go on."

I glowered at Taft. She chuckled, shook her head, and drained her beer.

"She is suggesting the route no one ever takes," explained Wensem, his voice deadpan.

"You boys ain't scared now, are you? I thought you were hard. Trail-worn," said Taft from around her beer-sized whiskey.

"Maybe, but we're not stupid," I said coolly.

Arms crossed across her chest, Samantha waited.

I looked slowly from Taft to Wensem and then to Samantha before closing my eyes and breathing out the answer.

"She's suggesting the Broken Road."

TWO

My old man was fond of saying, "fools rush in where the wise fear to travel." He was usually referring to some business deal, but the words echoed in my mind as I walked with Samantha toward our boarding house across town in the Campbell neighborhood.

The dust of the day had died down, and it had left a clear evening. Above us, the purple sky was broken by pinpricks of stars and tempered by the gas lamps that lined the streets. A few clouds—black shadows in the sky—ducked behind the towers to the south of us.

The narrow alley outside the tavern was lined with carts and stalls, hawking everything from food to fabric. The scents of roasting meat and simmering broth made my stomach rumble. The sound of a horn drifted from somewhere far away.

Samantha was kind enough to wait as I bought flatbread stuffed with peppers and spiced venison from a dauger, his stall immaculate, the sizzle of onions and peppers a song on the evening breeze.

"Is the Broken Road that dangerous?" Samantha asked when we started moving again. The warmth in her voice belied hints of nervousness.

"Depends who you ask," I said through mouthfuls as I limped along. The vendor had done a perfect job. The meat was tender and spicy with a rich gamey flavor that overpowered any dust that happened to cling to it.

"What do you mean?"

"Well, there's more rational folk like myself who don't buy into all the supernatural nonsense but have their own reasons to avoid the Road, and then there's the superstitious roaders who believe the crazy stories."

"Like what kind of stories?"

I chuckled. "Again, depends who you ask."

We walked slowly down the street, letting ourselves meld into the crowd. Ancient brick buildings seven or eight stories tall rose around us. We passed under raised glassed-in walkways that allowed Syringans to pass between buildings without having to press through the crowds on the street below. Most were covered with graffiti: curses in Strutten and even a few in Cephan, a few rough branch shapes left over from last year's Auseil decorations, the five-fingered hand with the sword in the palm—the symbol of the Purity Movement—was intermixed with circular symbols I didn't recognize, a strange horned eye, undoubtedly the symbol of yet another of the territory's strange faiths. As if on cue, a column of Curwenites marched along in their blue jumpsuits, following a twisted icon held by a dauger at the head of the column. It was a bizarre construct welded together from smaller statues scavenged from other faiths. A pair of large gray bufo'anur dressed in the battle robes of mercenaries-for-hire grunted displeasure as they passed, but we paid them no mind. You see weirder things in Lovat. Besides, we were in no hurry.

"You won't find the route on any map, not anymore. The road, or what's left of it, stretches from Meyer's Falls, north of Syringa, to Colby, a small village north of Lovat. The early stages stretch from the eastern passes and edge very close to Victory's territory."

Samantha's raised an eyebrow as I mentioned the reclusive nation to the north. Victory was a mystery to almost everyone on our side of its wall. The hermit-state had little contact with the outside world, save for its port city of Empress at the end of a long ferry ride from Lovat. Travelers weren't permitted inside, and its southern border was patrolled by masked guards in soaring gun towers. A no-man's-land extended a mile south from its wall, and anyone caught inside would be shot on sight and left as carrion for the eagles, hawks, and ravens.

Somehow, all manner of rumors trickled out from behind its thick wall. Some folks believe the nation living within is a utopia, untouched by greed, and the wall a device to keep out the sinful. It's a nice thought, but I've met Victory traders, and they're as touched by sin as any other caravaneers. Other stories go to opposite extremes, describing Victory as an authoritarian police state, secretly amassing an army that will someday break forth from its gates bent on conquest.

Regardless, I prefer to stay well away. Victory can remain isolated, and I won't take Bell Caravans near its gun towers. Better to leave well enough alone.

"How close?" Samantha wondered as she slipped beneath a pole of dried trout draped over a human merchant's shoulders.

"Close enough to see the wall. Maybe not close enough to see a patrol."

Samantha shuddered. "Are they real? The patrols?"

I nodded. "I've only seen them once and they were far from Victory. Near Grovedare, actually."

"What were they doing? What did they look like?" she asked, ever the researcher.

I thought about this, trying to dredge up the memory. "I don't know what they were doing. I didn't go near them. What did they look like… well, they were a platoon of six, dressed in black leather head to toe, with masks hiding their faces. They wore the sun and crown symbol of Victory on their chests, otherwise I wouldn't have known who they were."

Samantha frowned.

"They didn't threaten me," I said. "Didn't even acknowledge my existence. Don't know if I wasn't close enough or if I wasn't worth their attention. I'm not sure, honestly. It was strange. That's all I remember."

"A lot of religious orders sport similar garments," said Samantha. "I have heard of northern covens wearing suns and stars, and suns and bird, and suns and clouds—"

"You suggesting what I saw was some march-of-the-witches or something?"

She shrugged. "Maybe. Just pointing out it might have been something other than a patrol from some elusive nation."

We walked in silence for a few moments, letting the noises

of the evening shoppers fill the space between us. The chatter of voices dealing in Strutten, the common tongue of the land. It was a pleasant sound, and it made the evening lovelier. It was also nice to inhale the warm air and not get a snoot full of dust.

I thought on what she said. For years I had considered the patrol to be something from Victory, but she could be right. She was probably right.

I cast a glance in her direction, and caught her brown eyes looking at me. She grinned and then looked away, suddenly interested in the goods hanging in a stall.

Every little thing about her can set me off. The way she tucks hair behind her ear, or how she'll talk at length about a dead cult that once terrorized a corner of the territory, to the way she chews on the nail of her smallest finger when she's puzzling over something. If she was anyone else, I would have rushed in, but I was still unsure how the Reunified church would react to a fellow like me making moves on a priestess. Probably poorly. Many are allowed to marry, even have children. But the Reunifieds frown on clergy fraternizing with anyone outside the church, especially without a ring and a promise.

"I'm sorry," I said. "I know you wanted to be back at Saint Mark's by now. Had I known any of this would go down, I wouldn't have—"

Samantha laughed, cutting me off, and smiled that smile. "You had no idea. I'm sure the seminary will find a replacement for my classes until I return. They have to be getting the same reports on the monochromes in Lovat that we're getting. They know what's going on. Even so, I wired the bishops a few days ago when the span closed. They're aware."

"This isn't the way it usually goes."

"The brothers and sisters at the priory don't mind. Anyway, it seems every moment I step through the threshold I'm holding a lecture on this or that. Yesterday someone asked me to explain the hierarchy of the Firsts, as if that was a simple question with an easy and straightforward answer!"

She laughed and I laughed with her though I only knew a little about the theory. She had tried to explain it to me once and I got so lost that it all became a jumbled wash.

I finished my flatbread and threw the wrapping into an over-stuffed trashcan that a pair of alley cats and a strung-out pitch-fork addict were fighting over. That amiable silence fell between us again and I found myself mulling over the Broken Road.

I didn't know a soul that had traversed it in recent memory. Even if I could convince my company that it was safe, it most likely wasn't even passable. The Big Ninety was getting increasingly rough as time wore on and that had been a well-traveled road for generations. Who knows what years of neglect could do to a long abandoned route?

It was Samantha's turn to break the silence. "So even if Victory isn't the reason, what are the other stories? What am I missing? I doubt the patrols are enough to keep caravans away."

"You're right," I said, keeping my eye open for another cart selling something else to munch. I could go for some noodles. If there was one nice thing about being stranded in a city, it was the food choices. "It's more than just Victory. Really, it—"

"Depends who you ask," Samantha parroted, with a titch of annoyance in her voice.

I laughed and shrugged. "Everyone has a reason. Probably the most obvious and likely is bandits. They're a problem on the Big Ninety, but they're an even bigger problem off the main thoroughfares. The Broken Road is a place for the less reputable merchants: slavers, pitch dealers, organ peddlers, outfit goons, smugglers, those types. The tales deviate from there though. I've heard tales of roving bands of cannibals. Some claim they come from a city full of them, a city not on any map."

"A hidden city full of cannibals? Please," Samantha said, rolling her eyes. "Stories about hidden cannibal cities exist in both Hasturian and Curwenite lore. Though I doubt the Hasturians give any weight to the tale anymore. Who knows about the Curwenites. The chaos faiths are… complicated. Their beliefs seem to shift around as much as their idols do. With both Hasturians and Curwenites active here, it'd make sense that a similar tale could figure in the local folklore."

I shrugged. "I didn't say I believe them."

"I appreciate you letting me know. When we first set out, I felt so lost. It's like Wensem, Hannah, you, even Taft—you all have your own language. It's not something I am used to."

"Well, you're welcome. We'll make a roader out of you yet," I said and grinned.

She slowed, and then stopped and turned to face me.

"What is it?" I asked.

"What do you believe, Wal?" Her voice was laced with that tone that meant she was in priestess mode. She was serious. I looked down at my boots, and then at a hawker selling beads over her shoulder.

"I—I... Carter's cross, I believe that my company won't follow me down that road. I believe that superstition runs deeper in my crew than they'll admit, and they'd rather sit around this dusty old town than risk that journey. I believe that my relationship with Shaler is tenuous at best, and I need to keep her from taking me before the caravan authority, or Wensem and I could lose our whole company. Broken Road or not, that's what I believe."

I flicked my eyes back at hers and swallowed the lump in my throat.

She studied me for a moment before nodding slowly, and continued down the street. What had just happened? I hobbled after her, the pace exacerbating the ache in my right leg.

When I caught up with her, it was like we had never stopped. She was still full of questions. "So, cannibals, bandits, and Victory patrols..." she let her voice drift off.

I relaxed. "There's also tales of ghosts, spirits, spooks, and so on. The souls of the dead haunting laagers and raiding chuckwains. Fairy tale stuff. It's garbage. Oh, there's also the mist, that one is interesting."

"The mist?"

"Not sure how to explain it. They say it's like a creeping fog that overtakes caravans. Folks get lost in it. End up hundreds of miles off course, or die in the mountains. Rangers come across them after the spring thaw. Whole wains full of food, clothing and supplies, but the caravan party is missing, their bodies found starved to death not even a mile away."

"And what do you think?" she asked.

I thought for a moment and said, "Sounds like amateur mistakes leading to tragic consequences."

We arrived at our boarding house and I hobbled up the stairs, my right leg stiff, my knee popping. When we got to the porch, I leaned against the railing, taking a breather.

Months earlier, during all the trouble in Lovat, I had fallen and dislocated my knee. I had been told to stay off it or it wouldn't heal right. So it didn't heal right.

"Look, please keep this between us. It's bad enough with Taft talking about it, but Shaler's hell-bent on getting to Lovat as soon as possible. If she got wind of the Broken Road, she'd have us out there before daybreak."

"I won't say anything," Samantha promised.

I found myself wishing Applehome's crossing hadn't collapsed. It would have made things a lot easier, but between the military action at Grovedare and the Purity Movement using it as a catalyst to advance their own agenda, it left a lot of caravaneers stuck or out of work. Waiting out the standoff seemed like the best option. We might go broke in the meantime, but there wasn't much more we could do.

Shaler might be persuaded to let me out of our contract, and maybe Bell Caravans could take up the route between Syringa and Hellgate in the meantime. I hadn't been to the canyon city in a long while, and I had friends there whom I wouldn't mind calling upon. It wasn't the most lucrative work—traffic flows west, we always say—towards the spires of Lovat—but it would be work.

Rumor had it that Hellgate was getting some pretty decent restaurants as well.

My stomach growled again.

Samantha said something, and I turned to see her waiting for a reply.

"Sorry," I said. "Didn't catch that. Lost in thought. What did you say?"

She paused and seemed to study my face.

"Nevermind," she finally said.

I waited a beat. "You sure?"

"Yeah," she smiled. "You get some rest. I'll see you in the morning."

I watched her leave, my eyes tracing the sway of her hip as she ascended the stairs to her room. By the Firsts, she was beautiful.

I could handle a bandit assault, an unruly road, I could lead a caravan, but when faced with this particular woman I stumbled.

I always feel like I'm somewhere lower, somehow beneath her, struggling to catch up.

As she disappeared behind the door to her room I found myself once again wishing things were different.

My room was much as I had left it. The small single bed. The counter with the wash basin and mirror. The window with thick blue curtains that looked out on an alleyway. The small leather knapsack containing all my worldly possessions lying near the foot of the bed.

I stood before the basin, taking a swig from the flask I had tucked into my coat pocket, before discarding the coat and flask in a pile near my pillow. The vermouth inside was warm, but it was better than the swill at the tavern. I was glad I had taken a room on the lower level, grateful I didn't have to face another flight of stairs.

"What's the plan, old boy?" I asked my reflection.

He had no answer, so I collapsed on the bed.

I scratched at my chin. My beard had grown thick over the last few weeks and needed a trimming, but I was too annoyed to take the scissors to it right now. My dark brown hair also could've used a cut. It lay shaggily around my square face. I knew I looked shabby.

It's amazing how everything goes out the window when plans are interrupted so suddenly. It's like losing your balance, and trying to find your feet again. Though, I supposed, it could be worse. Could be a lot worse.

Pushing myself off the bed and pulling my shirt over my head, I added it to the pile in the corner, then began washing the day's dust from my face, neck, and chest. I watched the clear water in the basin darken and studied my reflection again. Not sure what I was hoping for. Answers? Some epiphany? I got nothing. Epiphanies are for prophets, not a broken caravan master.

I rubbed my shoulders, my fingers tracing over the knot of scar tissue from the old gunshot wound on my left arm. Memories threatened to resurface, so I buried them beneath another swig. The vermouth burned. I sat onto the bed and rubbed at my knee.

On some level I knew I hadn't really recovered from Lovat.

My experiences still haunted me, following me like my shadow. When I closed my eyes, I'd see the faces of friends and monsters alike. Living and dead. I couldn't shake it. Somewhere in the back of my mind, I knew it was partly why I was drinking more, and partly why I didn't want to risk the Broken Road.

I had lied to Samantha.

Convincing my company would be easy. They were trail-hard and could handle a little superstition, but could I? Could I protect my people? Too many souls had already been lost on my account. I couldn't handle losing any more. Safe sounded a hell of a lot better than the unknown right now.

It was hard to face the truth of it: somewhere beneath Lovat I had lost my edge. A chunk of me was missing, and it wasn't just physical. The caravan master that had walked into that city wasn't the same man who had hobbled out.

Wensem could see it. Maybe Hannah, we had traveled together enough. Samantha might be aware as well, but she had never traveled with me before. I was certain Taft had no idea.

No, I needed something safe, somewhere safe. I'd find it tomorrow. Enough sulking. Time to get out of the city and back onto a road, any road. Any road besides the Broken Road.

"Tomorrow," I said to myself.

Tomorrow.

Shaler might allow me to duck out of the contract if I threw enough money at her, and if I caught her in a good mood. It had been a simple enough contract: six cargowains, a load of fresh apples, some pears. A few weeks with the current road conditions. But it wasn't like we were hauling spices that could wait in an alley. Produce goes bad. Her haul had a time limit, and its expiration was quickly approaching.

Maybe she could find a company to risk the Broken Road. Even if she agreed to change our terms, any amount paid for backing out would put us in the red.

My thoughts were interrupted by a knock at the door. Samantha had gone to bed, so I assumed it was either Hannah or Wensem. I was feeling hungry, and could use some food, maybe get a drink before turning in.

I pulled on a fresh shirt and rose, putting most of my weight on my left leg.

"What's going on—" I began as I opened the door, but my words caught in my throat, my stomach flipped.

Margaret Shaler stood outside the door flanked by her cousins. She scowled like she had come to do battle.

Carter's bloody cross.

THREE

W e have a contract!"
Margaret Shaler's rage broke like a rainstorm, her voice thundering, face twisted and angry. I had dealt with difficult clients before, but nothing like this. Irrational, spiteful, and quick to anger. When she met my crew, she had been very vocal with her dissatisfaction. They were too old, too fat, and too green. They weren't good enough for a Shaler caravan. She couldn't stand that our company slept under tarpaulins at laager instead of inside the big plastic prairiewains she was accustomed to. She called my crew barbarians, and refused to leave hers behind. Plus, Taft had taken to calling her Maggie instead of Margaret. I'm sure this amused our chuck, but Shaler had been incensed. She wondered aloud why her father had hired Bell Caravans instead of one of the bigger companies, like Frankle out of Hellgate, or Merck if he so desperately needed a Lovatine company. My initial contract had been with her father—some self-proclaimed pillar of the farming community who operated a farm north of Hellgate.

He had sent a telegram saying that I would be dealing with

his son, but some accident on the ranch had kept the kid from coming. That left me with Margaret Shaler—his only daughter.

Maybe she had something to prove: she was bullheaded, angry, and her temper was explosive. She cared little that the way was blocked, and lately she was threatening to cut off the deal. I was considering letting her.

"Look, I realize that," I began, trying to calm the situation. "But you have to understand the situation. Caravan companies are being turned back every day. Go to the gates! Talk to the caravan masters and listen to 'em. There's no safe route to Lovat. Not right now. Not until this all blows over."

Shaler huffed and glowered at me. She was younger than me by a few years, but certainly taller. Probably still firmly in her twenties. She was too thin to be a beauty, too angular. Her prominent teeth peeked out from behind a pair of too-small lips. In her anger, she seemed to waver like a shambler. A strand of straw-blonde hair had fallen in front of her face. It whipped around as she spoke, adding to her intensity.

"I have promises to keep, I have deliveries to make, and I can't sit here idle. The contract is binding and subject to the authority of the local magistrate."

"I know. I have signed hundreds of them. Doesn't change the fact that all trade on the Big Ninety is stopped while this trumped-up dispute goes on. Until it's resolved, we're stuck," I shrugged.

Shaler pushed past me into my room with her two cousins trailing behind. The eldest was just old enough to grow facial hair, the other barely into his teens. I was so wrapped up in the discussion that I couldn't remember their names. I try to memorize the names of everyone in my company, but the vermouth was teaming up with the heat from this argument to do a number on me.

I turned as Shaler sat on the bed, her back straight, her knees locked together. It was the only space to sit in the small room. Her towheaded cousins stood awkwardly to one side, looking nervous. They were even less comfortable in this situation than I was.

"There's other trails," she spat, her lips twisting into a sneer.

"Sure, there's tons of trails. Eventually we're going to come to the river and what we're going to need is a crossing. With Applehome gone, that leaves the Grovedare Span as the only safe east-west span. That just happens to be where thousands of Syringan militiamen are currently having it out with the Lovat constabulary."

I thought of the contract. How do you plan for military action and terrorist road seizures occurring at the same time? If at all? No amount of travel padding would allow for something that disruptive.

Shaler mumbled something under her breath about the reliability of Lovatine caravan companies and glowered. Had I known her father's representative was so headstrong, I would have turned him down. I had assumed it would be the Shaler boy. Margaret's older brother was a jovial—if a tad dense—sort of merchant. A few of the caravan masters I knew had spoken fondly of him. So I had signed the contract with her old man, promising to meet up with his crew in Syringa and guide them to Lovat. Wensem had been wary about signing a deal without meeting the merchant coming along for the run, but the money was good and I was eager, so I jumped at the chance without talking things over with him.

He hadn't been pleased.

The year before I had taken a job with an importer named Wilem, Black & Bright. It seemed like an easy enough job, but by the end of it, I found myself enveloped in a vast conspiracy involving a bizarre cult led by a creature named Peter Black. The decision had led to the ritual slayings of some of my close friends, almost leading to the deaths of Wensem and his newborn son. Deep down a tunnel beneath Lovat, Black had been killed. That much, I remembered. Beyond that, things were foggy. A murky mess of gunfights, tentacles, and torrents of water, and then I was waking up, choking on the street. I still can't make sense of it. The doctors tell me it's shock.

Nearly a year later, the deaths still haunt me.

"What about the river road?" Shaler asked, bringing me back to the trouble at hand. "The Low Road, I believe you roaders call it."

She spat "roader" like it was a curse.

"South?" I blinked. She knew her trails. On some level I was impressed, but I was too busy trying to save our hides to linger too long on what a rancher's daughter knew about the roader life.

"Yes, south. You call yourself a caravan master?" She snorted what could have been a laugh and crossed her arms. "I have wainloads of apples and pears, and they're especially perishable in this heat. They're due in Lovat in a week." She emphasized the last word and threw her hands in the air. "I'm already losing contracts with the city's importers. The longer we stay in this abhorrent scratch of a city, the more danger it puts my cargo in. Last I checked the contract, it lists you as the party responsible for the safety of the cargo. Black and white."

She jabbed a finger at me.

"If I had known—"

She cut me off. "Spare me the excuses. I am done arguing. We'll take the Low Road. Tomorrow. Hopefully we'll still make Lovat before the cargo rots. Any losses will come out of your final payment."

All this for some fruit? She was willing to risk the lives of her family's employees and my company for fruit?

I shook my head. "We can't. The Low Road is blocked as well."

"I beg your pardon?" She blinked at me. Seeming to study my words, wondering if I was lying.

"The road is blocked," I said evenly.

"They didn't say anything about that on the monochromes."

I nodded. "I know, this is recent. My scout just came back this morning. The Low Road is a good thought, Miss Shaler." Take note, this is what's called bootlicking. Usually it works. Usually.

I continued. "It was my first thought as well. The crossing is secure, the route is safe, and while it's longer, it's better maintained than the Big Ninety and it has no passes to climb, so it's almost as fast."

"So what's blocking it?" one of the cousins asked. He turned his eyes to his boots when Shaler glared at him.

I explained the situation with the Purity Movement in Destiny. The two cousins looked at one another, worried looks crossing their faces. It was good to see that there were Shalers capable of emotions other than rage.

Again Shaler threw her hands into the air in exasperation. "I'm done. I've had enough of this bullshit. I go to the magistrate tomorrow."

She made a move for the door, but I stepped in front of her. Things were getting out of hand.

"Whoa, whoa. Let's calm down," I began, my cool slipping. The last thing I needed was to deal with the Syringan magistrate. "I've tried to be nice, and I have tried to be accommodating, but you should really read the rest of your damn contract! I am not just responsible for your haul. I am also responsible for the lives of the people within the caravan, both my crew and your company. It's my job to make sure everyone arrives unharmed to their destination. It's why I can't risk the Big Ninety right now, or the Low Road, or the damned Broken Road. We won't travel it! Not under my mastering. I'm sorry you might lose your shipment, and we'll cover the cost as a token of goodwill, but that's far better than losing your people, wouldn't you agree?"

She stared at me in silence for a long moment, and I had difficulty reading her expression. Outside the boarding house, the wind picked back up. Raspy promises of more choking dust.

When she finally spoke, it was with a cold emotionless tone and narrow eyes. "What's the Broken Road?"

Carter's cross!

I thought over the words that had just passed through my lips.

I wanted to kick myself.

I had been so worked up that I had inadvertently done exactly what I was worried one of my crew would do: I spilled the beans on the Broken Road. By the Firsts, how could I be so stupid?

"It's nothing. Just road slang." I tried to act indifferent, running my hands through my hair and doing my best not to scream at myself.

She didn't go for it.

"You're lying," she said, her voice flat.

I rubbed the back of my neck nervously as I looked up at her. The words poured out of me in sputtering bursts. "Yeah. Yeah, it's a… a lie. Sorry. Look, I mentioned it as an example because it's not safe. Certainly it's less safe than both the Big Ninety and the Low Road combined. Hell, it's probably not even passable—it hasn't been maintained for years. At best it's a bandit trail, used by smugglers and thieves. At worst, well… depends who you talk to. That's it. It shouldn't even be considered on the best of days with plenty of time."

"Where is it?"

Why wasn't she listening to my warnings?

"North," I said. "Starts up near Meyer's Falls. There's a crossing there." I paused. "If you can call it that." My stomach was in free fall.

"Bandit trail, you say?" She paused, rubbing an eyebrow.

I nodded, hoping the mention of bandits would dissuade her. Most merchants had a healthy fear of robbers. Can't really blame them. Thieves in masks stealing your livelihood—that's unnerving.

Truth be told, you stick to the major routes, you could easily go your whole life without seeing one. The cities do a fine enough job keeping them off the main thoroughfares through patrols. The real danger on a trail is the weather and the wild animals, and those stretches where the trail doesn't have the funding of a city or a road town to maintain it. Cargowains get bogged down in mud, wheels and axles snap. You could lose an ox or a mule to a hidden pothole.

"Then we'll take it."

"No, no, no," I shook my head. "Look, I'm serious when I say it's not safe. Bandits are common and the road itself is fraught with trouble. Not to mention that it runs parallel to the Victory wall for a spell. It's dangerous country. Lawless."

She studied my face, her expression hard.

"I have my security. You have that maero and his crew for your own. We'll be perfectly safe. You have a contract to fulfill, Bell. If there's a route we can take to get my shipment to Lovat, then we're going to damn well take it. You'll do your job." She paused, paced, and then spun on me. "Isn't that why my father hired you? Isn't Bell Caravans supposed to be one of Lovat's finest?"

Damn, I thought. Why couldn't I keep my trap shut? A knot had grown in my throat, and I really wanted a swig from my flask.

"My crew won't work the Broken Road," I countered.

"Then you'll find a crew that will," Shaler snapped back.

I set my jaw.

It's now or never, I thought to myself. Time to stand your ground and be the leader you were before Lovat.

I took a deep breath. "No."

"What did you say?" Shaler took one step towards me, and

stared down. I could smell her dinner on her breath. Something heavy with garlic.

Stepping back, I looked up at her, my voice calm. "I said no. It's too dangerous. My first job is the safety of the caravan. I won't do it."

"Fine," Shaler said, looking over her shoulder and motioning with her chin for her cousins to follow. "Magistrate it is. Wake him up. I'll settle it tonight."

Syringa's magistrate had a rough reputation. He was a hard anti-caravan man in a caravan town. A curious dichotomy, but if there was anyone who fit that unusual shape in the universe it was him. He had been elected after a few roughnecks from one of the larger companies had wreaked havoc on some local establishments. Trashing bars, roughing up merchants. The city, in turmoil, had voted him in. He was known for being a ball-breaker and a tough old bird, who more often than not came down on the side of the merchants rather than the caravan companies who fed his city. Roaders hated him. It wouldn't bode well for me. On paper she had the right of it. Delays due to unforeseen consequences weren't a part of the contract. If there was a route we could take and I wasn't taking it, I'd be delaying the caravan's progress. A breach of contract.

Under any other circumstances, at any other time during any other year, she wouldn't even have mentioned the contract. They were usually just formalities, done to keep merchants happy and make sure the company got paid. It was rare that they were enforced. A handshake, a smile, that was all it normally took. This sort of thing happened to other companies, not to me. In all my years on the road, this was the first time I had a client using a contract as a weapon.

Staring at Shaler, I tried to go over the fine print as best as I could remember it. Damages. Something about refunds. All written in legal Strutten I could barely comprehend.

She knew it better than I did, and she'd trap me with it.

My options were limited. The simplest one was to disband the company and try to reform in Lovat, which would require fleeing and would probably keep me from operating in Syringa in the future. I didn't like the idea of being on the run again. I'd had enough of running in Lovat to last a lifetime. I didn't want to make it a habit.

"Look," I raised my hands in a gesture of peace. "Maybe we can avoid the magistrate and work something out."

She put her hands on her hips and tilted her head to the side. "Like the Broken Road."

"Maybe not that, but something. You want a drink? Let's get a drink and discuss this like professionals."

"No!" she exploded. "I am done discussing anything with you! I'll settle for a late arrival, but my produce will be on the road in one day's time or I'll drag you before the magistrate. Do. You. Understand. Me?"

FOUR

Wensem's eyes were narrowed. He sat upright in his chair, his posture tense as he waited for me to finish. When I did, he slowly shook his head and spoke flatly. "The Broken Road. By the Firsts, what did you get us into?"

"Look, we don't have a choice," I said.

Wensem didn't respond. He just stared at me from across his beer. The tavern we had holed up in could seat maybe six people, eight if they were real small. Right now, it was just three of us: me, Wensem, and a dauger bartender with a flat lead mask. Outside the morning wind had begun to blow, and it howled against the wooden walls of the bar, whipping through the loose slats with thin whistles.

Wensem still hadn't said anything. He hardly blinked. I squirmed in my chair, feeling awkward under his blue-gray gaze. He had to understand, right? Had to see that Shaler left me no other choice. I ran a hand through my shaggy hair, traced the tips of my fingers around the rim of my glass and avoided meeting his eyes.

"I'm serious," I finally said. "You didn't see her. She was pissed. She threatened to take us to the magistrate. Was going to have our assets, our license, everything seized. She'd do it too, and the magistrate would let her. He doesn't like us very much."

"You."

"What?"

"The magistrate. He doesn't like you very much."

He wasn't wrong. There was a minor incident. I had approached the magistrate complaining about failure for completed payment by one of Syringa's beloved merchants. I don't know if it had been a bad day for him or what, but he wasn't cordial. He had said something offhand. Then my mouth got the better of me. He snapped. I snapped back. Suffice it to say we never got full payment and I spent a few nights in jail.

"Regardless, it didn't leave us with much of a choice. She was ready to walk right up to O'Conner's blockade. I'm not taking any of our people near those freaks. I'd rather risk the rumors than face down the Purity Movement."

Wensem breathed out a sad, resigned sigh.

Silence settled between us and we slid back into our game. Wensem staring at me, while I did my damnedest to avoid his gaze.

I couldn't take it. "Look, I know it was rash, but what other choice do we have? She insisted on the Broken Road. I didn't have a reason not to take it. Not a good one at least."

Silence. That stare.

I continued. "Ghosts. Cannibals. I mean, come on!"

Nothing. He just looked at me, his lips turned down. His

shoulders straight. His crooked jaw set. My words disappearing in the dusty air.

Finally Wensem stood, breathing out another one of those sad sighs. It felt like a punch in the gut.

"You know... I realize you have been through a lot. But this is supposed to be a partnership. Me and you. Together. Not... this."

He waved a hand and took a sip of his beer. My stomach tightened. Would he walk away? His eyes smoldered betraying the anger beneath the surface. The ice had cracked.

Still silent, he finished his beer and turned slowly to push his way out of the tavern and into the blowing dust outside. "Come on," he said. "We need to tell the crew."

Roaders are superstitious types—old trail hands who believe in omens, signs, and wonders. Superstition is a wild thing that grows like a weed. The longer you leave it unattended the more it multiplies, eventually pushing out the good, making room only for itself. This is why superstitious old codgers are more common than superstitious young people. They've had plenty of time to let their weeds grow.

There were grumbles. Voices lowered in discussion. Finally three of them, the oldest, and except for Hannah, my most trusted, asked for their stipend. I paid it. I smiled and shook their hands, and wished them well, but down deep, a small ball of worry lodged in my stomach. I knew what their departure meant for me.

Shaler wanted to get on the road and we didn't have time to hire replacements. That left us trudging down the Broken Road missing most of our security. Not something I'm keen on doing even on safe roads.

I was left with a company of six, counting Wensem and myself. I wondered if those three who had left weren't really the smarter ones. I found myself secretly jealous of their ability to just walk away.

"I don't like this, boss," said Hannah. Her voice snapped me out of my reverie.

She walked next to me at the head of the company's column, heading north out of Syringa. Behind us stretched the cargowains of the caravan, single file, trundling along like a procession of overweight boars.

The day had broken much like the last: hot, dry, and dirty. The sun was high in the sky, nearing mid-day. Syringa was already miles behind us, her small towers a hazy sketch against the sky. To my right—east—the peak of Syringa Mountain wavered as a dirty, bronze smudge against the washed-out blue of the sky.

"I don't like it either, but she had the law on her side and I let the route slip."

I turned and looked at her. At twenty-six, Hannah was one of the best scouts in the territory, and I was glad she was on my side. She was human: small and lean, all muscle. Her face was heart-shaped with a button nose and friendly green eyes that matched an easy smile.

She wore the heavy boots of a roader, along with dark rugged canvas pants, a shabby knit shirt, and a yellow patterned keff draped around her neck. She usually wore a brown leather jacket with a heavy hood to keep the rain off her dark hair and the sun off her shoulders, but had foregone it in the heat.

"Kind of stupid, wouldn't you agree?" She rattled off their names. "Norm, Rosebel, Horace—we lost some good people, boss."

"Shaler threatened to break the company if we didn't take the route."

"Could she have done that?"

"In Lovat, no. Here…" I let the sentence drop.

Hannah frowned and looked over her shoulder at the caravan stretching out behind us. The gearwain led the column, followed closely by Shaler's shambling prairiewain. Its plastic shell looked like a cheese box on wheels, and the contraption bobbed on the road like a ship at sea.

"She have something to prove?" Hannah asked, turning back to me.

"Doesn't everyone?"

Hannah chuckled and wrinkled her nose. "I suppose. She just seems awful willing to put her people's lives in danger over wainloads of fruit."

"They don't sell, then they're in for a hard winter. Let's remove the Shaler family from the picture; if those apples don't get to Lovat, well, then Lovat is in for a hard winter."

Hannah let it drop.

"Is Wensem upset? That was most of his detail who left."

"A little," I said, thinking of the way Wensem had walked off earlier. Me and you. Together. With his crew three short, it left all of Bell Caravans driving wains and guarding the laager. Under normal circumstances we split the responsibilities. Guards guarded and drivers drove. It keeps the crew fresh. A tired roader is a roader that makes mistakes. I had felt his eyes on me as I had broken the news to the company. Watching from the back of the group. We hadn't spoken since the tavern.

Wensem's primary responsibility was security. I was in charge of the day-to-day: routes, logistics, repairs, that sort of thing. Hannah was the only roader who remained from Wensem's part of the crew, and she was technically shared between the two of us.

Hannah breathed out, shifting her rifle to her shoulder. "Well, the day ain't getting any younger. I better get to what you pay me for. I'll see you in a few stages, but I might be a bit late to laager. I want to be thorough."

"All right," I said. We shook hands. "You stay safe. Watch out for rogue shamblers."

She laughed. Shamblers are a strange animal. They look like naked humanoid figures: neckless with malformed heads, sightless bulging eyes, and pallid gray skin. Solitary and slow, they were more nuisance than threat, occasionally stumbling through a laager or running into the side of a cargowain. They were usually herbivorous, wandering the high desert looking for scrub brush, but occasionally they would find a prairie bird or small mammal to munch on.

"I doubt we'll have much to worry about until after the crossing at Meyer's Falls. But it never hurts to be sharp." She looked at the sky. "Heat makes people crazy."

Despite her height, her legs were long and carried her well. I watched her move into a jog and disappear down the road. Hannah was right, it was three or so stages with bone-dry ground from Syringa to Meyer's Falls, and not a rain cloud in sight. The miles would blow by. Besides, it was after Meyer's Falls where the real journey would begin. It wasn't much in itself: a small fort, a tiny town, an undersupplied waystation. Its crossing was hardly deserving of the designation. No massive span crossed a deep flow of water. That far north, the river doesn't yet meet up with the fast-flowing tributaries from the eastern and western mountains. During wet seasons the river might rise to waist high, but with this drought, most caravaneers could probably walk across the river with barely a splash.

I stopped and watched my caravan roll past, inspecting the column. Our gearwain led the caravan, followed by Shaler's personal prairiewain, and behind its domed roof rolled her six cargowains laden with the fruit bound for Lovat. All in all, we were a caravan of nine counting Taft's chuckwain, which brought up the rear behind a small cart driven by our hired blacksmith, a human-dimanian half-breed named Clara Charron. One cart. Eight wains. Sixteen souls.

This is your caravan, I thought blackly. These are the people relying on your leadership, decision-making, and protection.

It's common practice to register your route with the local caravan authority. Departure date, manifest, crew, expected arrival date, what caravansara you'd be unloading with—mundane roader stuff. When I informed the Syringan clerk of our route, the bufo'anur behind the counter had laughed, thinking I was joking. When he realized I wasn't, his expression turned grave.

"Sixteen people on that road?"

I nodded.

"You're a bunch of fools. It'll eat you alive, if the locals don't get to you first. Last legitimate caravan registered that route was... one second..." He checked his ledger. "Over seven years ago."

"No choice. Client demands."

The clerk looked down to see who it was and winced at the name. "You know, they won't come after you. The authorities. Your party goes missing on that road, ain't nobody going to look for you. You're on your own, friend."

On our own.

As the caravan rolled past me, his words rang in my ears. They hung over me like a storm cloud.

I waited for the chuckwain. On previous caravans—before I had hurt my knee—I would have walked toward the rear of the column, opposite its flow, but these days it was easier to just wait. It hurt less.

As the chuckwain rumbled past, I pulled myself up next to Taft and extended my right leg off the edge of the bench seat. Behind me, a clutch of chickens angrily clucked in their cages. The aching throb that had filled my knee eased somewhat and I gave it a rub, trying to loosen it up.

"Morning... or what remains of it," Taft greeted me, lifting a blue enamel mug into the air. "Coffee?"

"I'd love some," I said. My stomach was rumbling.

"Kettle's behind the seat," she motioned with her head, keeping her eye on the solitary ox pulling her cart. "I'd give you the reins and pour it for you, but ol' Bart here is temperamental. And for now he ain't decided on you."

"He talks to you?" I asked with a smirk.

"More like I talk to him. Not much else to talk to back here."

"You keep him in line then, I can get myself coffee." I leaned back to pour myself a fresh cup from the metal kettle, then snatched a cheese biscuit from an enameled plate. It was still warm.

"I still think this is a bad idea," I admitted, taking a bite of the biscuit. It was soft, with hints of sharp cheddar cheese and pepper. It hit the spot. Honestly, I longed for some of her sausage gravy, but that'd have to wait.

Taft laughed. "You sound like every other superstitious roader. The stories about this road are a bunch of silly school-boy gossip. Ghosts. Cannibals. Death squads," she laughed. "All a bunch of bullshit. It'll be as boring as any other trail. Mark my words."

I sighed.

"Though I am a bit confused. Why'd you suggest it to Maggie?" Shaler hated Taft using the familiar name with her. Preferred "Miss Shaler" or just "Shaler." Taft reveled in getting under her skin.

I shook my head. "I didn't," I said. "Well, not direct—... er... intentionally. She was pressing the Low Road and threatening to take us to the magistrate, I was explaining about the Purity Movement's seizure and... well... it just rolled out. Last place on earth I want to be is taking a trip down the Broken

Road with an angry client bent on making record time. It's how mistakes happen, how people get killed."

"Why not the mountain trails?" Taft asked. "The ones south of the Big Ninety? Why not suggest those instead?"

"You're kidding, right? We actually want to get to Lovat. If we were only on foot I might've risked it, but the trails through the southern mountains are spotty, they twist and turn like snakes. Takes months to get cargowains through them, and if the weather turns, we'd be stuck till spring. I don't want to winter in the mountains."

"So it's the Broken Road." Taft glanced over at me as I took a swig from the piping hot coffee. "You ever been?"

I shook my head, swallowing the brew, wondering how she made everything taste so good. "No, for obvious reasons I've always avoided it. I've been a Big Ninety caravaneer for as long as I can remember. But I know the route well enough based off some old maps."

Taft laughed. "Maps? Maps! Some caravan master you are, letting a client force you into going in blind. Why'd I sign on with you again?"

I winced, but rolled on. "Never had a reason to take the Broken Road, so like most, I… avoided its existence. My world was the Big Ninety. I grew up along the trail, saw the caravans roll by, saw my father help the masters."

"What's he do?"

"He's a wheelwright."

"Ah, a wheelwright's son. Explains the tattoos," she said, nodding at the ink on my forearms—matching black wagon wheels. I had gotten them years before, when I spent a few nights in Hellgate.

"Yep, bit of the past, bit of the future," I said, motioning with the mug at the rolling caravan that stretched out before us.

"How about you?" I asked through a mouthful of biscuit. "You ever been down this way?"

Taft's laugh seemed to catch in her throat and her voice took on a strangely serious tone. "Once or twice. Long ago, before your time. Before it was called the Broken Road."

Silence fell. I didn't press it.

After half a mile or so, Taft emerged from the silence to slap me on the back with a meaty hand. "History is history. Best not dwell on it."

"That's something we can both agree on," I said with a nod. "I'm going to go find Sam."

"She's riding with Tin up in the gearwain. Wanted to be at the head of the company."

I groaned, thinking of the walk to the front of the caravan.

Taft laughed. "You can hobble faster than this caravan rolls, Master Bell. A walk up to the head of the company would do that bum knee some good. Don't give it more time to seize up."

"Thanks, doc," I said, slipping off the chuckwain and hobbling alongside it. "I'm keeping the mug!"

"I'll charge you for it," she called as I picked up my pace and left her at the rear.

Much to my dismay, Samantha had come along. I had explained the situation before we left Syringa. I explained the dangers, the rational ones, and told her it would be best for her to wait for the Big Ninety to open up and take a carriage back to Lovat. It wasn't worth it to risk the trip. She hadn't budged.

"I came with you eastward and I'm going to return with you westward."

When I tried to tell her she could do some good in Syringa with the missions, she only laughed. "I can do some good with a rolling caravan as well."

She wanted to get home, sure, but this trip allowed her to experience life on the road and see a part of the Territories that few folks in Lovat even realize exists. Nothing I said dissuaded her. For my own sanity, I asked that she carry a weapon, at least a rifle. She refused, unmoveable. Samantha hated guns. In a lot of ways, she was more bullheaded than Shaler.

I continued to limp up the column, passing the row of creaking cargowains.

A typical cargowain is between fifteen to twenty feet in length and stands about a shoulder high. Usually reinforced, they can carry several tons of cargo. When loaded with that burden, they move slowly, hardly faster than a walk. In healthier times, I walked up and down a caravan's column day and night, checking on wainloads, conversing with drivers, examining the state of the animals pulling the heavy loads. Making all manner of major and minor decisions. Now, with the bum knee, I was slower. It took a lot out of me to walk up the length of a column.

This morning I had committed the names and faces of Shaler's crew to memory. Some of Shaler's other hires were friendly enough. Chance and Range—the cousins whose names I had forgotten at the boarding house—both gave me a friendly nod from behind the reins of their oxen. Chance drove a cargowain while Range drove Shaler's personal prairiewain.

I wiped the dust off my face. Opposite me, on the other side of the column, Wensem was arguing with two of Shaler's men: the Lytle twins. They were both strong-shouldered and broad-chested, their dark skin further darkened by a latticework of tattoos that crawled up their arms and necks, as if fighting to hold in their muscle. Their faces were shadowed by stubble that hid the crooked lines of their lips. They weren't tall; Wensem stood a whole two heads taller than either of them.

They didn't like taking orders from a maero. They argued with Wensem about everything. I watched as Wensem spoke calmly, nodded, then gently placed a big hand on each of their shoulders. I couldn't hear what he said, but whatever it was, it worked. The mouths of both twins closed firmly, and one gave a curt nod and walked back toward the chuckwain.

Wensem was good with people. Even those that didn't like him. His cool and collected demeanor worked well when pitted against unruly roaders. In many ways, he was a better leader than I could ever be. I wished he had been there when Shaler had walked in the previous night. Maybe we wouldn't be here now.

The other drivers ignored me as I hobbled alongside them. No one spoke to me, and that was fine. I needed to stay focused on our trip. As I passed the prairiewain, I could see Shaler through one of the plastic windows, reading a paperback while she lounged on a small bed.

A throb began to burn brightly around my right knee, but I did my best to ignore it.

The scrubby brush of the high prairie was slowly giving way to the tall bunchgrass of the foothills as we gained altitude. To the northeast the long narrow trunks of lodgepole pines intermixed with fir and stands of birch and cottonwood. It'd be nice to get out of the dust, have some trees to block the winds that howled across the high desert plateau.

Three stages. Three days to Meyer's Falls, and then the journey truly began.

I picked up my pace, sensing the end was near and wanting to get off my knee for a stretch. Pulling myself up into the rear of the gearwain, I picked my way past our supplies to the front, where Samantha and Ivari Tin sat in conversation. The gearwain was the one piece of equipment Wensem and I purchased before heading east from Lovat. Our first big acquisition for the company. We had the name "Bell Caravans" stenciled in red paint on the side in our native Strutten, a crude symbol of a bell with a wagon wheel at its mouth splitting the two words.

Wensem had chosen the name. Said it had a nice "ring" to it. He thought that was really funny. I recall that he was drunk at the time.

"By the Firsts!" Tin shouted, grabbing his chest when he spotted me crawling up from the back of the wain. "You scared the bloody hell out of me, boss. I thought you were a bandit."

Tin was a young dauger; a member of the territory's masked

race. I have never seen a dauger without a mask, and for that matter, didn't even know anyone who had. As a people, they keep them on in all but the most intimate situations. Only other daugers are allowed to see a dauger maskless. I've heard all manner of rumors as to what's underneath.

Their masks play an important role in their species hierarchy. Precious metals denote richer families, while more base metals are worn by poorer ones. With his mask and family name, Tin's station seemed clear. He was probably glad to get out of the city and its class rankings and into open country.

I had hired him at the caravansara in Lovat, and he was eager to prove himself as a roader. Dauger don't take to the life as often as other races, but like everyone else out here Tin had an axe to grind. I had been impressed. He had done well on our trip from Lovat—quite well—and had the makings of a proper caravaneer. It was good to see he had remained with us, even after harder men had cashed out. If he could keep his wits about him, he might become a regular.

"Hah!" I said. "We're a long way from bandit country yet."

I sat down behind the seat that stretched across the front of the wagon, on a crate of tarpaulins we used at laager. Samantha turned around and smiled a warm smile that made my knees weak. She wasn't wearing her normal attire. Instead, she had opted for roader clothes: a lightweight ivory-colored shirt and brown canvas pants that hugged her curves. Her wild hair was pulled back into a thick ponytail, and she wore a brick-red keff as a hood to keep the sun off.

"How's the knee?" she asked.

"Hurts," I shrugged. "You liking the—"

"Is it really that dangerous?" Tin interrupted, his voice tentative. "The Broken Road?"

"Honestly?" I sighed. I was tired of lying. "I have no idea. When I registered our route, the clerk told me the last record they have of a legitimate caravan coming this way was seven years ago."

"Seven years…" said Samantha, looking at me warily.

"As I said, it's a route usually avoided." I tapped Tin on the shoulder. "We'll break around midday for some food. Still some miles left, but I'll let you make the call."

Tin nodded quickly, eager for the responsibility.

"Look, take your time slowing the caravan down. Give the yahoos behind you time to realize we're breaking. You rush it, they're liable to drive their oxen right into your ass, and then we're in a huge mess. Understood?"

"Yes, sir."

"How's the caravan?" said Samantha.

"Seems fine enough. Just came from Taft, she has a fine batch of coffee brewed. The cargowa—"

"Coffee?" Tin interrupted again. "Taft has fresh coffee?"

"You want a cup? I can take over for a spell." I was eager to spend some time alone with Samantha. We hadn't found much time to talk since setting out from Syringa.

Tin nodded and offered me the reins. I took them and we switched spots. As I settled in, he leapt off the wain and ran down the line.

I chuckled, and watched him go over my shoulder. "He's a good kid."

I looked over at Samantha and caught her smiling at me.

"What?" I asked.

"It's nothing," she said.

"Right, and I'm Hastur himself. What is it?" I gave a little tug on the reins, slowing the oxen a bit as we rumbled over some small ruts.

"It's nice seeing you in your element, is all. That's partly why I wanted to come along. When we came from Lovat I hardly saw you, I ended up spending most of my time talking theory with the other clergy. I wanted to see what drew you to caravanning."

I laughed self-consciously at the idea of her observing me. "Not sure there's much to see."

"Sure there is. I can see how much you care, how much you want your people to enjoy the road like you do. It's nice, and it certainly beats wasting away in the priory in Syringa talking with the sisters and the brothers. I'm seeing a side of you that up until now I had only seen at a distance."

I frowned slightly. "I wish it was under better circumstances."

"I know this isn't the route you want to take. I know you're worried but I doubt most of the others can see it. You look confident. The way you move, the way you speak. It encourages them. Your crew look up to you."

"Yeah?" I said, feeling unsure. "I guess I'm just doing what needs to be done."

"Sometimes that's all you can do," she said, turning away to stare across the vast and empty hills. I knew what she was thinking about: the tunnel. My memories were murky, but clear as day I could remember her standing in the shadows, gun in hand, doing what had to be done. I couldn't ever repay her for that, not properly.

I reached over and squeezed her knee reassuringly. It had taken a lot for her to do what she had done. She turned and gave me a sad smile, and her eyes sparkled as she asked, "Have you been able to remember what happened? Has anything else come back?"

I shook my head. The whole experience was convoluted. I had been in shock and spent a few days in a coma. As a result I could only piece together parts of it, only remember flashes. It felt like big chunks of memory had been torn from me. Sequences were missing.

"Nothing," I said. "I mean, I remember Black dying, crushed by the tunneling machine. I remember Wensem fighting someone, I remember knowing you and your brother were safe. Everything else…" my voice trailed off.

We rolled along for a while. Quiet, enjoying one another's company despite the difficult memories. I tried to focus on the road and not think on the ugliness from the tunnel. I had spent enough time worrying over it. My friends were safe, I was safe. I don't think I could have asked for a better outcome.

"I hate to ask this again," I said, breaking the silence.

She seemed to anticipate what I was about to ask. "So don't."

"Sam. It's—"

"I said no and I meant it. I won't carry one. You know that."

I also knew how good she was with a gun. I could feel her tense up next to me.

I pressed a bit further. "Even Taft has a—"

"I said no," she said, a bit of heat creeping into the words.

"Okay, okay." I held up my hands, letting the reins drop into my lap temporarily. "Just figured I'd try one last time."

She gave me a smile, but it lacked the warmth from earlier. I wished she understood where I was coming from. I had asked her about the gun before we set off, hoping she'd carry one. I had no idea what lay ahead, and bringing her into unknown territory made my stomach sour.

We settled back into silence.

The miles slowly rolled by. Thick stands of trees, dense mounds of tangled brush, fast-moving streams, and peaceful little lakes all slowly passed as we moved along. The tension began to slowly bleed out.

"Did you speak with Wensem?" Samantha eventually said.

"No. He looking for me?"

"Not directly, but he was bickering with Shaler's thugs. The Lytle twins. Figured you might be able to help."

"I saw them arguing. Think they're trouble?"

Samantha nodded. "They didn't seem keen on a maero giving them orders. Had a bit of an air about it. They were being snippy when I saw them."

"They'll need to learn to deal with it. He's in charge of caravan security, they're guards. They were hired by Shaler, but when it comes to the caravan, orders come from Wensem or me. It's not their call, it's his."

I realized as I said it that Wensem hadn't been making any calls. If anything, I was forcing him to follow my orders like a regular hireling. No wonder he was frustrated.

"Well, you might want to find them, maybe lay down some ground rules?"

Wensem seemed to have everything handled, but I didn't need the potential of insubordination looming. It was about to become dangerous enough without these two kicking up dust.

"I'll find them," I promised.

We fell into silence as the gearwain moved forward. I was lost in my thoughts. Already the potential for trouble burned within the caravan, and we didn't even have one stage complete. It wasn't a good sign. The road would get much more difficult the farther we withdrew from civilization.

I couldn't shake the sense of dread that was ever so slowly filling my chest.

FIVE

We crawled across the bone-dry plains, fighting the occasional dust storm and laagering beneath stands of trees. We had only one broken wheel, an easy repair I was able to do myself. We met a few other caravans while at laager for the night; companies working the road between Meyer's Falls and Syringa. Most of them were smaller parties of three or four people, sometimes a half-feral dog, and a cart with an ox or a bison tugging at it. Otherwise, it was miles of dust and days of walking and endless empty skies.

When we arrived at Meyer's Falls, Shaler requested we stop for a few days. "I want to make up for lost profits. Maybe sell a load to the other caravans."

"You sure they'll buy?" I asked, "Meyer's Falls is awfully close to Syringa, and they're overrun with apples and pears right now."

"I'm weeks delayed and losing contracts by the day. I need to try to make up lost profits," Shaler said as she leaned out an open prairiewain window. She rarely left the thing, preferring to issue orders from within. She only came out to relieve herself, and on occasion when the company met.

Now that we were underway, our discussions were more amenable. She could be pleasant enough as long as she got her way, and I went out of my way to see she did. I agreed to stop in Meyer's Falls, but had a request of my own.

"We don't know what the passes hold. We might be facing a drought over here, but the western mountains are dangerous and have a reputation to keep. The passes can get buried in winter and soaked in the fall. Wet roads means mud, and mud can slow our pace to a crawl," I explained. "We need time to do reconnaissance."

Shaler bristled. She had a deadline to keep. A promise to her old man. But when she saw the caravansara outside Meyer's Falls buzzing like a hive and filled with bored roaders waiting for the Big Ninety trade to reopen, she relented.

I doubted I'd find a veteran of the Broken Road, but at least I could try to learn more. Meyer's Falls was off the telegraph lines, and any foot messengers were as choked up as caravans. We knew little about what lay ahead.

Calling Meyer's Falls a town is generous. It is little more than a scratch in the wilderness, a small collection of buildings, barely civilization. Without the militia fort, I doubted it would exist as anything more than a waypoint. The fort sat at the center, leagues bigger than anything around it. It was composed of a ten-foot cement wall that encircled a single tall tower. From a distance, it always reminded me of a chess piece missing its battlements. Above it, a massive Syringan flag flapped in the breeze; diagonal green and blue stripes side by side on a white field.

A few small houses huddled like weeds around the fort, and between them a few businesses were scattered. They consisted of a message dispatcher, a bank, a general store, a restaurant named Gallea's, and the Three Flags.

On the outskirts sat the caravansara. Compared to most trading posts it left much to be desired. It was little more than a long, low-slung building with a hitching post and a barn that served as a livery. One large caravan company dominated the area, which forced the remaining four or five caravans to circle their wains and set up laager until they decided to move on. Trying to ply some trade in the wake of the closures, no doubt. This was probably the busiest the small town had been since the war nearly thirty years ago.

As a militia town, its main industries were guns, Syringan patriotism, and heavy helpings of beer. When the Big Ninety is open, only the circuit caravans move through here; the only thing in Meyer's Falls are surly militia soldiers, hermit hill farmers, and the poor folk who have to live here and deal with the others. It had to be three, maybe four years, since I had last set foot here.

I slid my handgun—a heavy .45 caliber Judge—under the glass partition across the counter, to the bufo'anur doorman. His massive globular eyes focused on me, then looked down at the piece, his expression inscrutable. I watched him file it into a cubby marked in crude Cephan and begin to fill out a small paper card.

"Name?" he said, his rumbling voice laced by a strange accent. The dry gray flesh beneath his wide mouth jiggled as he spoke. The sides of his huge face drooped under the weight of his cheeks.

"Waldo Emerson Bell."

He scratched my name down, tore off a slip and pushed it across the counter towards me. I pocketed it.

"Thank you, Mister Bell. You can claim your weapon upon leaving. Should you forget to claim your weapon, we'll hold it for a period one week. If the piece remains with us beyond a single week, the Three Flags reserves the right to pawn it or sell it in the store. Do you agree to these terms?"

"Does that happen often?" I said, genuinely curious.

The bufo'anur looked at me, his bored expression turning to one of annoyance. We were going off-script, and his eyes kept flicking to the tawdry romance paperback he had been reading before I had approached.

"Does what happen?"

"Customers leaving their weapons behind? Does that happen often?"

"We're thirty miles from Victory," he snapped. "What do you think?"

Admonished, I agreed to the terms and ducked inside the low door into the heart of the Three Flags. It was a militia bar, though you wouldn't know it from this crowd.

I lingered in the entranceway, allowing my eyes to adjust to the low light. The smells of fresh roasting meat, tobacco smoke, and the sour stench of beer filled the air. People milled about on the edges of the tavern, avoiding the tables in the center in favor of the shadowed corners.

I studied my fellow drinkers, moving between the tables and towards the bar. A tall olive-skinned man with dark sharp eyes held up the bar, drinking a black ale; farther down, two gray-skinned bufo'anur mercenaries wearing bulletproof vests split a bottle of whiskey and compared scars.

Most Lovatines were surprised when they first encountered the anur's much larger—and significantly less timid—cousin. Where the anur are a water people, the bufo'anur love the desert. The anur are small while bufo'anur are thick and muscular, dwarfing other races. The only other people in the Territories that could match their speed and strength had to be the long-limbed maero.

Two roaders, old acquaintances of mine, huddled over their drinks in a booth near a corner of the tavern, their faces lit with a golden hue from the oil lamp that burned on the table between them. This was a pleasant surprise.

Agata Levigne was a plain-featured, dimanian caravan master. Across from her sat sour-faced Berkus Mathison, a surly human Wensem and I had once worked with before founding Bell Caravans.

I felt sorry Wensem was going to miss this catchup session. He liked to reminisce.

I walked over to them. "Afternoon. Mind if I join you?"

"Wal!" said Agata, rising and embracing me in a big hug. Holding my arms, she looked me up and down, the way my ma

does when I step through her front door. I half-expected Agata
to tell me I wasn't eating well enough and I needed to relax more.
"How've you been?"

"Good. Good," I said, nodding as I slid into the booth next
to her and smiled at Berkus.

"Wal," said Berkus, his voice impassive. He extended a hand
to me, which I shook.

Apparently Agata and Berk were a couple, which was hard
to imagine. They were rarely seen together outside taverns and
worked different companies. A mutual acquaintance said they
had a son together, but I hadn't ever seen or heard mention of the
boy, and I wasn't going to ask. People's personal business is their
business, and I wasn't sure how much truth was in the stories.
Caravaneers are a gossipy lot. I always figured if it was important
enough, they'd let me know.

Agata was always warm and friendly, bubbling over with
laughter. Berk, on the other hand, was cold and quiet, staring
down unruly men with his heavy-lidded eyes and permanent
sneer. Wensem called him "Smiler" as a joke.

"Odd seeing you in Meyer's Falls," noted Berk, taking a drink
from a pale beer. I waved for the bartender.

"You trapped on the east side as well?" he asked.

"Yeah. I'm here for client work," I said, hoping they didn't
press it. I was tired of talking about Shaler and the Broken Road.

"Wensem still with you?" asked Berk.

"Yep. He's with the laager," I said. "What brings you two
here? You still running the eastern circuit, Agata?"

"Indeed I am," said Agata, drawing a circle in the air with

her index finger, as if tracing the route. "It's my twelfth year. Finished up here yesterday; heading east tomorrow. The normal load, sundries mostly. A few antiques I was hoping to pawn off on a caravan heading west."

"Good luck with that," Berk growled, burying curses in his glass.

"Indeed," I said. "You might find buyers in larger cities. I just came from Syringa."

"I haven't been there in months," Agata said. "How is it with the—you know—the news."

"Never seen the city so crowded," I admitted. "A lot of companies are trapped on this side of the Grovedare. The roaders are getting bored...." I let the sentence trail off.

"Now that you mention it, I've never seen the circuit so busy," said Agata. "I can't remember the last time Meyer's Falls had more than one caravan at laager, let alone five."

"Six," I said, tapping my chest.

We were interrupted by the bartender, who nodded quietly when I placed my order for vermouth on ice and ordered a second round for Agata and Berk.

"You still drink that vile stuff?" asked Berk. I nodded, and he shook his head and sighed.

Agata pulled the conversation back. "Usually in autumn the circuit trade drops, caravans return to their home cities for the winter. With so many folk trapped on this side, and with this late summer heat, we're still pulling a decent trade. Caravans are crawling over each other."

"I wouldn't be displeased with good business. Better than a lot of folk these days."

"Oh, I'm not complaining," said Agata. "Just surprised. Pleasantly surprised."

"How about you, Berk?" He liked rough jobs that required gunfire. He could keep 'em.

Berk grunted. "The First's writhing carcasses, damn this town, damn all these towns. They all seem to have more caravans than clients. I haven't found work in weeks! Hit all the northern towns, and now we're casting our eyes south. My crew's getting quarrelsome." He motioned to the two bufo'anur at the bar, now more than halfway into their bottle.

"You running a circuit, Wal?" asked Agata.

I shook my head, almost too embarrassed to answer. "No. Just the typical fare."

"Not Victory then?" joked Agata.

I shook my head again and laughed. "No. It's boring work. I'll probably run into you again."

Agata smiled.

"Carter's cross," Berk swore, suddenly slapping the table. "You hear about Seven Wains?"

I shook my head. "Should I have?"

"You probably didn't know them. They were a Hellgate outfit. Mastered by... what's his name?" Berk looked at Agata.

"Gilman," Agata said.

"Right, Gilman." Berk snapped his fingers. "Gilman... it's probably for the best, the guy was an asshole. Anyway—" He took a sip from his beer.

"What did he do?" I asked. Berk swallowed three times, almost draining the glass.

"Took the North Road," Berk said, his voice flat, eerie. According to some superstitions, calling the Broken Road by its rightful name can conjure up curses or raise demons. It's nonsense, but Berk is as superstitious as they come.

After a beat, he snorted. "I met up with him in a small town east of here. We were having drinks, a bunch of us talking about the lost routes. The Chubbuck, Blue Star, the old Sweetgrass Highway to the east, and the Meriwether Trail to the west. Of course, some shamblebait decided to sour the mood and pipe up about the North Road. Gilman stood up and announced he was going to blaze the trail, prove the stories were nonsense, and wire us when he got to the other side. We all told him to stay, wasn't worth it, said he was crazy. Nope, even the next morning when he had sobered up, he had made up his mind. He was going to brave it. Show us all how it's done."

"You know the stories," said Agata, her tone ominous.

"Starry Wisdom freaks wandering the hills, bloody hauntings, the ghost company," Berk said.

"I don't believe any of that shit," I said as the vermouth on ice appeared before me. "It's all trail talk. Lies. Superstitions. That's it."

"Cannibals," added Agata, ignoring me. "The forest of dead."

That was a new one.

"I beg pardon?" I said, taking a sip.

"Forest of the dead," said Agata. Her voice had a brittle sound to it. She was scared. "You haven't heard of it?"

"No," I laughed. "What in the name of the Firsts is that? Sounds like a monochrome serial."

"I don't know much more myself. Overheard a roader talk about it. Said it went on as far as the eyes could see, and it smelled like rot."

"What went on?"

Agata shrugged. "The… dead, I suppose."

I snickered.

"Would expect Gilman is there now," Berk said blackly. "We never heard from him. He never registered the route. Never sent the messenger he promised. What a fool."

"We told him to call off the stupid bet," said Agata. "He had nothing to prove to us. Why risk it?"

All this talk about the Broken Road was beginning to bother me. My stomach was churning. The heat in the tavern felt oppressive. It was probably the vermouth. Wasn't autumn supposed to be cooler?

I was tired of talking about this. Somewhere in the miles between Syringa and Meyer's Falls, I had made my peace with it. I'm a rational man. I don't go for these stories. I don't believe in ghosts, hauntings, gods, or the Firsts. I wasn't raised that way. The rules of the trail were simple: use all five of your senses. Stay alert. Keep a distance between yourself and other travelers. Never stop moving. Trust only your company. Rest only for short periods.

We'd keep to the rules and emerge at the other end.

At least, that's what I kept telling myself.

SIX

The noise began about a week down the Broken Road.

We had lingered at Meyer's Falls for a few days. Shaler's luck had been poor and she had sold nothing. Agata and Berkus left, leading separate caravans away from the town. I wished them well, but their story sat heavy on my mind. The tale of the fool who went missing while trying disprove the superstitious stories. Probably got himself killed. Would they be telling the same story about my company? Would the name Bell replace the name Gilman?

The heat lingered in spite of the blanket of clouds that settled over us and threatened rain. I worried that we'd be facing thunderstorms. We broke laager and began the hike westward. The Rediviva's level was what I expected—barely a trickle this far north—and the caravan crossed easily enough.

The road itself was rough, but manageable. Weeds had broken through its ancient crust and generations of weather had turned it to a scratch of gravel mingled with large broken chunks of crumbling asphalt. The chunks almost seemed magnetically attracted to the cargowain wheels for as many times as they smashed against them.

The road condition had slowed down the caravan, and we began taking shifts in pairs, walking in front of the column to push aside any chunks that could damage the wains. A broken wheel or a broken axel could set us back days, and with the perishable cargo, I wanted to make the best time possible.

We covered maybe ten miles a day, twelve if we were lucky. Shaler was annoyed, but there wasn't much she could do but sulk in her prariewain and make snide comments whenever I passed. At least we were moving.

Five days into our trip Hannah had returned, boots muddy, pants stained with road dirt. She wore her keff pulled up and around her head as a close-fitting turban. She met Wensem and me at the head of the column as we took our shift clearing debris. She had left a few days before the caravan, heading into the Broken Road to scout ahead. Her report started as expected. The road would continue to be rough, a few downed trees cross the trail, and then she mentioned something else. Something strange.

"I keep seeing figures in the distance," she explained.

"Bandits?" asked Wensem, shouldering his rifle.

"Not sure. If they are, they're strange-looking bandits. They wear these long robes that billow around them, and on their heads are these tall pointed hoods. All black. Haven't been close enough to see them real clear. They're like a shadow."

Shadow. I shuddered, thinking of my run-ins with Zilla— an umbra, one of the race of living shadows—back in Lovat. Her wicked straight razor, her murderous glowing gaze. All the people dead by her hands, so much bloodshed. Samantha had killed the damn thing, blasting a bullet into her head with the Judge that now hung at my hip.

"Could it be road priests?" I asked, pushing a chunk of asphalt off the trail with the toe of my bad leg. It hurt, but it was easier pushing with the bad leg and putting weight on the good one.

"I've never seen a road priest dressed like that," Wensem said. "At least not from any faith I know."

"Think they're from something new?" I asked. His anger had eased as the trail proved quiet. Wensem didn't meet my eyes for very long. Though our conversations were still short, I was glad that Wensem and I were talking again.

Wensem shrugged. "Maybe we ask Samantha."

Hannah continued, chewing on a strip of jerky as she spoke. "I've seen 'em five times now. Always in the distance. Always just... standing there. It's unnerving. Whatever they are, they were watching me, crouching along the ridges like some kind of gargoyles. It's best we stay on our guard."

"I'll tell the Lytle twins," said Wensem with a sigh.

"I'll talk to Sam. See if she knows anything about these... gargoyles. Hannah, thanks. You go get yourself a bowl of Taft's chili and take a load off."

Wensem nodded, patting the scout on the shoulder with a massive seven-fingered hand. She turned and began walking down the column towards the chuckwain.

"Think it's trouble?" I asked Wensem after Hannah had disappeared.

He shrugged, his eyes scanning the hills around us. "Could be."

"I don't like it."

"Could just be locals wondering what in the hell Hannah was doing by herself on the Broken Road. A woman alone like that can make backwood farmers nervous."

"You think there's farmers out here?"

Wensem shrugged and rubbed his crooked jaw. "Ground is ground. Just because caravans are scared of this trail, doesn't mean farmers are."

"Could be Victory as well, I suppose," I added, casting a glance northward toward Victory's wall. It was thirty-five miles north, give or take. Thirty-five miles, but you could feel its presence looming like a monolith.

"If it's Victory I'll eat my hat," said Wensem. "Unless their patrols have had some serious uniform changes over the years, it's most likely a local. What did Berk say?"

"More like what didn't he say. 'Starry Wisdom freaks, bloody hauntings, and a ghost company.'" I did my best Berkus Matthison impersonation, allowing my voice to go deep and gravelly. Wensem cracked a grin. It was the first smile I had seen on his face in days and it disappeared quickly.

"The road looks to be clearing for a spot. I'll go talk with Sam. You tell your troops and send them up here. It's about time for someone else to take over the debris for a spell."

Wensem frowned. "This is a partnership, Wal."

"Sorry... what did—"

He cut me off. "You keep throwing around orders. Yeah, I'll go tell my crew, but let's do less commanding and more asking.

Might be your name on the wains, but I am just as responsible for the outcome of this caravan as you are."

He turned and walked away before I could respond.

The road ahead looked remarkably clear of wheel-smashing chunks, so I stopped and let the gearwain catch up, pulling myself up behind Samantha. She was reading a book with yellowing pages and a wrinkled red leather cover. She brought it with her from Lovat, and had been studying it and scribbling in a notebook.

"How many times have you read that?" I asked. My stomach growled, and I fished around for a piece of jerky in my coat before remembering I had given it to Hannah. I'd have to make a visit to the chuckwain myself, soon.

Samantha smiled and turned on the bucket seat to look at me. She was covered in road dust, but it seemed to suit her just fine.

"About three times since Lovat. Working on my fourth pass right now. How's the trail looking?"

We crested a hill and the Broken Road stretched out before us, a gray ribbon winding through jaundiced hills. A line of ponderosa pines began to creep in from the North, and in the distance we could see the hazy mountains on the horizon.

"It's smoothing out, actually. Seems the roughest parts are in the valleys, where the rain settled and was able to erode the roadway." I changed the subject. "Hey, I have a question for you."

"Shoot," Samantha said.

I glanced at Tin, who was focused on guiding the ox over the road. He was still green, and a bit jumpy, but the whole caravan needed to know. Secrets can be poisonous.

"Hannah has seen, um… someone watching her." As I expected, Tin tensed a little and glanced over at me before turning his eyes back to the road.

"Trouble?" Samantha asked, her voice laced with trepidation of her own.

"Not sure," I admitted. "These folk have an odd description. Wensem and I don't think they're bandits, or Victory patrols, so I'm not sure if it's anything to worry about. Might have a religious bent to it; figured we'd ask you."

"I told you having a priestess along would prove handy," said Samantha.

I chuckled and ran my hands through my hair.

"What's the description?" asked Tin, his voice cracking as he studied the land around us.

"Hannah said they wore black robes, and they had tall pointy hoods. She's never seen them up close, mind you, always from afar so they're silhouetted against the sky. They watch her from atop a hill or a ridge, but by the time she gets to where they were standing they've disappeared."

"Creepy," said Tin, drawing out the word.

I nodded and looked at Samantha, who had begun to chew the nail on her smallest finger as she thought about it.

"Well, my first assumption would be Reunified road priests, though they don't wear pointed hoods. We can rule out Deepers, Curwenites, and Eibonians as well. None of them go for black," she said. "She's sure the robes were black?"

"Yeah, she saw them five times over a period of three days. Always black, always in hoods, always in the distance, watching, and then—poof—gone." This discussion was even starting to make me a little nervous. Seeing strangers on the road wasn't uncommon, but the actions of Hannah's gargoyles seemed deliberate. The weird costumes and our isolation this far down the Broken Road didn't help.

"Hasturians maybe?" asked Tin. "I have a cousin who converted. He wears robes all the time. His are yellow, though."

"No, it doesn't sound Hasturian. Not wearing black. Also, no hoods," said Samantha her voice distant; thinking. "Interesting."

I waited, but Samantha didn't have any more answers in her. At least not right now.

"Well, if something comes to mind, let me know. I'm gonna pass the word down the caravan. Make sure everyone's keeping an eye out. Could be scouts. If they're bandits, they're funny dressed ones."

I moved to slip off the gearwain when the noise began.

It was a feeling at first. A rumble deep in the earth that quavered up my feet and legs. I could feel it in my knee.

"B-boss," said Tin, his voice cracking.

"What's that?" I heard Samantha say.

It came low, like a deep mechanical hum, but rose into a weird undulating chuckle as it filled the air. It was impossible to tell its origin. It echoed across the rolling hills like thunder.

The sound had a wavery, raspy quality, but several octaves beneath the rasp was a heavier sound, like metal moaning, bending, and then tearing. It rose in waves, growing louder and louder.

The oxen began to bellow.

My ears ached.

It repeated itself over and over, like the beat of some giant chaotic set of drums. I could feel it shaking the ground.

"Hold up!" I shouted at Tin, who was staring upwards at the clouds, eyes wide behind his mask, searching for the source of the impossible sound. I couldn't blame him, but the ox that pulled the gearwain was spooking. If Tin lost control, we could lose the whole column.

Another undulation and tearing sound boomed through the sky. The gearwain rattled.

Panic had started to crawl its way through the company. The lead ox moaned in fear. A bad sign. Oxen aren't the smartest creatures. If we could keep the lead in control, the others would follow. If we lost him, however....

I stood and tried to shout to the column behind the wain. My voice was drowned out by the noise.

"HOLD UP!"

I waved my arms.

The gearwain kept rolling as the sound moved across the sky. I could hear a few screams, tiny in comparison to the titanic sound that echoed around us. I could see the column screaming, but couldn't hear their voices. These were horns from heaven, or the territory splitting in two, or the Firsts returning to re-Align the world.

Turning, I pulled Tin from his seat, sat him down atop a pair of barrels, and took hold of the reins. As I pulled back, another ripple of noise crashed around me. It vibrated up the reins. It quivered through me and settled in my belly, hammering around in some alien pattern. The ox fought me. I leaned back, pressing both feet into the buckboard and feeling pain ripple up from my right knee.

The animal slowed as I seized control.

Then the sound stopped.

Mid-wave, it just ceased.

Silence fell, it flooded the emptiness, as vast as the sound had been. After a few moments a few oxen bellowed. Sound eventually began to dribble back into the world, wind hissing against the pine branches, the warble of a wren from the bushes, the hum of cicadas, and eventually the distant calls of crickets.

"Carter's cross," I heard Samantha curse.

"What was—" Tin began, his voice full of terrified awe.

As the caravan slowed to a stop, a cold trickle of sweat ran down my spine.

SEVEN

When I finally pushed myself upward, I guessed I had slept maybe an hour—two if I was lucky. I felt foggy from the lack of real sleep. Sometime earlier in the night— heart pounding—I awoke gasping and hadn't been able to sleep since. I barely remembered the dream. Something about hooded figures among shadowed ruins, yellow demonic faces peering from fallen monuments. A man in red. Coyotes.

It was still early. The sun hadn't broken the horizon, and the sky was still the bruised purple of pre-dawn. A thick gray early morning fog was slipping quietly into the camp as the air chilled. The caravan smelled of sweaty oxen, Taft's hastily prepared pork shoulder from the previous night, and whiskey.

Some of the crew lingered near the fire at the center of our laager, their bodies silhouetted from the orange glow, engaging in hushed discussion. Others were sitting up huddled beneath their tarpaulins, knees drawn close to their chest, shadowed lumps in the darkness.

Rough night for all of us, apparently.

I rubbed the sleep from my eyes and scratched at the thickening beard on my cheek. I needed a shave. I wondered if Hannah had found fresh water during her scouting the previous night, or if I needed to open a canteen. If it was the latter, I'd skip shaving. Shame to waste fresh water.

You couldn't call the silence over the laager calm. Tensions still ran high, but the silence was preferable to the chaos that had erupted after the noise died away.

You couldn't blame them for their panic. It was frightening.

"It's angels blowing the trumpets of the second coming!" one wain driver said.

"No, it's the Firsts! The stars are right again and they are returning to devour the world! It's the Aligning all over!" shouted another.

"You're all wrong," said Chance Shaler. "It's a Victory weapon being tested beyond the wall. My dad said they had something like that. They're coming for the Territories!"

The more rational members of the party tried to play it off as a natural occurrence; thunder, but that explanation was somehow worse than the others. Nothing natural sounds like that.

I didn't know what to think.

Pulling my gun-belt close, I double-checked that the Judge still rested in the leather. The cold metal touched my fingertips and my thumb played over the hammer. At once I felt my nerves ease. With it I felt safer. I felt in control.

Pushing myself off the ground with a grunt, I strapped my belt around my waist, letting the holster slap against my thigh as I limped closer to the central fire.

Hannah, Taft and Samantha looked up as I approached. Hannah extended a bottle of whiskey, jiggling it slightly.

I took it, and sat down on a log next to Taft. When a caravan rests at laager, the wains are pulled into a circle. Tarpaulins are usually extended inward from the wains, overlapping to form a circle around the central core. At the center, however, a space is always left open for the fire. It makes a nice mobile lodge, and keeps the heat in and the smoke out.

"Trouble sleeping?" asked Samantha. She sat to my right and reached a hand out to rub my back. It was a friendly gesture, but I found myself wishing it was more than that. I could really use someone to lay next to at night. I had lost track of how long it had been.

"Yeah," I said. I considered mentioning the dreams, but I decided to keep them to myself, at least for now. Last thing I wanted them to see was fear.

I took a long pull from the bottle. The liquor rushed down my throat, burning as it went and shocking me out of my grogginess.

I choked, and Hannah laughed.

"Easy, boss," she said. "It ain't your vermouth."

"Shame," I said, clearing my throat.

"Right night to start," said Taft, extending a massive hand towards me.

I passed the bottle to her, and the group sat in silence for a moment as Taft took two long chugs. Two large bubbles traveled up from the neck to the base.

Hannah yawned and took the bottle back from Taft. "I had a hell of a night. Fell right to sleep, but it was a fitful rest. Screwed up dreams," she said, smacking her lips and yawning. "Weird faces. Ruins. Creepy shit. Even if I could get settled down, my dreams kept dragging me away from any rest."

Frowning, my eyes flicked up towards the scout. Dreams, and much like mine. Knowing that she was having similar dreams was unnerving.

"I feel like I walked fifteen miles in my sleep," Hannah added.

Out of the corner of my eye, I noticed Samantha catch my reaction. I met her concerned look and paused for a moment before turning back to Hannah. "I'm sure it's just shock after experiencing what we—"I paused, losing my words for a moment. "Experiencing what we experienced. It's bound to shake all of us, mess us up in the head."

Telling her I had the same dreams would only further increase the tension, and right now it was thicker than the strange autumn heat. I hated lying, but the last thing I needed was my crew losing their nerve over snaps in the brush, or jumping whenever an ox started.

"Right," said Samantha, drawing out the word. I could feel her eyes watching me but refused to meet them.

"You know back in Lovat, when the King Tide comes in and Level Two floods? There's those deep thrums that sound throughout the city?"

Hannah, Taft and Samantha all nodded.

"It's loud as hell, and scary if you don't know what they are. I'd wager that noise is like the King Tide, just a natural occurrence, like thunder. Some fluke meeting of winds from the north and the south working against these clouds and this unusual heat," I said, trying to sound cheerful.

"There was nothing natural about that sound," Taft said, her voice slurred. She had hit the bottle immediately after the sound had ceased hours earlier, and clearly she hadn't stopped since.

"I agree with her," said Samantha. "That was weird, Wal. Very weird, and very wrong. Thunder rolls like a wave, and even the King Tide has a pattern. That sound, it was random, it had no pattern, just that undulating moaning metal...." She shuddered.

"I don't believe in coincidence," Taft said. "We're on the damned Broken Road, Hannah starts spotting shadowy gargoyles on the hills, and then that noise? It's not right. Not natural."

"We're making a lot of assumptions here," I said, though my voice sounded weak in my ears.

"Think it's Victory? Maybe the Firsts?" asked Hannah, looking over at Taft. "I've read prophecies. I've heard the Deeper evangelists on the street corners."

"Whoa, whoa, whoa," I started, taking a deep breath before I tried to find an explanation. "Before we start going there, maybe we should pull it in a little."

"What do you mean?" Samantha asked.

"Well..." I breathed. "Maybe someone is trying to scare us."

"It certainly worked," Samantha said flatly. She crossed her arms across her chest and stared into the flickering flames.

I had no response. I was out of my element. Cougars? No problem. The occasional bandit? Easy. This? I read the clouds, study the road, fix wagons, make sure everyone arrives to their destination safe. I don't thwart monsters... at least, I'm not trying to make a habit out of it.

A silence fell around the fire and we all took turns taking swigs.

Finally Taft drawled. "Look, we're all tired. We're obviously upset. It's a good couple hours before sunrise. Maybe we should try to get some more sleep? The sooner we can get off this damn road and into Lovat, the better."

"Hear, hear," said Samantha, rising and disappearing into the shadows.

"See you in a few hours," said Hannah.

Taft gave me a drunken salute before half-falling towards her bedroll.

I continued to stare into the fire, a solitary figure in the middle of the laager. Sixteen souls. Sixteen people looking to me for leadership. It weighed around my neck.

I repeated my rules to myself:

Keep a distance between yourself and other travelers.

Never stop moving.

Trust no one but your Company.

Rest only for short periods of time.

Never rest in the same place.

Rest.

I needed rest.

For the next few hours of early morning, I existed in a state between sleep and waking, not quite cognizant but also not getting any rest. An uneasy, restless limbo.

When I finally rose, I felt even worse than I had earlier that morning. The camp looked much the same. The sky was brighter now, a moldy blue instead of a deep purple. A lone figure was stoking the central fire, one of Shaler's wain drivers, a dimanian fellow named Rousseau. I could smell bacon sizzling and beans simmering from the direction of Taft's chuckwain. It baffled me that anyone could drink that much and still have the faculties to prepare a meal before I was even alert.

For the second time that morning, and with a heady feeling of déjà vu, I pushed myself up and pulled my gun belt on. I scratched my cheek, yawned, stretched my arms and felt my spine pop. My right knee cracked along with it, a churlish reminder of the past and of the fact that I wasn't a young man anymore. I grunted.

Groggy or not, the lightened sky made things seem better. My stomach growled. I needed about a gallon of coffee and a pile of beans, eggs, and bacon.

The camp was waking around me. Roaders were rolling their bedrolls. A few were laughing and joking as they brushed their teeth with canteen water.

I sought out Taft.

"Morning," I said, sleepily sliding into an empty chair at a folding table. Taft set up a few tables around her chuckwain every morning, noon, and evening.

"Makes it feel like home," she would say as she spread gingham tablecloths. I was always impressed by what she kept in her wain. Changes of clothes, crates of all shapes and sizes, tables, chairs, and enough food to feed our small troop for months if need be.

"You'd be surprised what I keep in here," she would say with a wry grin.

This morning, my greeting got no response. Instead, Taft's wide face peeked around the corner of her wain. She was not grinning. Her face wore the serious expression of someone heavily hungover. She said nothing as she slid a plate of breakfast before me.

I dug into it, eager to fill the pit in my stomach. Three fried eggs, bacon, cheese grits, a hefty helping of pinto beans in a tomato sauce, and of course, one of Taft's enormous biscuits. As always, everything tasted incredible.

The food was a nice escape. I tend to think better with a full belly. I was glad to have a proper chuck. Wensem and I had only hired a few other chuckwains before, and usually the results were disappointing. Their cooking tended to be bland or lazy, their coffee always terrible. Taft was different. Her skill with the griddle was second to none. She could make a mint with a cart in Lovat, and both Wensem and I knew it. The food she had prepared coming east was fantastic, and I was glad when she accepted our offer to return with Bell Caravans when we headed west.

A real hot breakfast goes a hell of a lot farther than three-week-old, weevil-infested hardtack soaked in burned coffee.

Wensem strode up. He was naked, a wet towel draped around his neck and shaving cream suds dripping off his crooked chin. Maero don't go for modesty the way humans, dimanians, or dauger do. Don't see a need for it. The idea of a standard of modesty was bizarre to them. After years on the trail with him, I was used to it, but I doubted Samantha or the Shalers would be.

"You should wear pants when we laager," I said around a mouthful of biscuit. "These are east-territory people. They don't know many maero. Shaler's crew gets all awkward when you stroll past in the morning."

I had expected a joke, or that he'd complain about me giving orders again, but instead, he made a grunt. I looked up.

"What's up?" I asked. Wensem's face was drawn and serious, his long eyebrows were furrowed. He wasn't concerned unless there was something to be concerned about.

He breathed out heavily as he sat in the chair opposite me. "Problems. Ivari Tin is missing."

My appetite disappeared.

"What do you mean, missing?"

"He's not in his bedroll. Not at the camp. Hannah went to fetch him for breakfast and he was gone."

"He ran off?" I asked. I was worried a few of the company would follow suit and head back to Meyer's Falls.

"Doubt it. Boots, bedroll, rucksack, they're all here—he's not. Only thing missing is that scattergun he fancied."

"Maybe he's hunting," I said.

Wensem frowned even deeper. "Who goes hunting naked?"

"Carter's cross," I threw my fork down onto my plate with a clatter. "You sure he's not out taking a crap or something?"

Wensem shook his head sadly. "I'm sure. I circled the laager a few times and didn't see a sign of him. He's missing, Wal."

"By the Firsts," I swore, pushing my breakfast away from me

and rising from the table.

Taft's face poked around the chuckwain. "I hear him right? Ivari is missing?"

I ignored her question. "Wensem, gather everyone up. Shaler, her boys, the twins, Sam, everyone. We'll find him. We have to find him."

Twenty minutes later, the caravan—minus Tin—was gathered. Even Shaler had emerged from her prairiewain to hear my announcement. There were deep circles under everyone's eyes. Unkempt hair. Shoulders slumped. Eyes unfocused. The signs of exhaustion were there.

Wensem was the last to join, standing in the back next to the twins. He had pulled on a pair of brown pants held up by suspenders but neglected a shirt. In the early morning light his skin looked even paler than normal.

"Bad news," I began, letting the words sink in. "We're missing a roader. Our gearwain driver, Ivari Tin, isn't at camp. Everything's here except his shotgun."

Gasps.

Hushed whispers.

I waited.

"Has anyone seen him? Can anyone remember the last time they saw him?"

"I saw him last night," said one of Shaler's crew.

"I saw him at supper," said Rousseau, a thin dimanian with

two large curving horns that sprouted from his forehead.

"Anyone spot him after supper?" I asked, knowing the answer from the eyes that gazed back at me.

Silence.

"Okay. We have a roader missing and we're going to look for him. We'll find him. Tin missing means we're down to fifteen, so we'll split into three parties. Wensem will lead one, myself another, and Hannah the third."

"I scouted around the laager this morning. He's not near the camp. Not at any of the designated latrine sites," added Wensem.

"So he fled, you mean?" said Margret Shaler sourly. "Ran from the noise we heard yesterday."

"Now Maggie, we don't know that either," said Taft.

I could see Shaler's jaw clench and her fists ball at Taft's use of "Maggie."

"No—" I began, slipping in to try and stop an explosion from Shaler. I was interrupted by Wensem.

"I think he's gone. If he ran off he would've taken his gear. As it stands he's not dressed. Left everything behind but his scattergun. Boots, bedroll, rucksack, letters, all of his belongings are here."

"Maybe he killed himself," snickered one of the Lytle twins. The laugh caught in his throat as Wensem smacked him across the head.

"Enough of that!" I ordered, before Shaler could complain. "This is one of our own we're talking about. Let's show him some respect."

"Look, it's clear he couldn't hack it. A bit of thunder and

he flees—back to Meyer's Falls! I've heard similar stories," said Shaler with a sneer. I wanted to slap her. "We don't have time to waste looking, especially for a greenhorn dauger gone truant."

"He left his boots, lady!" said Hannah, her voice heated. "You don't hike any trail, broken or not, without your boots! You don't wander east, west, north or—Carter's bloody cross—south, naked! You expect us to just leave him? You know what? Screw you, lady."

"Hannah," I said, though I was grateful that somebody had said it.

Shaler stared daggers at Hannah for a few moments and then frowned, crossing her arms to stare at me bitterly.

"Look, I'd do the same for any of your crew. My first responsibility is the safety of this caravan. My company and yours. I won't let one of my crew go missing."

The company stared at Shaler, waiting. Finally, she relented.

"Fine. I'll give you one day. One. That's all," she said, throwing up her hands and stomping back to her prairiewain.

"You heard the lady," I said, clapping my hands and focusing on the task at hand. "Let's get to it."

EIGHT

We're not leaving."

I spat at the ground, hoping that emphasized the point.

"Wal," Samantha said, her voice almost a whisper.

"Carter's cross!" cursed Shaler. "Your roader up and left! He left. Fled! Couldn't hack it."

Her words were like a slap in the face, and I hope I didn't flinch. I stared down at the shotgun clutched in my hands. Hannah's group had found it, stuck among some raspberry bushes beneath a jack pine a hundred yards or so from the camp.

It was a bit shorter than a typical shotgun. The barrel was cut down so it would work better from the seat of a wain, and its wooden stock was plated in tin with an engraving in Strutten: To my son Ivari. Protect thyself but only as last resort. Love, Father.

Both barrels were still loaded.

"I gave you your day and another half-day. I spent another night in this damn laager. By my count, we've wasted almost two days on this deserter. Meanwhile, my cargo is rotting! Yesterday we threw out nearly a quarter–wain's worth. We're leaving. Today."

Glaring back at her, my voice rumbled. "Like hell we are."

I could hear her teeth grind as my words came out.

"Wal. Please," Samantha said again.

"You have a job to do," Shaler said.

"We have a roader missing," I said. I wouldn't let this happen again. Not to Ivari. Not to anyone. Memories of Lovat surfaced, poking through my clouded memory like jagged mountain peaks. Thad, Fran, August. Murdered. So many dead. I wouldn't let there be another one. I couldn't.

"We have a contract, Mister Bell."

My fingers tightened around the shotgun, my knuckles pale.

She didn't understand. She was reckless. Ivari looked up to me. I was supposed to keep him safe. Didn't she understand that?

"Wal!" Samantha nearly shouted. She placed a hand on my chest, and I looked down, seeing the spurs that grew along her knuckles.

"What?" I said, not sure what else to do. I felt a wetness in the corners of my eyes, and my voice was louder than it should have been.

"Wal. Step away," Samantha said, her voice kind, but firm.

The tension drove the party to silence. Shaler and I stared at each other, both drawing an unspoken line and daring the other to step over it.

"She's not worth it, Wal," Samantha whispered, gently pushing me back.

Tin's shotgun still clutched in my hand, I let her lead me away. As we moved from Shaler and the stand-off, my arms began to shake.

"Here, sit," said Samantha, easing me down onto a rock next to the smoldering remains of the laager's central fire. I looked past her, seeing Shaler arguing with her own crew before storming off to her prairiewain. She slammed the door shut and my eyes refocused on Samantha. Anger drained out of me like a leaky canteen.

Samantha squatted in front of me and met my eyes. Her dark hair was buried under her keff, but her large brown eyes locked me in.

"You okay?"

I tried to look away. I had lost control.

"Lovat wasn't your fault. You know that, right?"

I blinked, surprised. At once, I felt closer to her than ever, but also naked and exposed. I said nothing.

She leaned close to me. I could smell her. A mix of coffee, incense, road dust, and fresh flowers. "All of it was Peter Black's fault. You had no idea—how could you? He manipulated everyone. You know that. You fixed it."

"But—"

"No. No more. You miss your friends. Fine. You're angry. Okay. You took care of it. You took care of it. It's done."

"I hardly remember doing any of—"

"You took care of it…" said a new voice. Wensem. He stood behind Samantha, his lanky frame silhouetted by the flat gray sky. "…and you saved me and my boy in the process."

He folded his long limbs to squat down next to Samantha.

"You're a good man, you care for your people. Hell, you force yourself to memorize the name of every wain driver and caravan guard in the party, even though your memory is terrible."

I chuckled. It was a pitiful, wet sound, but it felt good.

"Ivari is gone," Wensem said. "I don't like it any more than you."

I envied his calm. His strength. I felt like a failure. I needed to protect my crew, and I had lost one of them.

My mouth dropped open in protest, but Wensem held up a finger. "Wait. No. Close that yapping mouth for a second and listen, dammit. You know he's gone. Logically, you know this. By the Firsts, we're all upset by it, but we did our best, we looked everywhere. He's gone. We could stay here wondering, or we could move on and get out of here before someone else gets abducted."

"You think he was taken?" Samantha asked.

I nodded. The idea had haunted me most of the day. It was the only answer that made sense. Boots here. Gear here. Shotgun taken, probably the only thing he had been able to grab. Whatever had taken him had been efficient and quiet. Hannah's gargoyles were at the top of my short list of suspects. Whatever caused the sound was next. They were probably connected. Wensem was right, we needed to move on.

"Bell Caravans doesn't leave a man behind," I said, but the fight had gone out of me.

"We're not leaving him behind. The trail is cold, there's nothing more we can do," Wensem said, not unkindly. "Our best bet is to press on, and hope we find something to lead us to him later."

"All right," I said, rising and dusting nonexistent dust off my jeans. My mind struggled to come to terms with leaving Tin's disappearance unsolved. "All right."

I turned to face the huddled mass of the caravan company and raised my voice. "Let's pack 'em up! We have half a day of light left, and I'd like to see six miles before the sun sets."

That night, the noise came again.

NINE

Sleep didn't come. I was too restless. I sat under a tarpaulin near the edge of the laager, keeping my eyes off the fire. I wanted them to remain adjusted to the darkness. If someone tried taking any of my people again, I would be able to spot them coming. I'd stop them.

The noise hung in the sky for about half the night. Wavering up from over the hills and cascading across the laager like a demon song. We endured it. The oxen bellowed. Men and women whimpered in their bedrolls. I realized how wrong I had been, suggesting this sound was anything natural, anything like the King Tide. This was much darker.

Eventually the sound died when the green moon hit its apex, its lurid light casting a morose hex over the camp. It deepened the shadows, and made it harder to see what was going on along the periphery.

Bodies moved about with each shift. I started with every cough and scratch. I clasped the handle of my Judge in a white-knuckled grip, its chambers loaded and ready.

The sunrise surprised me. Had I slept? The evening had become a long blur of minutes that melted into each other, creating a knot of time that was difficult to unravel. The morning was eerily quiet compared to the thunderous noise the previous evening. I stalked around the camp, counting the company. One. Two. Three. Four... a spike of panic when I couldn't find the fourth, a sigh of relief when he was found under a pile of blankets. My counting continued. Five, Six... and on until the entire company was accounted for.

No one had fled.

No one had left.

No one had been taken.

I turned and watched a pack of shamblers skulk over the distant hill, my arms hanging down my sides in a subconscious mimicry of their bearing. The pack was moving slowly in the direction of Meyer's Falls. I envied them.

I resumed my patrol around the laager, feeling as mindless as the shamblers seemed. As I passed the chuckwain, Taft stopped me, her mouth downturned in a rare frown.

"You didn't sleep," she said, hands on her immense hips. Wearing an apron, she extended a wooden spatula awkwardly at me, like a small branch from a massive tree.

"I got a little," I said.

She stared at me for a while before asking, "You hungry?"

"Always," I admitted, turning back and mentally counting the company again.

All here.

All minus Tin.

I slept little over the next week and a half. When I did sleep, the nightmares would return. The same images repeated again and again. Yellow demonic faces, hooded figures among shadowed ruins, and always that solitary man in red. Always him.

Days ran into one another. My mind fogged up with lack of sleep; coffee was no longer a luxury, but a necessity. Wheels clunked over rough ill-kept roads and jolted me back into reality whenever I lapsed into unconsciousness. The unusual heat stuck with us, and the sharp cloying scent of weary, sweating bodies hung about in the evenings. This autumn trip felt more like a mid-summer excursion.

I surrendered myself to routine. My nightly vigil. The morning walk around the laager to count the company, making sure all were there and none were taken. The day's steady travel. Repeat.

We had one wain driver run off, a guy named Wilkins. Pot-bellied and big as a barrel, he just jumped off his wain and sprinted away, hollering about the end of the world. Wensem and I had run him down, tackling him, trying to hold him until he calmed down. He bit at us like a wild thing. Raked his claws across Wensem's back, tried to gouge my eyes.

"He has come!" he yelled, his eyes bulging from his sockets, a wide grin splitting his lips. "He has come. He is horrible. Horrible beyond anything you can imagine—but wonderful…."

It hadn't worked. Eventually he thrashed so much that we let him go. Watched him leap up and run off toward Meyer's

Falls. Away from the column, away from his post, away from that awful noise.

"Can't you hear him?" he screamed before disappearing over the edge of the hillside. "He calls to you!"

We shifted duties after losing Wilkins. Samantha offered to take over driving his wain while Wensem took up Tin's duties driving the gearwain at the head of the column. The Lytle twins split their duties between the left and right side. Meanwhile I trudged up and down its length, hobbling between wains, checking on the crew and making sure everyone was awake, alert, had their weapons loaded and was ready for whatever might come.

The noise came and went, splitting the sky and hanging with us like an evening storm, then silencing late in the evening, leaving headaches and frayed nerves. A horrific accompaniment. During the few nights of silence no one mentioned it, afraid that talking about the noise would summon it.

In her scouting, Hannah spotted the hooded gargoyles only twice after Tin's disappearance. Both times more distant, black smudges under pines that vanished when they realized her eyes were on them.

At the halfway point we made camp in the ruins of an ancient town atop a hill. The land here was rolling, dry earth. The beginnings of foothills rose before us in the west. From our perch we were high enough to see the Victory wall to the north. A tidy gray line, etched across the tawny hills. We had been following its path west since Meyer's Falls, running a parallel route just thirty miles to its south.

The noise hadn't come that evening, so the whole company relaxed a little. We circled the wains into laager and made camp.

After a supper of the last of the salt pork and stewed black beans, seven of us sat around the campfire passing a bottle of rye that Hannah had generously offered. Samantha, Taft, Wensem, Hannah, and I were joined by Rousseau, the cargowain driver, and Charron the blacksmith. Unlike previous nights, the conversation came easily. No one wanted to talk about the noise, preferring anything that could serve as a distraction.

"Never seen the wall before," said Hannah. "It's big."

"You should've seen them build the damn thing! Folks came from miles around and watched—from a distance, of course. They had soldiers walking the whole line of it. No one from the south could get close," said Taft.

"You saw it built?" asked Charron, brushing her long hair out of her face. I hadn't had much chance to interact with the hired smithy. She was about my age, mid-thirties. She was mixed-race, human-dimanian her skin the color of coffee with plenty of cream added. Small nubs of horns sprouted from her forehead, elbows, and knuckles, like Samantha, but they were smaller than those of a typical dimanian. She was plain-featured and pleasant. And Carter's cross, was she good with a hammer. It was nice to see her interacting with the rest of the company. I hoped she would work out. A lot of the big importers used iron and steel cargowains, so having a good smith in a caravan meant we could take some of the more lucrative contracts.

Taft laughed. "Honey, I'm old as the damn hills. Yeah, I saw it get built. Hell, I was part of the reason it went up in the first place!"

"You were in the Syringa militia," I surmised. I knew Taft had a good thirty years on me, but I had no idea she had been a soldier. Hadn't pegged her as the type, to be honest.

Taft grunted and pawed at her chin with a thick hand. "A past life. Yes, I was in the Syringan militia. Enlisted when I was just a kid. Wasn't in it very long, mind you."

"Why did you leave?" asked Samantha.

"I was a member of General William Bowles' own brigade. I was at Crowsnest."

"You're kidding," said Rousseau, hissing as he drew his narrow lips together tightly.

"Crowsnest?" asked Samantha, confused. "What's that?"

"Don't they teach you about the Territories in Lovat?" asked Taft with a wide smile.

"Aren't you a professor?" I asked.

Samantha rolled her eyes and punched me in the shoulder. "Religious studies don't include Syringan history. Never heard of Crowsnest."

Hannah chuckled. "In Lovat, we call it Bowles' Folly."

Taft gave the scout a sour expression and put her hand on one of her sizable knees. "Hand me that bottle, Hannah, before I wallop you."

Hannah grinned and passed the whiskey to the cook.

"Before Crowsnest, Victory was a very different place. They

had a standing army, sure, but they were mainly woodsmen, farmers, trappers, and traders. Peaceful enough. There were caravan runs deep into their territory. I'll bet your old man knows companies who did runs through Victory, Wal." Taft nodded at me and passed the whiskey.

I took a swig and nodded.

She continued. "The circuits ran to a handful of small cities, enough they could support trade and keep a few companies profitable.

"Occasionally Victory forces and ours would cross paths and get in a tussle, but overall Victory had little to do with Syringa."

"Victory's capital is Empress," I said, interjecting. "On an island to the north and west, off-shore from Lovat. You can still take a ferry there, though apparently Victory is very careful about who they let in."

"It's the only open port," said Rousseau.

Taft took a swig of the rye and continued. "Syringa has a history of iron rattling. It's the smallest city in the Territories and little more than a trail stop between Hellgate and Lovat. It makes the Syringans ornery. I'd wager their aggression is them trying to assert themselves politically, pretend they're one of the big players."

Hannah chuckled. She never liked Syringa. Born and raised in Lovat, she had a bit of disdain for the smaller city. Referred to them as yokels.

"Well, about thirty-five years ago, Syringa was on the offensive again. Before any of you were born I'd imagine, your company excluded, Wensem."

She nodded at him, and he smiled a crooked smile and nodded back.

"Anyway, I was just a little thing then, skinny as a rail if you can believe it! I was serving in the Syringa militia like my old man did. Even joined the same outfit—Company A, Syringa Militia, under General Bowles."

"So why the aggression?" asked Samantha, her curiosity piqued. She drew her knees up to her chest.

"If I remember correctly, the Syringan Council wanted to claim more land for the city. The valleys controlled by Victory to the north were rich, fertile land. Perfect for farms and ranches, and the mountains were full of mines. I suppose with the land being so close to Syringa and so far from Empress, Syringa didn't see how Victory could really lay claim to it."

"Wasn't Victory an independent nation before the Aligning?" asked Hannah.

Taft shrugged. "Maybe. I don't know much about that. It's just myth and legend to me. All I know is Victory claimed it, and Syringa wanted it. The strategy to claim the valleys centered on Crowsnest."

"Where's Crowsnest?" I asked.

"If it's still around, isn't far from here. It's a border town. Or it was. I suppose that's why I'm gettin' all nostalgic."

"That, and the rye!" Hannah laughed.

Taft waved her off. "About halfway between Syringa and Lovat, then north." She gestured towards the wall. "If a force could take Crowsnest and march north you'd effectively cut Victory in half."

"So, what happened?" asked Samantha, staying on track. "I mean, Hannah said Lovatines call it Bowles' Folly. I assume it didn't end well for Syringa."

"That's putting it mildly. The problem was Crowsnest was an army town and a large garrison was stationed there—a direct assault would have been nearly impossible. So Bowles had this bright idea and he selected Company A to do it.

"Our orders were to wait until dark and sneak close to the barracks. We were given these big grenades, size of a pinecone. We were to throw them inside the buildings, and they were supposed to crack open and begin spilling this white cloud— flood the garrison with gas.

"It was nasty stuff, and it took a few minutes to work right. I can't remember what it was called… but it smelled awful, like swamp water and rot. Knocked you right out, though. Once the majority of the garrison keeled over, Company F would rush in and mop up the remaining forces."

"Chemicals? Bowles used chemical weapons on an enemy?" Samantha eyes were wide and her mouth hung open.

"He did, or at least tried to. Two hundred of us in Company A, bit less in Company B. When the majority of the garrison put in for the night, we snuck in. There was one problem, though," Taft grunted a bitter laugh. "Victory had made masks! They could filter out the chemicals! They'd built them using some old mining equipment. Impressive pieces of equipment and hard to come by, even now.

"So when the grenades crashed through and began to hiss, the soldiers woke and reacted, donning their masks as they were trained.

"Our strategy crumbled after that. Gas hadn't stopped 'em and they knew we were close. It was like kicking a hornet's nest. There was six hundred of them. They swarmed out of the barracks, wildly pissed."

"By the Firsts," said Rousseau, leaning in.

Taft took another swig before continuing. "We fled! Bowles at the head of the retreat. He didn't even issue an order, just hightailed it on his ugly ol' mare.

"Company B saw this all happen and off they were, too," Taft snapped her fingers. "Disappeared into the woods, and we didn't see them again. The Victory garrison ran us down. Killed more than half of the company."

Taft frowned. Charron gasped and covered her mouth with a hand.

"How'd you escape?" I asked.

Taft picked up a stick and poked at the embers of the fire. In the distance, coyotes howled. It was an oddly pleasant sound. She looked up at the group and finally shook her head.

"Let's just leave it as 'I got away.' I didn't return to the militia after that. A lot of soldiers didn't. Not that it mattered much. Syringa was lucky and they knew it. Those of us who ran weren't hunted down as deserters or anything. They knew Victory could've steamrolled them, and most of their militia was dismantled.

"Instead of all-out war, though, Victory went the opposite way. Began to withdraw. The caravan routes were cut off, then their army set up defenses all along the border and began building that wall. Only took them three years, if you can believe it. Thousands of them, crawling along the border. Pouring cement under guard by a legion of soldiers day and night."

"So did Syringa just pull back and lick its wounds?" asked Samantha.

"Pretty much. They sued for peace. Begged for forgiveness. Which Victory gave them, though any chance at an allegiance was impossible. Not sure what happened to Bowles. I heard he might've gone to Lovat, but who knows? It was a long time ago. If Bowles is still around, he'd be pushing eighty-five, maybe ninety." Taft shrugged and took a final swig before handing it back to Hannah.

"That's a hell of a story," Samantha said, leaning back.

"It was a long time ago," Taft smiled and looked at me. "I'm beat. I'm going to turn in, we have a lot of miles ahead and a peaceful night's sleep is too rare to pass up these days."

TEN

S omeone's coming," Hannah hissed, jerking me from sleep.
I bolted upright. Sleep cleared from my head almost instantly.
My scout stood at the foot of my bedroll, the light of morning
silhouetting her against the sky.

"Let's go," I said, rising and pulling the Judge from its holster.
I padded barefoot and shirtless following Hannah.

We stopped a few paces outside the circle. She pointed. In
the distance I saw a shadow. Large, black, a pointed hood that
swayed as it moved. A chill ran down my back and I shivered in
the early morning warmth. Was this one of the gargoyles? It had
to be.

"Where's your spyglass?" I asked, knowing Hannah kept the
contraption close at hand at all times.

She handed it over.

"Hard to see details in this light, but it's moving in this direction."

I stuffed the Judge into my waistband and brought the
spyglass to my eye.

Hannah was right. The brightness of the late morning cast

the stranger as a black smudge on the horizon. Difficult to make out—a dark pointed shape, nothing more. It wasn't moving quickly, but it was growing larger and coming this way.

"Check the camp," I said. "Count the company. Make sure we're all here, and get everyone armed."

Hannah said nothing, but moved off to follow my orders. After a few beats I could hear her rousing the laager.

Shaler appeared beside me like a specter. I was so intent on watching the approaching figure that I jumped. If Shaler noticed, she didn't say anything.

"What's going on?" she said, her voice heavy with sleep.

"Maybe trouble, hopefully nothing."

I pointed with the spyglass towards the figure moving in our direction. "Someone's coming."

Shaler raised a hand to shield her eyes from the light and squinted. "A gargoyle?"

"Not sure, it's tough to see. From this distance a man can look wain-sized. Its shape does match Hannah's description. It could be one of the strangers or it could be nothing."

"Do we stay here?" she asked.

"Yes. It's easier to defend ourselves up on this hill if there's trouble."

Shaler looked over her shoulder at the camp, her blonde hair whipping around and catching the light. My old man liked to say that time mends all wounds, and it seems he was right. Tensions had eased between Shaler and myself, at least for the time being. Sometime in the past week and a half, since Tin's disappearance, something between us had settled. We began to tolerate one another. There was some unspoken understanding. It had almost become pleasant.

"I'll have the Lytles arm my drivers," said Shaler, her icy blue eyes meeting my own briefly. She tucked a loose strand of hair over her ear as she glanced away. "Let me know if I can do anything else."

"You have enough weapons for that?"

"No."

"Wensem might have a few extra. Talk to him. Tell him I said to hand over anything we can spare, he can come find me if he has questions."

She nodded, turned, and left. No argument.

Hannah reappeared, filling the spot Shaler had just abandoned. We stood in silence, watching the swaying point of the hood.

"Everyone safe?"

"Don't know about safe, but we're all here. Word is spreading. Wensem is moving to that hill over yonder with his rifle." Hannah pointed to another shorter hill to the north and west of where we stood. A patch of raspberry bushes clung to the base of a stand of lodgepole pines. It was a good hiding spot. I handed back her spyglass.

We watched the approaching shape. After a while Hannah said, "Way I see it, this can go one of two ways. If it's just another traveler, you'll follow custom and be curt and quiet. If it's one of them hooded gargoyles, I reckon there might be a world of trouble."

I didn't respond.

"I'll keep an eye out," Hannah said after a couple more minutes of silence. "Go get your boots and a shirt on, boss. No one will take you seriously half-naked, even with that gun. Whoever that is, they're still an hour or so out. Grab some food. You've got time."

"Thanks," I said, and walked back into the center of the laager to my bedroll along the north edge of the camp. I found my boots and gun belt beside it; next to my undershirt, my faded black flannel, and my old jacket. I slipped the Judge back in its holster, then pulled on my shirt, stuck my feet in my boots, and pulled up my suspenders before draping my gun belt about my waist.

The nightmares had returned the previous night. I could still feel them as foggy, distant memories. But, unlike the days before, I hadn't woken up. Either I was growing used to the dreams, or exhaustion had overwhelmed any fear I had felt.

Sleep, good or not, had been needed. That morning, under the bright gray sky, my head felt clearer than it had in almost two weeks. I was nervous, but I was thinking straight.

Samantha approached me with a plate of bacon, beans, and runny eggs. She was wearing her brown trousers and a light jacket. Her keff was pulled up, covering most of her hair, stopping just shy of covering the horns that grew from her temples.

She greeted me with a nod. Samantha slept opposite from me at laager, on the far southern side near Taft's chuckwain and the mountainous woman herself. I wanted to suggest that she move camp nearer me, but couldn't figure out a decent excuse.

"That for me?" I asked as the scent of breakfast filled my nose and made my stomach grumble. I knew I should eat, but all I could think about was the approaching figure. My stomach, however, felt otherwise

"Taft said you'd be hungry."

It was already warm that morning, so I skipped my over-shirt. Instead, I wrapped my own gray keff around my neck, wearing it as a scarf for the time being. The light cloth fabric was a staple of most roaders' wardrobes. On the rolling plains, sunstroke could be as dangerous as lack of water or exhaustion, but just a little fabric kept you cool and the sweat out of your eyes. Even with the thick cloud cover, I was sure I'd use it before the day was out. The heat wasn't about to break.

Forcing myself, I took the plate from Samantha and mindlessly began to eat.

"Thanks," I said through a mouthful of food.

"Think it's trouble?" she asked, looking westward in the space between two cargowains to where Hannah nervously rocked on her heels as she stood watch.

"Not sure," I admitted. "Looks like the strangers Hannah's been seeing."

"I find it interesting that after the one night we don't have that noise rumbling overhead, someone is paying a visit. If it's Hannah's gargoyles, it seems weird they'd approach us now. Is it a coincidence?" asked Samantha as she chewed on the nail of her smallest finger.

"Maybe. Would be an awfully strange one."

"I wish I had my books. There's something here, there has to be. Something we're missing."

I shoveled a spoonful of beans and half a piece of bacon into my mouth and tilted my head. "Something religious?"

Samantha shrugged. "If not religious, at least historical. Hagen might know without looking it up."

Hagen Dubois was Samantha's wild-haired, single-horned, skinny older brother. He ran a religious curiosity shop back in Lovat. He was a good man and an even better friend.

"Be nice to at least find some evidence of that noise. It's so frustrating."

"What about the book you have with you now? Does it say anything?"

Samantha shook her head. "A Treatise on the Writings of Keziah? Very little. It claims to be a commentary on the Aligning, but it's nothing but spotty drivel. A madwoman's scrawl. It has a few passages on the Firsts, but nothing on strange hooded creatures. Most of her work was focused on 'the coming change.' It's widely believed that is the Aligning, though some Scholars have suggested it could be some future calamity we haven't seen yet."

"You've been hauling it around since Lovat. Why bring it?"

She smiled weakly and shrugged. "Been wondering that myself. I've been doing research on another cult that is believed to be operating in the Territories. It's strange stuff. At the seminary we've been referring to them as the "Nameless." They're mentioned a lot in some early pre-Aligning manuscripts, but they don't have a name. They operate in secret, pulling strings and manipulating the population for some unknown end. Keziah mentions them a few times."

"Sounds dark," I said.

She shrugged. "It's all legend and myth. Nothing concrete. They're not like the Children cultists we faced last year."

"Oh, well, that's a relief," I said, wondering if it was. Were they really only myths?

She ignored me. "I am supposed to teach a course on Aligning prophecies next spring, and Keziah's writings are a good example of pre-Aligning texts. I was hoping it'd do double duty for my research and my course prep."

Hannah approached, interrupting our conversation. It couldn't have been a whole hour already.

"What is it?" Samantha asked, her tone apprehensive.

"Good news!" Hannah said, cracking a smile. "It's not one of the strangers."

"It's not?" Samantha and I said in unison.

"Nope, you'll love this. It's one of yours, Sam. A Reunified. A road priest."

The crew huddled together along the western edge of the laager. I looked towards the raspberry bushes where I knew Wensem was hiding. I considered sending someone to fetch him, but figured an insurance policy would be useful. Just in case Hannah was wrong, or if this was some tricky bandit masquerading as a benevolent man of the cloth. I've seen crazier things on the road.

It made sense that Hannah and I had suspected it to be one of the hooded gargoyles. It was a small building built onto a wain with a tall pointed steeple. The cart rolled towards us, pulled by a pair of skinny oxen that looked older than the mountains behind them. As its wheels turned slowly over the uneven ground, the steeple swayed drunkenly, as if stumbling towards us. A haphazard red cross was painted on the front, big and bold.

Road priest chapels vary greatly. Usually there is enough space for four or five, and a small room at the front that served as bedroom, confessional, and pulpit. Larger, less mobile chapels could seat small congregations and often held normal service hours. Chapelwains such as this one were designed to move from road town to road town, caravan to caravan, spreading rust wine and the message of the Reunified good book.

"Ho there!" called the lone driver in common Strutten. He raised a gloved hand in greeting. He was a skinny, bent, human man dressed in thick brown robes and a wide-brimmed hat that covered his face in deep shadows; the typical road priest attire.

"Ho there fellow travelers! Fellow roaders! Caravaneers! Ho there! Saint Christopher's Blessings! The Lord's Blessings! Greetings! Greetings! Greetings!" He shouted as he pulled back on the reins to slow his oxen and bring his chapelwain to a stop. His voice had a singsong quality to it, and his Strutten was laced with an accent I couldn't place.

"Greetings, road priest," I said, stepping forward. "Strange road to find a man of the cloth."

"Is it?" The little old man frowned and bobbed his head, causing the brim of his hat to flap. It was still difficult to make out his features. He slipped effortlessly from the seat of his wain and walked alongside one of his oxen, patting the animal's meaty haunches. As he got closer, his face emerged from the shadows. Deep lines broke around his eyes and under his swarthy cheeks. His eyes were dark with large pupils, the whites tinged a slight yellow, an early sign of jaundice.

"Strange roads are as full of sinners as the unstrange. I'd say every road is worthy of a priest. Wouldn't you?"

There was a tension in his voice that made me pause.

"You come from Colby? Lovat?" I asked.

"No, no." The road priest shook his head. "Neither . I was up in the northwest corner, near the wall, then I crossed down towards the south and found this road. I didn't expect to see another soul for a few weeks."

He looked over his shoulder back the way he came, then turned back, his eyes slightly wide, shifting.

He's terrified, I realized. His joviality is all an act.

"Margaret Shaler, Shaler Ranch. Pleased to meet you, father," Shaler said, interrupting. She stepped forward, offering a slim hand to the road priest. "This is my caravan. We're from Hellgate, by way of Syringa, and Meyer's Falls. Our final destination is Lovat."

It was a breach of trail etiquette. When underway, roaders don't like shaking hands with strangers. With your hand grasped by someone else, it's too easy to put yourself at the mercy of a bandit. It's a very simple way to get yourself stabbed or kidnapped. We bow, wave, size each other up, and share a drink or two before we ever decide to shake hands. We also don't offer details upfront. As the rules say: Trust no one but your company.

It was obvious the road priest had ignored most of her

rambling. He sighed and studied Shaler's extended hand, then looked up at her face before sighing again and grasping her hand in a firm shake. "First time on the road, Miss Shaler?"

His tone was one of chastisement, friendly mockery. Shaler's skin flushed as she gave him a tight, bitter smile. I wondered if she wasn't preparing to bite his head off.

"I'm Jeremiah Norry, Reunified Priest of Saint Christopher's Road Chapel," he said. "I'm afraid I don't have a city I hail from, as I hail from the very road itself. It's a pleasure to meet someone so friendly for a change. Roaders can be an awful suspicious lot." He looked at the rest of the crew with mock-mischievousness, and I wondered if they could even see his expression under that big hat of his.

"What can I do for you fine folks? I can take confession inside Saint Chris', or if you want, I can offer thirsty souls a taste of my rust wine! Best in the north it's said, yes, it is!

"Or if the sintalk isn't something you're keen on, you can take a load off in the chapel and we can just straight talk. Though I'm afraid I only have room inside for a handful of you. Less than that if that big lass joins us," Father Norry said, eyeing Taft, who lingered at the edge of the group.

"I'll remain behind," Taft said, doing little to hide the edge in her voice.

"I'd like a sip of that wine, boss, but I need to get eyes on our trail," said Hannah, slapping me on the back.

I nodded and looked over my crew. "The rest of the caravan has plenty to do as well, so maybe just a cup of wine for the crew, unless someone wants confession."

Hannah looked over her shoulder. Charron raised her hand, as did both the Lytle twins. I figured the two of them had plenty of sin to confess.

"Well, let me fetch the bucket and y'all can drink while I hear confession," said Norry, disappearing into his chapelwain. He reappeared moments later, clutching a massive iron bucket in his gloved hands. A steel ladle clanged against the side as he moved down the steps in a waddle.

"As the savior before me, please allow me to give you weary souls the gift of wine," Norry said with a grunt. He sat the bucket on a small platform that unfolded from the side of the chapelwain and ladled out the homemade wine for the company.

"I'll leave you all to it," said Norry. He looked at Charron. "Come, lass, I'll hear your confession first while these hooligans drink my wine."

Once confessions had been made and each roader had their fill, Norry reappeared outside his small chapel. I finished up issuing orders to a few wain drivers and turned to face him as he approached. "Now let's trade stories like proper road folk. We can talk inside Saint Chris' if you'd like."

I wasn't too keen on stepping foot inside a chapel. I shook my head. "Let's stay out here."

Samantha was also suspicious of the old priest. While he had been talking to the twins, she had approached me.

"I don't trust him," she said, glancing backward.

"You think he's legit?"

"Oh, he's a road priest. He's just hiding something. You see the way he looks around? He's always looking west, back the way he came. Down the Broken Road."

"Yeah, I noticed," I said as the door to the chapel swung open and Norry followed the Lytles out.

Only eight of us now remained around the chapelwain. Father Norry, the Shalers, Samantha, Charron, and myself; the rest of the crew had returned to their various duties. It was already midday, so we likely wouldn't be moving until the following morning.

"Out here suits me just fine," said Norry. He lowered himself onto a set of fold-out steps that hung off the rear of the chapelwain. "We can stay out here. How do you like my rust wine?"

"It was good," Chance Shaler said, nodding stupidly. Another gaffe. The proper response for the gift of road wine is something like "Thank you father, may it be a blessing unto me." It's something real churchy. Honestly, I never get it right, but I certainly don't say "It was good."

Norry smiled weakly at him and seemed to study him for a long time. "This your first time on the road as well, son?"

"It is," mumbled Chance. He looked down sadly.

Norry smiled warmly, ignoring the mistake. "What's your name?"

"Chance Shaler."

"Ah, are you two siblings, then?" He looked from Shaler to Chance and then back again.

"Cousins," Shaler corrected.

"And who are you two? " asked Father Norry, looking at Samantha and then at me.

"I'm Samantha Dubois," said Samantha, the normal sweetness in her voice absent. I wondered if something about the priest's mannerisms bothered her. It was curious that she left off her Priestess title. She let her words hang there, as if she expected some recognition.

"I'm Waldo," I said. "Waldo Bell."

"Ah, it's your name stenciled on that wain outside?" asked Norry. "This your outfit?"

I nodded. "My caravan company. Miss Shaler's goods and cargowains."

"Seems like a fine group of souls. A fine group," Norry said, nodding. "I'm heading to Syringa myself, see if God's word needs teaching there. Though it's hard to find anywhere bereft of sinners in this age. It's all deplorable. Folks worshiping monsters, fish gods, squid, and then there's those Hasturians." He paused and flicked his eyes around at all of us. "You're all fine Reunifieds aren't you?"

Everyone but me nodded and mumbled yeses.

"Good, good." His voice grew thin for a moment and he seemed to be thinking about something. "You're headed to Lovat, you said?"

Shaler jumped in before I could respond. "Right. We were late heading out of Syringa. Got caught up in the traffic waiting for the Grovedare span to open up."

"It's closed?" He glanced at me and Samantha and chuckled awkwardly. "I am sorry for my ignorance. The northern territory is a wild and rough place. Few telegraph offices and no telephones. I've been on the trail for six, no... seven months. I have hardly seen a living—yes, a living soul."

Why had he paused at the word "living"? I was certain he was hiding something now.

"Well," Shaler said. "Lovat and Syringa occupy each side. A standoff ensued and they closed the bridge and all traffic along the road. It has mucked things up considerably in Syringa, as you can imagine."

"Well!" said Norry with a chuckle. "I am glad I decided not to take the Big Ninety! So which route have you come by then? Hmmm?"

"We pulled north up to Meyer's Falls and made crossing there."

"How was the crossing? Esther and Elisha—my oxen—aren't as strong as they used to be."

"It's dry. Little more than a trickle," I said. Norry was an odd duck, but I had met more eccentric road priests. The call of the cloth often attracts the strangest people.

"Ah good, good. What else of your journey?" Norry leaned forward, and I could smell the rust wine on him. I wondered if that was because he made it himself, or if he had done some imbibing along with the crew.

And underneath that, there was another scent, something I couldn't place.

"Well, things were quiet enough at the beginning," said Shaler. "Then a few weeks back, Bell's scout started seeing strange figures in the hills, and in the evenings, we began hearing bizarre loud noises."

"N-noises? What kind of noises?" asked Norry. His voice wavered.

"Strange noises, father," said Chance. "Ain't heard anything like them before. Sounds like a cross between bending metal and a… barking laugh."

Norry shuddered. His hands fidgeted.

Chance continued. "It's horrible. It followed us for a while, some nights lasting a scant few minutes, others lasting hours."

"We lost a roader as well," I said.

Norry blinked and whipped his head from Shaler to me. "A soul l-lost? Oh my, oh my. Oh, Saint Christopher p-protect him. What happened?"

"It was the first night the noise came," I explained. "The sound lasted well into the evening. The next morning, when we woke, one of our wain drivers was missing, a dauger named Ivari Tin. We found his boots, his shirt, even his shotgun, but he was nowhere to be seen."

Norry crossed himself and shook his head. "Poor boy. Poor, poor boy." He mumbled a prayer to himself.

"I—" he began, pausing to collect himself. "—I must admit, I meant it when I said I hadn't expected to see a caravan until I was closer to Meyer's Falls. Not with this road's reputation. I figured I could risk it. Road priests are welcomed by most anyone, bandit and butcher alike. Others, though…"

He looked off towards the rear of the small chapel as his voice drifted off.

"Others though, what?" I asked, wondering if he'd spin the same tale Berk and Agata had told me back in Meyer's Falls.

"Have you heard of Methow?" Norry asked, his voice cracking. He knotted his thick-knuckled hands together as he asked the question. There was fear in his eyes. This must have been what he had been hiding. I leaned forward.

"Should we have?" asked Shaler.

"This isn't the same stories of roving cannibal packs is it?" said Samantha. It was clear she chose her words carefully. "We heard those tales between Syringa and Meyer's Falls."

"Cannibals? No. No! Worse than that. Much worse," he said. Norry looked small in his road priest robes. He blinked. I wondered if he was fighting back tears.

"I just came from there. It's not far; few days to the west in a valley at the base of the mountains. Sits below an old copper mine in the hills. The Kadath, I believe it's called. You can see the headframe from the town, if you know where to look."

"Headframe?" slurred Chance, interrupting.

"The mining tower."

"And what of it?" said Chance, leaning forward, his eyes as big as saucers.

"It's h-hard to explain," Norry stammered, shaking now. His robes rustled around him. "I hadn't seen anything like it. Haven't ever seen so much... so..." His voice broke again. "...I f-fled, headed east, away from that evil place."

"What did you see, father?" I asked, a bit more firmly. If there was trouble ahead, we needed to know.

"I guess there's no easy way about it," the priest said more to himself than the group. He forced a weak smile and took a deep breath before continuing. "I saw a forest. A forest of the dead. A forest of bodies, impaled on stakes. Crucified on crosses. Hundreds, maybe thousands of them. I smelled the rot before I saw them clearly. I didn't dare approach. It's like nothing I've ever seen before. Like the town's population just… went mad… and began killing each another. Men. Women. Children. All ages. Naked, impaled. I couldn't bear it. When I r-realized what I was seeing… I fled." He sniffled. "What could I d-do? What could I say to a town that did such awful things to people?"

I looked at Shaler, who stared silently at the priest, her jaw set. I turned to Samantha, who looked both shocked and intrigued. I could tell she wanted to poke and probe at this story. See if it fit, if it was true. I did as well. It couldn't be true. It was more roader tales, right?

"You're sure it wasn't some ruse?" I asked, now understanding what Agata and Berk had mentioned earlier. A forest of the dead. If what Norry said was true, it wasn't a fantasy of some ghost-haunted forest, but a mass of actual crucified dead.

"I had been there before! To Methow. Just a few years ago! They were lovely, honest God-fearing men, maero, and dimanian. Working the land and laughing at the stories told about their old road. It's the thing I love about the northern towns. Fearless and hearty. Now…" Norry's voice trailed off and he began to weep into his gloved hands, his shoulders shaking in heavy sobs.

Samantha stepped closer and squatted next to him, looking at me as she reached out a hand to comfort the old fellow. Her face was drawn, the muscles around her lips tight.

Norry looked up, starting at her touch. "I was scared. I was so s-scared. I should have stayed. I should have pulled them all down and administrated last rites. Buried them like good Reunifieds. That is my duty as a priest. Instead, I ran. I left them hanging there. Their bodies bloating in the sun; food for the ravens and the buzzards."

"You did what any sane person would have done," said Samantha.

"M-maybe," Norry said weakly. He wiped his nose with the back of his hand. "I didn't take the cloth to be sane. I took it to do what's right."

He looked up, focused on each of us in turn, his yellowing old eyes filled with tears.

"Please turn back," he said. "Don't go the way I just came."

"We can't," Shaler said, almost too quickly. My stomach turned.

"You must!" Norry pleaded, reaching out and gripping one of Shaler's hands. She recoiled slightly at the old priest's insistence.

"We can't. There are clients waiting and orders to fulfill."

"Orders? Damn your orders! Are orders worth your lives?" Norry nearly shouted, turning to address us all. "Y-you can't go on, don't you see? We can't be out here. None of us should be out here. The road ahead is not meant to be traveled by living souls. It is a wicked place. Condemned. God is not here. God has long abandoned this road. God has long abandoned us."

Samantha tensed visibly.

Norry continued. "It's true what they say about this road. The Broken Road is gone. God has forsaken it, just as he has forsaken Methow. It is no longer a place of God." He met my eyes. "It is a place of perdition."

ELEVEN

A warm rain started to fall in the heat of the late afternoon. It would make the coming evening muggy and unpleasant. The caravan watched the road priest's chapel wobble away, casting its long, pointed shadow before it as the sun set. Eventually the crew scattered, leaving just Shaler and me standing vigil. The diminishing form of the chapel crested a hill and disappeared on the other side, heading east. Away from Methow. Away from the scene that had so tormented the terrified old priest.

"What a wainload of bullshit," Shaler said. She shook her head and sighed. "I wonder if he really thinks that story works on people?"

I was still sorting out my feelings. The rational Waldo Bell didn't believe the story, but something else inside of me did. It was strange. I tell myself I don't believe in the Firsts, I don't believe in gods or demigods, or any of that. It serves little use for me on the trail; it doesn't put food in my company's belly or boots on our feet. So why was I struggling with old Norry's tale?

It sounded like the sort of scene you'd see in a horror picture.

Hundreds of impaled and crucified victims left exposed to the elements. Like a warning. I shuddered again just thinking about it. My mind had gone immediately to Tin. Would we find him hanging among those bodies?

When I didn't respond, Shaler turned and looked at me with a sour expression. "It's foolishness. Just a drunk old man, driven mad from years on the road. He spends too many nights dipping into that rust wine."

I looked at her, seeing the hardness in the angles of her face. I blinked. It was difficult to tell what she wanted. For once, I had no response. Was I supposed to tell her everything was all right? That we'd find nothing on the road ahead? That Norry made up the tale? I couldn't answer that.

Memories of Lovat nipped at my heels. Specters of dead friends haunted the halls of my past. August, bright eyes behind his nickel mask. Tad's wide shrewd features drawn in quiet contemplation as he studied an interesting pair of spectacles. Fran's smile as she brought her flute to her lips and began to play. I had inadvertently pulled them into a scheme that had resulted in their deaths. What right did I have to lead another group of souls into the unknown?

My feet felt frozen. I was unable to move. If the priest was right…. The thoughts playing through my head for the last hour felt foreign to me. So wrong. It was hard to imagine I was really thinking it.

You should have never left Lovat. You aren't fit to lead. You need to turn around. Return to Syringa and wait out the closure. You have to run.

It was true. Accepting that made it clear to me. I didn't deserve leadership. Now more than ever, I wanted to turn around and go back. Too much. This was all too much.

I should have turned around when the noise, that awful moaning howl of rusty laughter ripped the sky. We should have stopped. Even when I had lost someone else, lost Tin—a member of my company—I had pressed on. Then came the priest with his tale of a forest of bodies. Would I listen to this last warning, or would I ignore it as well?

You want to run. I did. I did want to run. The thought reverberated through me. My chest felt hollow.

Shaler studied me, waiting for a response.

"We should go back," I said. The words stumbled out of me, my voice flat. Fear overwhelmed any guilt I had over abandoning Tin. I ignored the fact that I was leaving one of my crew behind.

Shaler sneered and stepped back, sizing me up.

Just leave. Leave me to my thoughts; let me figure out a way out of this, I thought.

"You, too?"

I stared back. Said nothing.

Shaler sighed. "You know, I'd expect this from Chance. He's young and stupid. I don't expect it from my caravan master."

Her tone was cold and her words sharp. But she didn't understand. Didn't know what I knew, hadn't seen what I had seen.

She was deaf to the warnings all around us. She existed in a world she only thought she understood, and she would lead us to ruin.

I had to fix this. It wasn't just the caravan or our livelihood that was in danger, it was our lives as well.

Swallowing, I stepped forward, raising my hands in a pacifying gesture. I needed to calm her down. We were on the other side of the big river that divided the Territories. We could push south. There were no roads, but we could make them. It would take time, but better a month or two than facing whatever was on this road. It would be better than risking our lives.

"No. We're not turning around, we're not going back. We're not getting off this road. We're going to move on. Press forward. We'll prove the tales are a bunch of bullshit, we'll blow past Methow—if it even exists—and press forward into Lovat. Simple as that."

"Miss Sha—" I began, the words catching in my throat before they slipped away from me. Something had cracked. And I fell through.

A monster had awakened. A writhing, gibbering, creature from ages past. A hideous yellow thing. Tentacles, eyes. A horrible beak that snapped as it thrashed about. I had been telling myself I didn't believe in the Firsts. Yet… I had seen one. Seen one with my own eyes.

Until this moment, my memories of the incident at Lovat had been foggy. Tin's disappearance had thinned the ice. Father Norry had cracked it. Something about the priest had cut through the fog. The fear that bubbled up from my conversation with Shaler had triggered something. A deluge. Clarity. I could remember what I had seen in that tunnel.

"I need to take a piss." Shaler interrupted my thoughts. "Get the camp in gear and pull yourself together. Tomorrow morning, I expect us to wake and move on. If you try to sow discord among my crew, so help me, I will see you and your company tried and all your assets seized for breach of contract."

She didn't ask if I understood. She didn't wait for a response. Her shoulder collided with mine as she brushed past me towards the camp. I turned and watched her go, long blonde braid whipping behind her as she stomped past Taft, her cousins, and Wensem.

Once she left, I crumpled. Slumping backwards onto the wet grass, I held my head in my hands. I felt overwhelmed. Cybill thrashed around in my head. Wensem's bloodied face seemed to rise up in the darkness. I could hear the thrum of ancient machinery, the low chanting of the cultists, and the clip of Black's hooves. It was difficult to breathe.

"Pull yourself together, Bell," I said.

A year ago I would have told you I didn't believe in the Aligning, or the Firsts either. But the tunnel... what I saw in the tunnel told me otherwise.

As if on cue, the noise suddenly returned. It roared its howling metal moan and filled my ears. Just like before. That creature vast and titanic. The hill shook with its thundering, and underneath it all I could hear the muffled shouts and cries of terror welling up from my company and the oxen beginning to panic.

"Not again," I said. "No. Not again. Not now. Not now!"

I lay back into the grass on the hillside and covered my ears, forced my eyes shut, squeezing them so tight they hurt. I shouted at the sky, "Not this! Not now! Please not now!"

The twisting, writhing, yellow form of the beast in the tunnel flashed in my mind's eye. Faces of dead friends flickered. A year ago they were living, breathing, people. People with families, jobs, hopes and dreams... and now?

Those who remained in my company were still alive. Terrorized by this endless roaring sound, but alive. They all had families, jobs, and hopes and dreams of their own.

It meant abandoning Tin to turn around and go back, or pressing on and risking more missing, more dead. What else could I do?

This was a mistake.

I realized it then. It was a mistake to leave Lovat. To take the contract and head north. It was a mistake to lead my company down this old Broken Road and leave the safety of Syringa for the unknown.

I had always known that there was something wrong about this trail and I had doomed us all.

TWELVE

How I slept with that awful noise, I have no idea. Early the next morning, confused and groggy, I awoke. I was lying in the grass near where I had fought with Shaler. I couldn't remember falling asleep. My body ached and a headache drummed away behind my left eye.

Above, a formation of geese cut the slate sky as they honked their way south. I could hear the rattle of pots and pans and smell the campfire scents of burning cottonwood and bubbling coffee.

The morning light was languid and shallow. Everything felt fuzzy and foreign, like waking from a whiskey drunk.

The world slowly sharpened as I pushed myself off the wet ground. I stretched a bit of the stiffness out of my back before I began hobbling towards the laager.

My knee was tight, and it pulsed and ached as I walked. My back felt sharp and there was a soreness in my thighs. Probably wasn't the smartest decision to sleep out on the cold ground.

Coffee sounded good. Coffee to wipe away the fog that gripped my head. Coffee and a plate of eggs, and maybe a pound or two of bacon. My thoughts lost to food, it took me a few more steps before I noticed the sound of a small commotion.

Stepping between two cargowains, I emerged on a hectic scene. People milled about with looks of concern on their faces. They spoke in hushed tones. Guns were drawn, and rifles rested on shoulders. Samantha was the first to spot me, and she shouted in relief before rushing over.

"Oh! Thank God! Wal! Where have you been?" She asked, wrapping me in a tight hug.

That was unexpected. It felt good. Warm.

"Sorry…" I paused, looking over my shoulder. "…I fell asleep outside the camp last night."

Samantha pulled away, and looked at me with those beautiful dark eyes. I smiled sheepishly and felt my cheeks warm before I looked away. She pulled my face back with a narrow finger, studying me for a moment before smiling, an expression of relief flashing across her face.

"We were so worried."

"Why?" I asked, confused. I rubbed at my temples, trying to relieve the headache. The same nightmares had haunted my sleep. The faces in the ruins, the man in red.

"Margaret Shaler is missing," Samantha said, her voice faint. "We thought you were gone as well."

That snapped me into reality.

"Shaler's missing?" I asked, blinking at her.

Samantha nodded. "Her stuff is all here, but she's gone."

My stomach twisted over. My fears from the previous night welled up.

"Just like Tin," I mumbled to myself.

"Taft saw her head down the hill last night. Said she saw you arguing, and then she marched off. No one's seen her since."

"Damn it." I should have been more upset, but my head was too fuzzy. "I don't remember falling asleep. The noise came, and now..."

"You too?"

"What do you mean 'you too?'" I asked.

"Everyone slept, despite the sound. None of us remember falling asleep, just waking. That's when we noticed you and Margaret were missing. Her crew is pretty panicked."

Taft and Wensem detached from the group and moved to where Samantha and I stood.

"I knew we'd find you," said Taft.

"Shaler's missing," Wensem said flatly, rubbing an eye with the heel of one of his seven-fingered hands. He frowned down at me.

"Sam told me. How's her crew?"

"Scared," said Taft. "But can you blame them?"

"We need to organize a search party immediately," I said. In the back of my mind, I knew it would turn up nothing, just like the search for Tin. But I felt obligated to try. Regardless of how we got along or how I felt about the woman, her safety was my responsibility.

"Hannah is working on that now," said Wensem. "Same as last time, three groups, circling in opposite directions, spreading out as they go."

"By the Firsts," I said.

This was the last thing the caravan needed.

Losing my client was disastrous. Shaler had been a pain in my ass, but I didn't wish her any harm. For her sake and my own, I hoped she was still alive. It'd make things a lot easier if we found her somewhere in the tall grass, or sleeping off a drunk in a thicket of pines.

I had the same hopes when Tin went missing.

My emotions from the previous evening still bubbled beneath the surface, threatening to overflow at the slightest provocation. The returned memories of Cybill were still bright and terrifying. I couldn't think about that. I'd deal with those memories later. I had a caravan to run. My crew was scared and looking to me for answers, so I forced the feelings out of my head, doing my best to focus on the situation at hand. What else could I do?

It had all gone wrong. Shaler's disappearance was also a financial burden. It meant Bell Caravans wouldn't get paid; if we didn't get paid, then this trip down the Broken Road was for nothing. My job—the contract I signed—was for the safety of the caravan, not just the cargo. If lives were lost, it was my responsibility, but getting away from the Broken Road was going to be difficult. We had left the high desert behind us, and the ground on either side of the road was soft. With the recent showers it'd be impossible to blaze a trail. We could abandon the wains, cut the oxen loose, but on foot we were even slower. We didn't have the provisions to survive months out here. Our safest solution was returning to Syringa without Shaler but that placed the caravan in a precarious position with the magistrate.

Shaler would have been the one to contact her father, have him wire payment to the caravansara. Even if I could get the cargowains to Lovat, there was little I'd be able to do. The contract was null and void, and Bell Caravans was on the hook. William Shaler—Margaret Shaler's father—had a reputation as a hard man. He'd hold me responsible.

Regardless of my own safety I had to find her and, with hope, Tin.

I left to assist the search parties, walking with Samantha and Chance. We picked our way up the edge of a gully, keeping one eye on the landscape and the other in the direction of camp. A row of trees rose up and hung out over the depression, emerging from the grass like the gnarled fingers of a buried titan.

It wouldn't do us much good to get lost now. The trees were growing thicker, the hills around us steeper and colored a deep green, not the dry brown of the plateau. To the west rose the snowcapped western mountains, pointing at the sky like sharpened spikes. The next stage of the route would be harder. The ground would soften and rise and slow us down, and the trees would creep closer, keeping us from seeing where we were going.

"Margaret probably just slipped away for a morning walk. Clear her head after the noise last night," said Chance, his voice wavering. The kid wanted to believe his cousin was all right.

Samantha and I exchanged a look. She was gone. Just like Tin.

We made a wide circle, checking the stands of pines, under the occasional willow, and poking our way through scratchy scrub brush. But we found nothing.

I could see the color draining from Chance's face we progressed. The look in his eyes shifting from nervousness to panic to despair.

In the end, we returned to camp empty-handed, where we found the other search parties waiting. As I had suspected, no one had found anything, not so much as a sock or a boot.

Wensem had searched her prairiewain and said it looked untouched. All it contained was a change of clothes, her jacket, and a small novel. As if she was ready to return at any time, except Shaler wasn't going to return.

She was gone.

I could see the end coming and it was too late to stop it. The moment had come and gone, and nothing I said or did would set things right.

The caravan clustered together and looked at me. Fourteen pairs of eyes watched me expectantly, waiting for some word from their caravan master. The responsibility sickened me. At that moment I hated the job.

The caravan stood speechless. I gathered myself as best I could. Tin's disappearance already weighed on my conscience. I tried not to think of this latest soul hanging around my neck.

I swallowed the lump in my throat and spoke, my words coming out in stutters. "M-Margaret Shaler is gone. She's gone, and with her the contract with Bell Caravans."

We had all been thinking it, but vocalizing it hardened it in everyone's minds. Made it more real. For a moment the group was quiet, a solemn moment of silence for our lost roaders.

It was Taft who spoke first. "What's your plan?" She folded her meaty arms across her expansive chest.

"I don't know," I said. My words flat. I felt helpless. I looked at Wensem, meeting his eyes. "Any ideas?"

He seemed to think about it for a moment, looking from me to the caravan in his slow methodical way. The buzz of flies and the bellow of one of the oxen were the only sound. Finally he sighed and spoke. "Well, we're closer to Lovat than we are to Syringa and it's always been our rule that we don't leave a roader behind. Shaler was a roader as much as any of us. We owe it to her and Tin to see if we can't find them. Exhaust every last option. I say we blaze forward. Find our people and then get ourselves home."

A surge of relief seemed to flood my chest. My eyes met Taft's. Wensem's words were so confident. I felt more sure of myself when I agreed. "Wensem is right. We have to find Shaler. The priest mentioned a town up ahead, maybe they can help."

"Yeah, we heard about that town," said Charron. "Dead people hanging around it! That doesn't sound like any place I want to go."

"Yes. The stories aren't pretty. I'd be lying if I said the path ahead would be easy." I thought of Cybill. "But we can face whatever is fearsome together. We need to find our people. If it was one of us we'd want everyone to come looking. Perhaps the townsfolk there can help us. I'd feel guilty for the rest of my life if we didn't find out for certain."

"And if we can't find them?"

"Then…" I could face jail time in Syringa. With my client missing, getting to a safe city would be my best option. "I imagine we finish the trail. Like Wensem said, we're much closer to Lovat than Syringa now. The ground here's too soft for our wains and blazing a trail on foot this late in the season would take too long. We don't have the supplies for it, anyway. As much as I don't like it, going forward seems to be our best option."

"So… forward unto Lovat," said Samantha, unsure. Her eyes flashed as they flicked up and met mine, but it was difficult to read her emotions. Fear? I wasn't sure.

"No way. That town is between us and Lovat! That forest of bodies! The city of killers he told us about," said Charron. She fidgeted nervously, playing with the stumpy spurs that grew along her knuckles.

"We don't know what's ahead," I said, hoping I sounded strong. "We only have stories."

"Road priests tell tall tales," said Wensem.

"Didn't sound like tall tales to me," said Samantha. "That man believed what he saw. He was sure of it. There is something out there."

"But we have to see if we can find Shaler. She's a part of our crew. Just like Tin. Just like any of you. Maybe that town up ahead has answers," I said.

"We have two missing people," said one of the wain drivers. "Our boss and one of your crew. I'd say that gives us plenty of reason to assume something's amiss!"

"You heard Wal," said Wensem, his normally soft voice

suddenly hard, rising over the murmurs. "We move forward."

He clapped his hands together trying to rouse the wain drivers into action.

"Well, I don't know about you lot," said one of the Lytle twins. He looked at Wensem, his eyes cold, his lips turned up in an ugly sneer. "My brother and me are leaving. We're turning back and getting off this damned road. We don't care if it takes longer. We don't care if we go hungry. We'll eat shamblers if we have to, we're just not going to stick around here. To hell with this trail and to hell with Bell Caravans!"

A silence fell. This was the end. I had seen it before, long ago. Before Bell Caravans had existed. In many caravans, time and time again. This was where it fell apart. The fear, the anxiety, it breaks into a crew.

"I'm coming with you!" said one of the wain drivers.

Others echoed his sentiment.

Charron also nodded her head. The Lytle twins stood, looking proud as more and more of the column threw in with them. I began to count who remained.

"Wait, what about Margaret?" yelled Range Shaler. "You're all just going to leave her? She's still out there. She might need our help! We have to find her!"

"Or we might end up just like her," said one of the Lytles.

"Nothing you folk pay me is worth my life," said a wain driver.

"Hear, hear," said Charron.

"Now hold on a minute!" shouted Wensem, but it was too late. His expression melted into defeat as he watched the caravan shatter in front of him.

I looked from him to Samantha, Taft, and Hannah before turning to Range Shaler. His panicked eyes met mine and I gave him a reassuring nod. I wanted to find his cousin as much as he did. My livelihood—and maybe my life—depended on it.

The Lytle twins had the right of it, of course. What they wanted was the most logical route. I couldn't blame them. Get off this damned road before anyone else vanished. It made sense.

Everything inside me said to go with them. Leave the lost behind and return to Meyer's Falls. That would be the safest course of action, the smartest decision.

But...

Shaler's cousins stared at me, expecting a response. I chewed the side of my cheek and ran my hands through my shaggy hair.

I had a responsibility.

As much as the logical part of me wanted to flee, I agreed with the kid. Margaret Shaler could still be out there, Ivari Tin could still be out there. Victims of this forest of the dead? I owed it to them to investigate. I needed to see this through. Some mixture of honor and fear wouldn't let me turn around. Bell Caravans didn't leave a soul behind.

"Range is right," I said and the kid thanked me with his eyes. My chest swelled, despite the fear I felt.

"Margaret Shaler could still be out there. She could be at Methow for all we know. Tin could be there as well. We owe it to them to check."

One of the Lytles chuckled and shook his head, spitting on the ground. "I don't owe them a damn thing. We did our due diligence. We're leaving. Weeks ago when that damned noise started, we should've taken that as a sign. But no! We had to press on. Shaler got us into this mess. Serves her right. Better that bitch than me."

He stabbed at his chest with a tattooed thumb as Charron and a few of the wain drivers nodded in agreement.

"Watch yourselves," said Wensem from behind them.

They both jumped at his voice.

"Go on then!" said the other Lytle. "Get yourselves killed. We'll have none of it."

"You're out of line," I said. I could feel my fists tightening as they hung at my sides.

One of the Lytles waved a hand dismissively. "Our contract was with Margaret Shaler, not Bell Caravans. I don't see a Margaret Shaler here. We're done. We're going to Meyer's Falls. Now." He turned to the group. "Who's with us?"

In the end, a majority of the caravan that had set out from Syringa left with the Lytles. They took most of the wains and the bulk of the cargo. Wensem and I had argued with the deserters over it, but in the end we capitulated. With most of the caravan leaving us we didn't have the crew to drive the cargowains so we begrudgingly let them go. Very little remained of the original caravan.

Eight souls.

Six oxen.

Four wains.

The gearwain still led the column, now driven by Wensem with Samantha riding shotgun. A single Shaler Ranch cargowain followed, driven by Ernest Rousseau. Behind him rumbled Shaler's plastic prairiewain, still driven by Range. At shotgun sat Chance. No longer were they soft young men. Their faces were drawn, masks of cool intent. Rifles always at the ready. Eyes flashing at any commotion off the trail.

Taking up the rear as before was Taft, the pots and pans clanging in the chuckwain as we rolled forward.

Our wheels turned, ours wains rocked, our boots stepped across the ancient gravel, and we all moved cautiously, fearing what lay around each bend. The foothills of the western mountains rose around us, and cradled in those hills was the town of Methow.

THIRTEEN

The smell hit us first. Riding on the wind with the noise, it swirled around us. Another menacing companion, another ill omen, another traveler on the Broken Road. Crows circled in the air ahead, their harsh cries mixing with the noise. A numberless mass of them, writhing in the air and forming an ominous cloud.

The scent was deeper, more rank and more subtle than the decay of vegetation that surrounded us. Something darker than the rot of the fallen autumn leaves blanketing the forest floor we picked our way through.

The noise was with us almost constantly now. It roared to life as we put miles behind us and faded as we rounded blind corners in the woods. The noise came and went like the wind on the high desert, carrying sound and smell instead of bone-dry dust.

Everything in me told me to turn around. Turn tail. Flee. Retreat like General Bowles at Crowsnest. There's intelligence in recognizing when you're beaten, in admitting it's time to throw in the towel.

That seemed to skip me. Something else drove me on, something deep and rank inside me. I wanted this over. I wanted to look in the faces of the people who took Tin and Shaler, and I wanted to end them.

I remembered the faces of the people I had killed, the cultists in the tunnels below the city. I could still see the look in their maddened eyes as they were cut down. They lingered on the edge of my thoughts, haunting me alongside friends I'd lost. The Judge hung at my hip, a heavy pendulum rocking with the roll of the wain. Would I be able to go through with it again? Would I be able to pull my gun when I faced off against this unknown? Could I kill again?

"Mankind often chooses war. It is in his nature." My old man's words rang in my ears. He was right, returning to Syringa meant this would haunt me forever. The ghosts of Shaler and Tin would hang with me, joining the others.

I couldn't have that.

My father was right. I chose war.

We ignored the smell of decay, the odor of death that slithered through the pines and aspen. The rolling hills fell behind us and forest began to thicken around us. Tall rangy pines and white aspen stands broken up by willows and cottonwoods replaced the open spaces of the rolling hills. Parts of the Broken Road were overgrown by bushes and brambles and we hacked our way through, clearing the road for the wains.

At laager the caravan barely spoke. We ate our meals in silence, our stomachs grateful but our minds tired from the desperate effort of ignoring the scent that threatened to wrench our meals from within us. What words were spoken were only what was necessary: check ins, the morning roll call, orders for the caravan.

Sleep wasn't easy. The nightmares were unceasing. I'd wake each morning in a persistent cloud from a night of restless sleep, my head muddled, my vision blurred. Exhaustion became a constant companion, almost comfortable. As constant as the sound that roared above us.

I began to hallucinate. I saw old friends, dead friends among the rocks and trees of the Broken Road. I saw the shadows of hooded gargoyles on the hills and ridges, hanging about like statues on an ancient temple. They watched our dwindling caravan like crows circling ahead of us, so many carrion birds staking claim over a dying animal too stupid to realize it was already a corpse.

Occasionally someone would spot a figure moving in the trees. A shadow that flickered and disappeared. Wensem and I tried to go after them a few times but found nothing, not even footprints. I started to wonder if the rumors of a haunted road were true.

Ernest Rousseau deserted us the day before we made Methow.

When he came to me, face drawn, I knew what was on his mind. I saw it in his eyes. I understood before he even began to speak.

"You know why I am here?" he asked, his voice the raspy

whisper of a dimanian who smoked too many cigarettes.

I frowned. A part of me didn't want to acknowledge his question. Rousseau staying behind with the company lent validity to my decision to carry on. Made me feel like my decision—despite my suspicions—was justified. He was one of Shaler's own crew, the only one remaining not related by blood. Recognizing he was about to leave cracked the weak wall erected around my decision. Doubt threatened to flood inwards once again.

"I can't handle it anymore. The sounds. The dreams. Now this—this awful smell." He inhaled, as if to lend credence to his choice, his face twisting.

My head snapped up.

"Dreams?" I asked, blinking. Trying to bring his face into focus.

He grunted and gave a curt nod. "Nightmares, more like. Strange ones. Wicked faces staring down at me from shadowy ruins. Hooded figures. Someone in red, with animals following him, licking at his fingers." He chuckled a dry laugh that sounded like the rattle of bones. "Sounds ridiculous when I say it out loud in the light of day. But at night..." he tapped his forehead. "That's a different story. Never had dreams like that before. They are ill omens, Mister Bell."

A chill slowly ran down my spine. Ill omens. My own dreams sprang into memory. Rousseau had dreams just like mine, just like Hannah's.

Mass hysteria was something I had read about, years ago. Usually sparked from a single event and especially common among close-knit groups, it could spread quickly. More so during times of stress or fright. I tried to think back to what we had all experienced. The sound could be our common event. The hooded gargoyles were suspect as well. But we seemed to be sharing dreams. Was that even possible? Something like that wasn't hysteria. Mass hysteria was one thing, this was mass hallucinations.

I tried to rationalize away the idea, but came up short. The thought made my stomach turn.

Rousseau didn't wait for a response. "I can't stay. I won't. As it stands, I will get nothing out of this. If I leave now—leave before we find something even worse—at the very least I will escape with my hide intact, probably my sanity." He paused and watched me for a few moments before he finished. "That's more than some can say."

His words were muffled compared to the commotion inside me. Hannah and I experienced the same dreams, and now Rousseau had too. The exact same dreams. The faces. The hooded figures. Ruins. The man in red, even the dogs.

"I understand," I said. My words sounded distant in my ears. It was true, I did understand. I could relate, and somewhere inside, I was jealous.

We always choose war.

"Under other circumstances…" Rousseau's voice trailed off.

I waved a hand dismissively. "Save it. We can blame folks for days, but I'm still the caravan master." My legs wavered below me, my right knee popping. I extended my hand. "I hope your future roads are led by better men than me."

Rousseau didn't meet my eyes as he grasped my hand in a weak shake before brushing past me towards the last Shaler cargowain.

I watched him pull himself up and coax his team of oxen forward. He broke the column, whipped around and began to move east.

Samantha appeared beside me, saying nothing. I could feel her hand on my shoulder. Light but purposeful. As if to say, it was okay. That everything would be okay.

FOURTEEN

Hannah was the first to scream. Then one of the Shalers, and finally Taft. The rest of us remained silent. Shocked. Horrified. Too stunned for sound.

The forest just ended. A quarter-mile scar was torn into the ground between the tree line and the source of the horror.

My body trembled at the sight. It was exactly what the priest had described. Bodies, hundreds of bodies impaled or crucified, left to rot under the sun. It stretched on before us; a waking nightmare. Crows and carrion birds fluttered between the corpses, while the sound of millions of flies and other insects added a dull hum to the scene.

None had been spared. There were naked men, women, even children among the dead. Bodies in stages of rot and decomposition were hammered to crosses of various shapes and sizes. Some of the corpses had been mummified and emaciated in the heat while others were bloated mockeries of their former selves.

"Oh Lord," Samantha said, standing next to me. She moved backwards, recoiling from the scene, hand over her mouth, eyes wide as she struggled to comprehend what we were witnessing.

Hannah dropped to her knees and vomited. Wensem looked like he might do the same. We couldn't take our eyes off of it. Here it was, a manifestation of evil. How could it exist?

This can't be happening. This isn't real! I thought, blinking against the midday sun. The noise that had dogged us relentlessly had dropped away, fading like the last note of a demonic symphony as we emerged upon the forest of the dead.

Father Norry's tale had sounded too far-fetched to be true, like a trail myth that gets passed around. Boogieman stories that always begin with, "I heard this story about a friend of a friend…"

Is this the war you wanted to fight? I thought. Could you win a battle against whatever could do something like this?

The forest of the dead spread across a narrow valley that cut north. Steep hillsides lined the valley, and an old mining tower— the headframe—loomed down at us from atop a small mountain opposite where we stood, like one of Hannah's gargoyles.

The Broken Road ran north through the horror and between the burnt foundations of buildings. It disappeared under a gate built into a hastily constructed barricade. Wood, scrap, and corrugated metal wrapped around what remained of the town, a huddle of buildings cowering at the center of the forest.

Is it keeping people out or folk in? I wondered, sure I didn't want to find out. I couldn't see anyone moving behind the wall. A few gray tendrils of smoke rose from behind the gate. The remains of a fire? Maybe there wasn't anyone inside those walls, maybe the town was now just a husk, smoldering in memoriam.

Summoning my courage, I took a step forward, moving into

the first stand of stakes. I looked at the bodies. Fresher ones were placed around the edges. As I looked towards the buildings at the center, I could see the corpses there were more decayed.

Someone gasped. "Wal, their arms, their legs, look at them!"

My eyes flicked to the nearest corpse, and then the next, and the next. I blinked at what I saw. Parts of the corpses, a hand here, a leg there, were severed, cut cleanly. Not taken by rot or torn free by wild animals, but removed surgically.

Intentionally.

A sense of déjà vu struck me and I dropped to my knees with a painful jolt. Peter Black, the mad cultist and supposed demigod followed a similar path in his effort to resurrect Cybill.

He had killed friends and acquaintances, took body parts for a perverse ritual. A ritual that we quashed in the tunnels below Lovat. He meant to make Wensem and his son his last victims before ripping out my heart as the final piece of the sacrifice.

Was this his doing? Some other wing of his cult operating outside the city?

My stomach heaved. Where had I taken us?

What was this place?

How could this exist… anywhere?

Heaving a third time, I emptied the last of my stomach's contents. The stench of death was overwhelming. The sight of disfigured and naked corpses too grisly to comprehend. My stomach continued dry heaving despite having nothing to eject.

I steeled myself and rose to check on my company. Samantha had collapsed. Chance and Range shook their heads in disbelief. Taft was nowhere to be seen. The moment we realized what we were witnessing, she retreated to the back of her wain, and refused to come around. Wensem was sitting back, his face buried in his hands, shoulders shaking.

I don't know how long we sat there. The sun marched across a now silent sky.

It was mid-afternoon when the first of us recovered. Hannah shakily stood, then poured whiskey from her flask onto her green keff and wrapped it around her face.

With her green eyes peering out, she looked like a wild bandit stalking forward. Rifle at the ready, she approached the scene.

"The priest was right!" said Range. He stood and turned his back on the forest of the dead, facing the party. "This is hell!"

"Who would do this?" asked Wensem, his soft voice wavering.

I shook my head, unable to answer. Fearing that if I spoke, I would be wracked with another bout of heaving I needed to wrap my head around the scene. I tried to count the bodies, looking over the forms as to not linger on any one for too long.

I lost count after two hundred.

Breathe. Look at this objectively. Tactically.

I stood, my knee popping with pain. Following Hannah's lead, I soaked my own keff in whiskey and wrapped it around my neck, over my nose and mouth. The liquor's smell was strong, and it went a long way towards masking the scent.

Drawing the Judge with my left hand, I stalked behind Hannah. The feeling of the gun in my hand was a comfort, something I could control. I studied the bodies with a coldness that made me feel hollow.

Stay calm. Remain disengaged, I told myself over and over as

I witnessed the terrible means by which these people had died.

The means of crucifixion were varied, but they all served the same brutal purpose. Somehow the impalements were harder to understand. I attributed it to the Reunified. Years of seeing their crosses had prepared me for the concept of crucifixion, if not the actual reality.

The most common cross was two pieces of wood hammered into an X shape, so arms and legs were spread wide. Some were just a single pole, while others were T-shaped. Others were the traditional cross, like the crucifix that hung around Samantha's neck.

What had the priest called this place? Perdition? It meant hell. I didn't believe in hell, at least not until this moment.

"Wal! Wal! Come quick!" Samantha shouted from somewhere to my right.

I ran towards her voice and found her along the eastern edge of the Forest, near the freshest corpses. She had also donned a liquor-soaked keff. The rest of the caravan arrived behind me, trepidation in their eyes.

Ivari Tin was hanging upside down on a single stake. Flies swarmed his body, and I tried to bat them away. His feet and hands were nailed, and his chest and stomach had been horrifically gashed open. He was naked, save for the tin mask that clung to his head, dented and bloody. Lifeless eyes stared from behind the slits in the metal.

"No, no, no, no, no," I said, as I dropped to a squatting position, my head pressed between my fists. My jaw was clenched so tight it was hard to breathe. Tears welled up in my eyes.

I beat my fists against my head. Strange guttural noises erupted from somewhere inside of me.

Something in me had hoped he was still alive. Hoped he was in hiding or held hostage waiting for rescue, but here he was: crucified. My arms were shaking, and when Samantha reached down for me, I pushed her away.

"No," I said coldly.

By the Firsts, I thought, by the Firsts, kid, I am so sorry. I am so, so sorry.

Something in me hardened. Something in me grew cold, and it scared me. I remembered the feeling from before, when I was in the tunnel facing Black's horde of cultists. When I raised the shotgun and fired into the back of the nearest one.

A red rage filled my chest. It flowed down my arms, into my stomach and legs, it numbed me.

Standing, I stared at Tin's body.

Samantha stood to one side with a look I hadn't seen on her face before. Worry? Fear? I couldn't tell. Somewhere in the back of my mind I wanted to reach out and hold her. Console one another. But that part of me wasn't in control. I wanted to find the bastards responsible and tear them limb from limb.

"Let's get him down," I said, my voice cold. "I won't have any member of my company treated this way."

"I'll fetch some tools," said Hannah, retreating from my cold rage.

"What about my cousin?" Chance asked. "What if she's out here hanging just like him?"

It was a valid question.

"You and your brother spread out and look for her. Fire your gun if there's trouble." I said.

The thought that Shaler was also out here sickened me further. There was little affection between the two of us, but no one deserved this. I couldn't imagine how I would inform her father if we found her here.

"I'll help as well," said Samantha.

The three of them set off, moving quickly, keeping liquor-soaked bandannas and keffs held tightly over their faces. They glanced at bodies but didn't dwell as they moved among them.

When Hannah returned, it only took a few moments to remove the spikes that held Tin inverted on the simple cross.

We lifted him down, and wrapped his body in an oiled tarpaulin. We made sure we were careful but he was stiff as a board and it was difficult to get him into a peaceful position.

"Careful with his mask," I said as we bent his arms in place. "Respect his customs even in his death. We'll do right by our dead."

This was the first time I had to deal with a dead member of the company. Samantha and the boys reappeared as we were finishing up.

"Anything?" I asked.

Samantha shook her head.

"She's not out there," said Range. "That's good, right?"

"I hope so," I said, my tone flat. I meant it, but summoning emotions for Margaret Shaler was difficult.

"We'll bury him in the woods, back the way we came, away from this place." I looked at Samantha, and she looked back with her large dark eyes. "He was Reunified. Sam, can you oversee his burial?"

She nodded, and bent over him and began to mumble some prayers. I left her to it and turned my gaze back to the Forest of the Dead, regarding it with a loathing I now found frightening. How many of these had come here like Tin? How many of these bodies were friends, husbands and wives, sons and daughters of someone out there, someone wondering if they were still alive?

When Samantha finished, the company lifted Tin and carried him back to the wains in silence. A pitiful funeral march. His final resting place was under an old cedar rising high above the pines that surrounded it. No one spoke as we tore into the ground, our spades and the distant sound of the carrion birds the only noises. We took turns digging the grave, making sure it was deep enough so Tin's body wouldn't be found by the coyotes or a herd of shamblers. The cedar's roots slowed our shoveling, and we had to use saws and axes to break through the thicker roots that blocked our downward progress.

Once we laid him to rest, we discussed the marker. We considered a cross, but I felt there was something perverted about having your grave marked by the instrument of your death. So we opted for a simple wooden plank, with "Ivari Tin, Roader" carved into its face.

As Samantha led the final prayer, I stewed, focusing my rage into something sharp and hot. Prayer finished, I moved back to the gearwain and began gathering weapons. Fresh shells for my pistol, two knives, one for my boot and another for a leather bandolier that I draped around my chest.

"Wal, what are you doing?" Samantha asked, her voice laced with concern.

"I'm hunting," I said. My voice cold.

"About damn time," said Hannah, holding her rifle in the crook of her arm, checking it was both loaded and ready.

"I'm coming," said Wensem.

"Wal," said Samantha. "Don't—not yet. Let's think about this logically. Let's be smart."

I looked at her and saw the fear in her eyes. She was remembering Lovat. I didn't respond. Instead I put her at my back and marched through the Forest of the Dead, toward the cluster of buildings at its center.

Strands of long gray smoke still drifted up into the sky above the enclosed buildings. Someone had to be in there. Someone had to have seen us arrive and find the body of our roader. Maybe this was the lair of Hannah's gargoyles? Visions of panicked hooded figures struggling for escape fueled me onward. I wanted to kill whoever had killed Tin, empty my gun in their chest and end this. I drew the Judge, raised it high into the air and emptied the chamber at the sky.

BLAM! BLAM!

Pause.

BLAM! BLAM! BLAM!

"You there! You inside! We're coming in! Do you hear me, we're coming in!" I screamed. I reloaded as I did so, then repeated my challenge, emptying the gun at the sky and marching angrily towards Methow.

By the third reload, we stood before the gate. No faces

appeared over the wall, no one returned fire. No one shouted pleas for mercy.

But there was something. Something beneath the buzz of bugs and the caws of the birds. A muffled sound. Crying? A sniffle? The shuffle of feet on gravel?

Something.

A crude hand-painted sign hung on the solid gate that broke the outer wall. Thick red letters spelled out a warning in a raw, shaky hand.

HELL HAS COME TO METHOW

DO NOT ENTER

TURN AWAY

To hell with that.

FIFTEEN

I looked for a way inside. Two cinderblock towers roughly fifteen feet high flanked a gate made of corrugated metal screwed into plywood. Other objects were hammered into the wavy facade to keep visitors from getting too close. Spikes. Barbed wire. Sharp jagged scraps from all manner of found and reclaimed material. The barricades on either side weren't solid, more a pile of objects. Glass spikes lined the top and more barbed wire looped through the defenses.

Whoever was inside wanted to keep everyone out.

It'd be easy enough to climb, though I'd probably end up cutting myself and contracting something from the rusted material.

There was also the matter of not knowing what was on the other side. It could be anything, the hooded gargoyles, a tribe of murderous, blood-thirsty cannibals, a cult similar to Black's Children, a mess of bandits, or worse—something like that creature I had seen in the Humes tunnel, something far more fearsome. I wasn't about to go poking my head over the edge.

"You going to let us in?" I shouted at the wall.

I considered firing again, but I wasn't carrying an unlimited supply of ammunition. Wasting them for dramatic purposes began to feel foolish.

"ARE YOU?" I screamed. My breath heaved in and out of my chest, and my fingers twitched at my sides. Remembering Tin's body only enraged me further.

No answer.

More sounds seemed to come from behind the gate. A shuffle. A sniffle. A cry? It was hard to tell.

My companions flanked me. Wensem's face was drawn and his feet were planted wide apart, but his shotgun was resting at ease on his shoulder. He was here for security. He wasn't up for a rampage, not yet at least. I had seen him snap only three times before, twice on the trail and once deep beneath the city of Lovat. Wensem was a slow burn—a dormant volcano—and Firsts help you when he went off.

Hannah's mood mirrored my own. She rolled her shoulders and shifted her rifle between her hands. Her green eyes flicked about, scanning the top of the wall and the roofs of the small collection of buildings visible on the other side. Scouting.

It was hard to tell how many structures were still erect behind the barricade. Gambrel and flat-roofed buildings rose from behind the defenses like tired old veterans. Old. Worn. Missing shingles patched with strips of bark or clumps of sod.

Garrets stained from centuries of grime stared down at us in judgement from the roofs like clouded eyes.

Samantha joined us, standing behind me and to my left. If I turned my head I could see her just over my shoulder. She reminded me of one of those cartoon angels in those kid serials that played on the monochrome. Agents of goodness whispering in the ears of the protagonist. Offering sensible advice to oppose the devil on the opposite shoulder.

I wasn't in the mood to listen to advice.

"Maybe no one is home," said Wensem in a soft drawl.

"Bullshit. I heard someone," I turned and shouted at the gate. "You hear me? Carter's cross! Do you hear me? I hear you! I know you're in there!"

I slammed the butt of the Judge against the corrugated metal. My harsh bangs echoed inside and disturbed a line of crows perched atop one of the buildings.

"Wal..." said Samantha. She made a noise like she was clearing her voice, but I could hear the concern in her words. "... maybe you should ease off a bit."

Ease off?

They killed one of my crew—a member of my company—and hung him on a stake like some animal. Who knows what they were doing to Shaler! The Forest was the work of madness, pure evil. Whoever was behind this gate was responsible and they would pay. I decided that the moment I laid my eyes on this whole bloody spectacle.

My breath came out in ragged sharp bursts. I ground my teeth together until my jaw hurt.

"Wensem."

"Yeah, Wal?"

"Get the dynamite."

"Wal!" Samantha shouted.

We kept a small cache of dynamite in the gearwain to clear rock and mudslides in the passes. It was handy for trail work. It'd be handy for invasion work as well. A stick or two would make short work of this door.

"Wal... I don't know if..." Wensem began.

Samantha was more forceful. She appeared before me and gripped my shoulders leaning into me. Her eyes blinked rapidly as she stared into my own. "Wal! No. You can't do this. We don't know what's going on. It's horrible, yes. It's the worst thing any of us have seen, but you can't just start blowing things up! There could be people in there, Wal. There could be innocent people."

Innocent? The idea struck me as bizarre. Innocent? Had Samantha not seen the death surrounding this town? Did Samantha miss the fact that hundreds of corpses hung from torture devices a scant few feet from where she stood? Was the smell not enough? The graying color of rotting flesh? What innocent person could live in the center of all of this?

"Sam's right, Wal. We don't know what's going on here. There's a lot of questions and no answers," Wensem said.

I said nothing. I turned and pulled back. Samantha, who was leaning into me, stumbled and fell to her knees in the mud. I needed to get inside. Even if the place was dead, I needed to see. Right now it was the curtain and I had to pull it back, reveal the horror on the other side. Innocent or not. I was ready for blood.

"Fine," I spat, flashing Wensem a sour look. "If you won't help me, I'll get it myself."

I returned with a few half-sticks of dynamite and the fuses

needed to set them off. I worked in silence. My eyes focused on the work at hand. I cut fuses. Stuck them into blasting caps. Checked my lighter. All while trying to ignore the glares from Samantha and Wensem and the scene of death surrounding me.

"This isn't necessary," Samantha pleaded. "If there are people inside all this will do is potentially kill a lot of them."

Looking up at her, I frowned, my voice coming out in an exasperated huff. "That's the idea, Sam."

With a crack my lighter snapped on and I lit the fuse of the first stick of dynamite. With a loud hiss, the fuse caught and the spark began to slowly eat its way toward the blasting cap.

"I'm going to blow this gate to hell if you don't open it up!" I shouted. "Do you hear me? I am going to blow your barricades! Then what will you cower behind?"

For a while the only noise I could hear was the caw of the birds and the sizzle of the fuse and the low murmur of Samantha mumbling a prayer. I held the dynamite out in my right hand, let the sparks waterfall over my wrist, felt it singe my skin. The scent of burning hair mixed with the odor of rot and decay.

"Wal, please," Samantha pleaded, her voice now anguished. "Don't do this."

I ignored her. I looked at Wensem for some support. Instead he nodded in agreement with the priestess. Hannah looked similarly displeased.

Always alone, even in a group.

Pulling back, I moved to throw the lit dynamite at the base of the gate.

"Please! Please don't," came a wavery voice from the other side.

I halted.

The dynamite sizzled in my hand.

"We're opening up the gate. Don't blow it up! Please!"

Taking a deep breath, I paused. Examined the explosive in my hand. Who was behind the gate? Who was I sparing? A beast or Samantha's supposed innocents? I wasn't sure.

After a few moments I pulled the lit fuse from the half-stick of dynamite, tossing it to the muddy ground. Stomping the flame out with my boot, I tucked the stick into my belt.

"Damn right you're going to open it up," I mumbled.

Samantha stood near Wensem now, tears in her eyes, her brows drawn. Her hands were balled into fists, making the spurs along her knuckles look more like claws.

As we stood there, we could hear noises from behind the gate, the movement of a heavy mechanism and the whine of metal on metal. Eventually the gate swung outward and my party stepped back to make room.

An older man with thin arms, long graying hair and a weak beard that did little to hide an even weaker chin emerged pushing the massive door open. He held a stained rag that I think was meant to be white.

A flag of surrender.

Behind the door more people appeared, gathering in a small huddle in the middle of a square that made up the center of the cluster of buildings. Old people, males and females, a mix of humans, maero, and dimanians. Children ranging from two or three to about fourteen clustered between them. Few in the group were my age. None seemed to be in their twenties.

A forgotten town of the old and the young.

They all had dark graying skin, drawn pale lips, yellow eyes, and dirty hair. Their clothing was tattered, colorless, matted with mud and who knows what else. In withered hands with cracked nails they all clutched tattered off-white cloths.

The scene blew over me all at once like a Syringan dust storm. I was no conquerer. These people were defeated before I arrived. They weren't strong enough to take care of each other let alone accost one of my roaders.

A wave of pity overwhelmed me and I yanked down the keff covering my face. The rage bled out of me. I wanted to help these people. Take care of them. Feed them. Clothe them. But why were they still here? Why would anyone remain?

Everything felt frozen.

I couldn't even begin to comprehend what had happened. Judging by the state of the place Methow hadn't operated normally in months. Maybe years. The structures were as dilapidated as the inhabitants.

How long had they been here?

"Please," came the wavery old voice from somewhere in the middle of the crowd. "Please don't hurt us. Please."

At once I realized I still had my Judge extended. They stared at me nervously. My hands shook and it wasn't easy to lower the gun and slip it back in its holster, out of sight.

Embarrassment rapidly filled the spaces abandoned by my rage. It was no wonder these folks hadn't rushed to open the gate. They weren't in any state to defend themselves. They probably thought we were bandits.

"Who is in charge here?" I asked—gently—breathing out the last of my anger as I took in the haggard group.

"I am," came the same voice as before. A human male with a bent back and a sagging face shuffled from the center of the crowd, a dirty cloth of surrender clutched in his ancient gnarled fingers. Small black eyes stared at me from under long eyebrows below an exposed pate. Unlike the man at the gate, this fellow was clean shaven, the corners of his mouth drooping like the tired limbs of a willow and his cheeks sagged like a bulldog's.

Crossing the space between us I extended my hand in both apology and friendship. I gave an embarrassed smile. I reacted without thinking and ended up the fool. Once again, Samantha was right. I would need to work to show him we weren't a threat.

The old man recoiled at my gesture and I forced myself to pause. Breathe. He's scared, I told myself.

"You should not have come," he said suddenly, staring at my still awkwardly extended hand. Abashed, I lowered it.

"We were traveling along the Broken Road and it brought us here."

The old man made a noise, and looked at me only for an instant before he gazed over my shoulder, across the Forest of the Dead, to the spot where my wains and the rest of my crew squatted against the tree line.

"You should not have come," he repeated again.

"We hadn't planned on coming," I admitted, running my hands through my hair.

"You bandits?" he asked.

"No, roaders," I said.

"Haven't seen your kind in a while."

"No, I reckon you haven't." I looked around at the crowd.

He stared at me, saying nothing. Finally after a few more seconds of awkward silence the old man sighed and then spoke. "Come, come in. Come in," he beckoned us inside. "Ill wind today. Ill wind brings ill fortune."

I looked over at Wensem and he gave a slight nod. We were heading in.

"I'll stay out here," said Hannah, her eyes glancing about. "Make sure we're not followed. Make sure no one is coming. Watch the wains," she nodded back to the rest of the party before adding, "ya know."

"Be careful," said Wensem as he, Samantha, and I tentatively moved past the gates and into the small compound. The gate was closed behind us, closing us off from the Forest and my crew beyond.

I was fairly sure if this was a trap, we'd be able to both outfight and outmaneuver these people. Hell, the old man could hardly stand. I couldn't see any of them overpowering us.

The old man stopped in the center of what I gauged was a town square. Six old buildings of various sizes squatted around the perimeter. Citizens gazed down at us from windows and from doorways. What roads once existed between them were blocked by makeshift barricades constructed out of brick, steel, mortar, wood, and stone.

The largest structure crouched at the north side of town. Its looming three-story presence occupied a single side of the village and looked like the remains of a small school or a hospital. The imposing white walls had faded to a dingy dirty gray and were streaked with mud. A few of the windows were boarded shut. Another bent figure watched the gathering from behind the gloom of the double doors.

Behind the big white building the foothills rose in the distance. Their crowns were dusted with a light snow despite the heat still felt in the valley. The old mining headframe stood vigil.

The crowd of villagers milled about us, studying our clothes, eyeing our weapons, our healthy complexions. Emotions of fear and envy seemed to flicker on all the faces, young and old. I felt like an adventurer meeting a tribe of wild folk.

"How many are there?" I asked Wensem quietly. He'd know the number.

"About a hundred, maybe hundred and twenty," he responded. He paused, looking around. "Mostly children and old folk."

The old man finished conferring with his cadre and turned to face us. He straightened as best he could and studied us for a moment before speaking. When he did his voice still carried that far away, foggy tone.

"You should not have come."

"Yeah, we're understanding that," I said. "Look, I'm Waldo Bell of Bell Caravans, this is my partner Wensem dal Ibble—"

"You a maero?" The old man asked Wensem, his already small eyes further narrowing. They flicked from me to Wensem and then to Samantha and then to… I wasn't actually sure. Somewhere in the sky? He reminded me of the pitch addicts in Lovat. The drug-blasted minds… even when they're sober it's hard to get a straight answer out of them.

Wensem didn't respond, he just gave one curt, respectful nod, and shifted his shotgun onto another shoulder. He was an imposing figure. Especially compared to most of these people.

"—and this," I continued, "is the Reunified Priestess and Professor, Samantha Dubois of Saint Marks' in Lovat."

The old man made what seemed to be a respectful grunting noise and nodded his head, still not making eye contact with any of us. The whole town seemed nervous and distracted. I wondered how much my enraged gunfire scared them. Based on their body language probably a lot.

A few silent moments passed before the old man finally spoke. "Now it is my turn for the introductions. I am Donal Feeney, mayor of Methow, or—what remains of Methow."

He frowned at the town around him.

"Mister Mayor," I said respectfully.

"Let me introduce you to the town's remaining council members. This lovely dimanian to my left is Councilwoman Sarah Eustis. She's served Methow for going on twenty years now."

A small dimanian woman of considerable age with straight spiky horns growing from her brow and one single horn sprouting from the back of her head nodded in greeting. Her face was drawn, and her eyes nervously studied our movements. Her eyes flicked around as if she expected one of us to attack.

What had these people gone through?

Mayor Feeney continued. "The fellow looming over in the Big House is Councilman Enoch Boden. He doesn't come out much. Catches chill easily and sun stroke even quicker. You'll likely meet him later. Old as dirt but he's an amiable sort."

"Pleased to meet the council," I said, giving my best caravan master smile.

"Finally, the maero charged with protecting the town: Sheriff Joul dal Habith."

Joul dal Habith was a maero with dark-gray skin and a thicker frame than any maero I had ever seen. Like most of their race he was at least as tall as Wensem but he was twice as wide. He seemed to carry himself with a bit more presence, too. He seemed less dreamy, as if he was more in the moment. It was clear who was the master of Methow, and it wasn't Feeney.

"Please to meet you," he said in a rumbly voice. He extended a thick seven-fingered hand with fat grubby fingers that enveloped my own.

"Indeed. Sorry about the scare," I said. I swallowed my emotions as I spoke. "We found one of my crew… in the forest… I—er—I overreacted."

"Dreadful. By the Firsts. So dreadful," he said with a shiver. "I'm sorry. I'm so sorry. Your reaction makes sense. I had a similar reaction when I found one of my deputies out there. I'd worry about the sanity of any person if they came across the Forest of the Dead and took it in stride."

There was something off about this guy. He seemed oddly sane and pleasant for being surrounded by so much death. The almost absent way in which he talked about the scene outside didn't sit well. The stench alone was a constant reminder. How could all this become normal? How could you face something like this and learn to talk about it so casually? How could these people not be driven insane?

"What happened here?" I asked.

"Well—"

"We will tell you," said Feeney, interrupting. "We will. Come. Come. We don't have much food but we can offer you coffee or tea. That we seem to have in abundance. We will drink coffee and we will talk."

The wizened old mayor turned and addressed the gathered crowd. "Go back to your homes, citizens. We will meet at the usual time. No need to be gawking at Mister Bell here. No need. Not for now, at least."

The sheriff, the mayor, and Councilwoman Eustis walked before us, leading us across the empty square and toward the big, off-white building at the northern side of town.

The words "Sunflower High School" were carved into the granite stone around the main entrance. Over it, hand-painted in red were the words "Big House."

We lagged behind as the leaders of Methow took to the steps.

"This is too weird," said Samantha. "Something's not right." She paused and then added with a bitter smile. "Outside of the obvious, I mean."

"Well, I don't think any of them are strong enough to hurt us. The sheriff might be trouble, he seems the most calm about this whole situation. The clarity in his voice, the smile, it was…"

"…weird," said Samantha, finishing the sentence. "It was weird."

"Let's talk with them and see what's up. Maybe they can point us in the direction of Tin's killer."

Samantha hugged her arms and frowned. "I don't like this, Wal."

"I don't either."

"Mister Bell," called the sheriff from down the hall. "We're in here."

We walked towards the sound of his voice into what had once been a teacher's lounge but had now become a kind of nerve center for the town. A crude drawing of the village was scrawled and annotated on a chalkboard dominating one entire wall while papers and notes were stuck with push pins into cork-boards along another. Long dead sodium lights hung from the ceiling dripping with cobwebs. It was clear the town had been without power for a while.

Lamps stained black from ages past were lit and scattered around the tables and on top of bookcases, immersing the room in a dull gray light. A wall of windows was boarded shut and only slivers of light could be seen through the slats.

"You should not have come," said Feeney yet again. He and the two members of the council took seats and beckoned for us to sit opposite of them.

The sheriff folded his arms across his chest and leaned against the windowed wall, becoming a silhouette.

The shadowy man we had seen lurking in the doorway of the Big House upon our arrival slipped into the room behind us. He came around the side of the table and took a seat next to the mayor.

"I'm Enoch Boden. I'm sorry I couldn't have greeted you personally. Health isn't what it used to be," he said and smiled at me. He wore a heavy hood despite being indoors. His features were barely discernible beneath the shadow.

Boden was a tall man with a weak smile, swarthy olive skin, and sharp bird-like eyes. He was human and seemed like he had once been handsome. Like the sheriff he looked healthier than most, though that wasn't saying much. The homeless and addicts of Lovat look healthier than these people.

Like the mayor and the councilwoman, Boden had a scared rabbit look to him and the absent dreamy quality to his tone.

I waved a hand dismissively and introduced myself, Wensem and Samantha. We sat across from the council in rickety chairs and studied our hosts.

"Coffee? Tea?" asked Feeney.

"No thanks," I said. The scent from the Forest was dulled somewhat within the walls of the school but its memory lingered. I doubted I could keep much down.

"You should not have come," Feeney said again, still in that dreamy voice.

"Right," I said. "You mentioned that. Something is seriously wrong here."

"Mhmm," the mayor said.

"We heard rumors," Samantha interjected. "A road priest told us about the Forest of the Dead. We weren't sure it could be believed. Then…"

Her voice trailed off.

"Oh? We had a priest once. A Reunified one. Nice chap. He was taken and impaled over a year ago. Along the western side of the Forest. Dreadful. Liked acorn bread. His sermons were often too long. I miss him. He was a good bridge partner," Feeney said, his sentences more stream of consciousness than anything cohesive. He stared at a spot over my shoulder. The two other council members stared at their folded hands and said nothing.

I looked at Samantha and caught her brief frown before I turned back to the Methow council. "Why are you still here? Why haven't you left?"

The council looked at one another and frowned. Heads shook and shoulders shrugged sadly. I waited for some sort of answer. Eventually it was the sheriff who spoke up.

"We can't," he said.

"We can't," echoed Feeney.

"But why?"

Feeney began to speak, and his answer made my stomach sink.

SIXTEEN

W e're trapped."

I blinked and opened my mouth to ask a question but I was cut off by the mayor's wavery voice. "Methow used to be a prosperous town. Sure, we were a little off the beaten path but we made enough to support the families here and we were slowly growing year over year. The Kadath copper mine was doing well, and there were a few successful logging crews working the slopes. Even with all the rumors surrounding the Broken Road our harvests were large enough to attract the occasional caravans.

"I lived here my whole life, all sixty-three years of it and I didn't believe a word of the stories about where I lived. I had never seen a bandit or a ghost or a cannibal. We used to joke about it."

"Kept the riffraff out," Councilman Boden added with a shadowed smile. "It is kind of how folk talk about Lovat's weather. Rains all the time. Clouds going on forever. Dreadful place."

Samantha, Wensem, and I all smiled and nodded. Lovat's weather was always the first topic of conversation with visitors. You either adapted or moved.

"So how are you trapped?" Wensem asked softly. "We came up to the town easily enough. The road, while rough, is passable."

"Everything has changed. It started with the landslide."

The sheriff interrupted. "About five years ago a landslide cut off the Kadath. It's built in a narrow gulch near the top of the mountain. The slide destroyed half the mining camp and killed many of the miners. The Kadath closed down after that."

"We should've taken that as a sign," said the mayor. "Our prosperity was turning. Then last fall, little over a year ago, the nightmares began."

I felt a cold tremor down my spine. Samantha and Wensem also seemed to shift uncomfortably.

Feeney continued. "The nightmares spread through the town. Fathers, mothers, children—whole families were affected. The screams came. Eventually we were all screaming, even if we bottled it up inside."

"What kind of nightmares?" Samantha questioned, leaning forward almost eagerly.

"It varied slightly per person. Some saw ruins. Some thought it was Methow but it seemed ancient. Dry stones lifting from a desert. Ancient towers broken by siege machines. Hooded and shadowy figures moving about broken battlements, yellow leering faces in the cracks of walls. We thought those were the worst but some began to dream of a figure... we call him the Red Man. He wears dark red robes. You never see his face. Only his form, his bizarre shadow... it was wrong somehow. I have no words to describe it but it was wrong."

I shuddered visibly.

"Are you... having these dreams?" asked the old man in a creaky voice.

"Yes," Samantha, Wensem, and I said at once. We looked at one another, eyes wide.

"Exactly those dreams," said Wensem. "To the letter."

A knot formed in my guts. We'd need to discuss this after our meeting with the council.

Councilman Boden jumped in next. "The dreams were bad, but we thought maybe it was a side effect of our isolation, a small community dealing with the stories about the Broken Road."

"Then the noise came," said Feeney.

Boden nodded. "It was... I don't know how to describe it. It was familiar and yet like nothing else. Part scream and part laugh. The miners said it sounded like a tunnel machine tearing itself apart. Otherworldly. Awful."

He shook slightly, and turned to gaze absently towards a corner of the room. The sheriff shifted uncomfortably. "People began leaving town after that. First a few wains here and there, and then whole caravans of them, good people, honest folk."

"Scared folk," said Councilwoman Eustis.

The sheriff agreed. "We searched the mine. Nothing. Some folks thought it was Victory. So we checked the hillsides and found nothing. A few believed it was the devil being tortured by angels. Others theorized the Firsts returned and were wreaking havoc on some elemental plane of existence we couldn't comprehend. We never found the cause."

"How long ago was this?" I asked.

The sheriff shrugged. "Beginning of this year. Maybe... six

months? Eight? Time has gotten funny. Sleep comes too easy..."

Feeney seemed to snap back into reality and continued his story. "Dreams and noises stole the sleep from us! We sleep, yes, but we do not rest. It makes us tired and sluggish. I cannot remember the last time I slept a full night. I always loved how quiet this area was. Things were so easy, so simple then. This valley was once home to almost a thousand souls. After the night scares came and people left we dwindled to a few hundred, a handful of what it was before."

"Not long after that the disappearances started," Eustis added.

"This is eerily similar to our own experiences coming here." I looked to my friends on either side of me. "We've had the dreams, we've heard the noise, and we've had people go missing."

"Why'd you keep coming?" asked the sheriff.

I was wondering that myself.

"To find our people," said Wensem. "We don't leave a caravaneer behind."

"Is that who you found in the Forest?" asked Councilman Boden.

I nodded.

"Our first went missing in the early summer," Feeney said. "It's been a hot year. The weather has been unpredictable. Seasons are funny now, they don't follow themselves liked they used to. We got snow a few months ago. Mid-summer and snow! Then rain washed it all away. Then this damnable heat."

Feeney's voice drifted off and he seemed to examine a space in the air between us. Like his words had gotten stuck in a spiderweb and couldn't shake free.

"Mister Mayor?" I finally asked, but noticed the shake of the sheriff's head. A warning? Feeney seemed to ignore my question but after a few more moments he slipped back into his story.

"Young Walter Brenton was the first we saw dead. He was a dimanian smithy. An apprentice but eager, hardworking, and always wanting to improve. There was no job he'd turn down. His teacher left a few months earlier when the nightmares began, but Walter had remained. Still working for the community, mending what needed to be mended, fixing what needed to be fixed. He was a good lad.

"After the noises came he started to break down. More than the rest of us. We'd find him in the corner of his shop when things grew quiet. Curled up in a ball, shaking. Rocking back and forth. Hands pressed tight against the sides of his head. It was too much for him. After a few weeks he packed up a cart, kissed us farewell, and set off eastward down the Broken Road to seek his fortune and to escape the racket.

"Two mornings after he left, we found him."

I cringed, knowing where this story was going.

Feeney's eyes moistened as he continued. "Two hunters found his body hanging just outside of town. He was impaled. Half his right leg missing."

Feeney paused and fell into his awkward silence. He stared at a space in the air in front of him, his eyes unfocused.

These people are slowly being driven insane.

"What did you do?" asked Samantha.

Feeney slipped out of his haze and seemed to become lucid for the first time in our meeting, his eyes burning with anger.

"We brought him down, of course!"

I said nothing, not sure how to react to his sudden clarity. Eventually he drifted back into his sleepy tone and continued.

"We left the poor boy in the doctor's office and made preparations to bury him. The next morning, however, he was gone. Missing from the table. His grave remained empty. That's when the abductions started in earnest."

The sheriff jumped in at this point. "Started simple enough. The disappearance of Walt's body... then one of the men who helped pull him down from the stake, dimanian by the name of Clément, disappeared. Went to bed with his wife and when she woke up he was gone."

"Did he run away?" I asked.

Feeney's eyes narrowed. "No. They both showed back up. Impaled outside town. The doc examined both of them. Walt was much the same as before. Clément had been sewn up, and when the doc opened him up he found him as hollow as an old stump. Strange words were written over his body in blood... It wasn't Strutten."

I shuddered and felt Samantha's hand reach for my own. I gripped it, and we shared our warmth with one another. Somewhere in the back of my mind I realized that in brighter times I would have relished the touch. Now it was just keeping us grounded.

"Same as before we pulled down their bodies, only this time we buried them the same day. Two more people disappeared that night. They showed up a few days later, with Walt and Clément alongside of them, exhumed from their graves. Re-impaled and hanging among the freshly disappeared.

"We kept taking them down. Letting them die in peace, offering them burial."

"It didn't work though," said Councilwoman Eustis. "They would be dug up and impaled again the next day and more people would disappear. They closed around the town."

"The town thought it was someone on the inside doing it," said Boden. "People were getting into fights. Accusations were made."

"More people tried to leave," said Eustis. "We'd watch them go, and they'd show up staked as well."

"We couldn't leave," said the mayor. "We were trapped."

"Finally we realized when we didn't touch them, no one else would go missing. The disappearances would slow and then almost stop," said the sheriff. "The noise would come. The nightmares would remain. But nothing would happen to our people. We'd all wake in our beds. We'd all be able to go about our business."

Feeney snorted a bitter laugh. "That was the start of the Forest. The saplings, as it were. Those too afraid to remain, or those brave enough to try and leave, would be impaled along the edge of the town."

"It didn't take long before we couldn't bear it. How could anyone? How could you go about with the naked corpses of your neighbors hanging right outside?"

"You can't," I said flatly.

"You can't," agreed the mayor.

"We all did it," said Boden. "Together. We took down the bodies. We broke whatever chaotic code our kidnappers follow."

"It was a punishment," said Feeney. "We all know it. We all know it."

"Punishment?" I asked, knowing I wouldn't like the answer.

A silence fell across the table. Four pairs of eyes blinked at us. I could feel my throat going dry and my heart thumped quicker inside my chest.

Feeney took a ragged breath and his hands shook. For once he met my eyes. They were deep pits of terror.

"Enoch, would you mind putting on the kettle? My nerves…"

With a nod, Enoch Boden rose and tottered off, disappearing from the room and moving toward a kitchen somewhere inside the Big House.

"Sorry, I need to catch my breath," said Feeney. "It's not an easy thing to talk about."

Samantha withdrew her hand from mine, placing her hand on the quivering old man's. "I cannot imagine it's very easy even up to this point. I am so sorry."

"You shouldn't have come here, it's not safe," said Feeney again. He looked brighter, more lucid. He was actually meeting our eyes with his own.

"Our choices were limited," I said. "If I could take it back, start over, I would have never come down the Broken Road."

"It used to be a safe place," said Eustis. "Really it did."

She patted down her wild hair with a hand while looking at the tabletop.

"Maybe it will be again," I said.

"I should finish the story. So you can understand. You need to understand…" Feeney said and took a deep breath. "We set about doing a mass burial, a rescue party of a sort, all of us, the whole town: men, women, children, the young and old, the sick and healthy. There were about four hundred of us left. Not much, but more than the victims hung around the edge of the town. Enough to do the work. It took us only a few hours. We removed the bodies, gave them a proper funeral and cut up the stakes and buried them as well."

He took a deep breath that seemed to catch in his throat. When he spoke, the words rolled out, dark and ominous. "Then the children began to go missing."

The thought made me sick to my stomach. I glanced at Wensem. He was a new father, his own son a little over a year old, and I could tell the idea bothered him greatly. His chest moved slowly.

"Three disappeared the following night, two the next, one the night after that. All crucified or impaled next to exhumed corpses on fresh stakes. It was clear then… we had no power in this. Nothing we could do would make it stop. If we left we'd be taken and killed. If we pulled down the bodies we'd be taken and killed. Now they were taking and killing our children…"

"There's bodies out there with three or four holes in them," said the sheriff. "People we pulled down only to see them re-impaled. We only did what we thought was right. We only wanted to give our people a proper burial! Take care of our folk… our kin. Biggest mistake we could've made."

"So we stopped," said the mayor. "What else could we do? We pulled in, little by little, tearing down houses and fences to build barricades. Methow was never a big place, but we had enough empty buildings we worried could become refuges for our tormentors… so we burned others, hoping it would help us see whoever was coming from afar. It didn't stop 'em. If anything, it gave them more clear land for their stakes.

"The nightmares never went away, the noise returns every now and then, and sometimes folks disappear. We no longer open our gates. We don't give in to compassion anymore."

The mayor stopped as Boden returned bearing a tray of cups. He seemed to drift off, his eyes getting glassy and his tone shifting back to that bizarre dream-like quality.

"Thank you, Enoch," he croaked, taking a cup of tea and sipping with loud slurps. Finally he looked up at me, his dreamy expression returned. "You should not have come."

I agreed with him. We should not have come.

We were trapped.

SEVENTEEN

Seven sets of eyes stared back at me and I forced down a swallow. My throat was dry and my hands were clammy. I needed to break the news to my crew. Mechanically I recounted the information the council had shared as my head continued to swim. Even as the words came tumbling out I wasn't sure exactly what to say.

One thought clanged around incessantly: we were trapped. Mayor Feeney was clear on that. Folks who tried to flee ended up in the Forest of the Dead. If we tried to leave now, would it only put my people further in harm's way? We already pulled down Tin...

Trapped.

I hated that feeling. I needed my freedom as much as people need air to breathe. It's common among roaders. There's probably some psychological term for it, but I'm no clinician. I'm part drifter. I can't be locked into a place for too long. Drives me crazy. Whatever it is, it's rooted deep in my gut. It's what pushed me to escape that jail in Lovat. What sent me down that wild road that ended at the hooves of the Black Goat and those damn cultists.

"So we're stuck," said Hannah. She looked up at me with her jaw set, her bright eyes narrowed but sparkling with ferocious energy. "We have no place to go. If we leave we'll be taken and killed."

"Seems that way..." said Samantha. "When people tried to flee they were later found crucified or impaled."

I sat on the back of the gearwain facing Methow's Big House, my legs dangling. Samantha sat next to me and Wensem stood to my left, leaning against the side, his shotgun slung lazily over his wide shoulders. Behind us was what remained of the caravan's laager.

We set up camp in the center of Methow. The laager, a fraction of its former size, with only four wains, was now more of a square and less of a circle. The gearwain sat at the north side, the remaining Shaler cargowain to the west. Taft's chuckwain sat solidly in the south, her lone ox resting. Shaler's plastic prairiewain filled out the eastern side. Extended tarpaulins huddled over the center around a hastily constructed fire that belched white smoke.

After our meeting with the town leaders I ordered all of my people inside its barricades. What remained of the Shaler caravan moved quickly, rolling to a stop as the heavy gate was swung shut behind. It was a false sense of security. People went missing with or without the gates and barricades, but it was better to look at the haphazard constructions than at the impaled bodies.

The citizens of the besieged town emerged from their ramshackle structures to stare at us with sunken eyes. They gazed out from under awnings, from cracked and dirty windows, from gaping doorways that reminded me of hungry mouths.

"The rumors are true. This route is cursed," said Range absently. Neither of the two boys said much. They had picked their way carefully through the Forest, eyes glancing at each body, hoping they wouldn't find Shaler's corpse among the profane versions of trees.

"None of this makes any damned sense whatsoever," said Taft, the big chuck crossing her arms across her chest. She was still looking a little green. Her eyes glanced over my shoulder toward the gate we had just come through. "It's like a disturbed ghost story told around a campfire. We're sharing dreams. Horrific noises thunder in the sky. People go missing and turn up impaled in a forest of bodies. It's like some damn horror picture. It doesn't make sense."

"No, it doesn't," I agreed. "That doesn't mean we don't take precautions. Losing one person was tough, two was unbearable. We're not going to see another one of our column go missing."

"You can't promise that, boss. How do we know we haven't already angered whoever's doing this? How do we know it's not out there, waiting to snag another one of us?" asked Taft. Her normally smiling eyes looked vacant and sunken. She seemed nervous and on the verge of panic.

Had they all given up? Had I? I brushed the question away and tried to focus on the discussion at hand. Tried to remain strong.

"We don't," said Wensem. His voice was soft, but deadly serious. I turned and looked at my partner as he continued. "Truth is, we're lost. Our backs are up against a wall. Is it dangerous?

You bet it is. But we've been in tough spots in the past. We'll figure out what to do. We have before, and we will again. Bell Caravans will emerge from this. Trust me on that."

He sounded confident. More confident than I felt. Could we really emerge from this? Was there a caravansara at the end of this trail? I looked in Wensem's blue-gray eyes and tried to read the emotion in them. His words had more hope in them than I could begin to muster.

"So what do we do?" asked Range. The young man looked wild, his dirty hair splayed back and to the side, and he stood with his chest puffed out like a rooster. His fingers were clamped so tight around the stock of his rifle that his knuckles paled. Next to him stood Chance, head down, his pointed boots digging at the packed earth.

"I don't rightly know," I admitted. "I'm still working that out."

"Our cousin could still be out there," he said, his voice edged with concern.

I nodded.

"I don't like being stuck here, boss," admitted Hannah. The scout looked over at Range, then at Wensem, and back at me. "Hard to see an enemy coming when you're cowering behind barricades and barbwire."

"As Wensem said, we'll figure this out," I nodded. "I don't like it either but we're not cowering behind any barricades. We're going to be proactive. We're going to set up a watch. I want eyes on the outside at all times, I want to see who or what is coming before it gets here. We've spent too long huddled at laager and too little time watching the angles. Wensem will set up a watch schedule and we'll speak with the leadership to get the locals involved." I turned and looked at the figures milling around the edge of the small square. Could we trust them? Feeney seemed on the edge of losing his mind. The sheriff hadn't seemed willing to help. The two other council members seemed worthless. "We're all on duty."

The mayor and Councilwoman Eustis walked up. The sheriff, who had been at our side since we stormed the gate, was strangely absent. I introduced them to my company and then dismissed the column to finish setting up the laager.

"How many were you when you started out?" asked the councilwoman, her blue eyes watching my caravan return to their work. Only Wensem remained at my side.

"Sixteen."

Seven remained. Seven. Less than half.

"Did the others get taken?" she asked.

"No. Most of the company left after the disappearance of our client, taking some of our security and the majority of our cargo. They felt a return to Meyer's Falls was safer than proceeding. We had another one turn around a few days before we came across Methow."

"They were the smart ones," mumbled the mayor.

"Yeah," I admitted. "Yeah, they were."

The mayor seemed to refocus on our laager. "How long will you remain here?"

"Good question," said Wensem, looking at me with an eyebrow raised. It gave his crooked face a strangely comical expression.

"Way we see it, we're as trapped here as your people are. No sense in trying to leave any time soon. I'd rather not see any more of my crew on those stakes."

"We don't have food—" the councilwoman began.

"We have plenty," I interjected. "We plan on sharing as much as we can. Your barricades will give us some advantage, some protection. My duty is to protect my caravan. The way I figure it, the best way out of this is to put a stop to whatever is doing this. That way we can be sure to leave unmolested."

The mayor snorted and then nodded, his mind as absent from the gesture as it was from my words.

"Where's the sheriff?" I asked.

"Important business," nodded the mayor. He hummed. "Yes, very important business."

Wensem and I made eye contact. It was odd for the sheriff to be absent from this discussion, and I hadn't spotted him along the edge of the camp. Was the sheriff involved in this somehow? It couldn't be that easy, could it?

"Here's the list of folks who volunteered for guard duty," said the councilwoman, handing over a scrap of paper with about seven names printed in block Strutten. Wensem took the paper and nodded.

"Thank you. Tonight we'll set up a ring of torches around the town. Light up the Forest like an Auseil holiday party. We'll be able to spot anyone coming."

"You think it'll help?" asked Eustis. The councilwoman scratched behind one of the horns that sprouted from her scalp with an index finger. The horn was sharp and black. "We have never seen the kidnappers. They arrive. They take. They disappear."

Wensem grunted but said nothing more.

"It can't hurt," I said. "It'll help our guards feel more at ease."

"And if they see this... kidnapper?" asked the mayor. "What then?"

"Then we kill them," I said.

A short while later I found Taft by the chuckwain preparing dinner for the caravan. Trail food: rice with onions, peppers, and strips of dried beef in brown gravy. There was a tinge of dimanian spices and the whole mixture smelled delicious. My stomach rumbled.

"See what you can do to feed these people," I said. "We should have plenty."

Taft paused and looked at me without saying anything, her hands on her expansive hips. I half expected a protest, but she just turned and looked at the people milling around the edge of the square. Finally she nodded. "I'll start some potatoes boiling and see what I can do to extend this meal. How long you plan on feeding the town?"

"Long as we can," I said. I wished we still had a few cargowains of Shaler's produce. It would have really helped. "It's the least we can do. They're giving us shelter."

"And we're sorting out their problem," mumbled the chuck.

"That's the way of it," I said, taking another quick whiff. It was a much more pleasant odor than anything else in recent memory.

"We can hold out for a while," said Taft. "I did prepare to

feed seventeen of us for more than a few months on the trail. It won't last forever though. Notice how they stare at our animals like they're walking banquets?"

I nodded. "Yeah. I also noticed there's no animals here. You'd expect to see dogs and cats in a place like this… but, shit, I haven't even seen a rat. A place this filthy should be crawling with them."

Taft nodded.

"Well, let's get some food into them and maybe it'll keep them from our oxen."

Taft wagged a heavy chef's knife at me. "If one of those dirty buggers even thinks of touchin' Bart I'll shoot 'em well before any mountain monster can get to them. You know I will!"

I chuckled, it felt nice.

Samantha walked up, arms clutching her elbows.

"You have a minute, Wal?"

"Sure," I said.

We moved away from the chuckwain to a corner of the town devoid of people or prying ears.

"What's up?" I asked.

Samantha met my eyes and then looked away. "I feel like I am missing something."

I blinked.

Samantha continued. "I think Taft was wrong when she said none of this was making any sense. I think it does make sense. There is some connection here. Some connection to… something."

"Someone, you mean?" I asked.

Samantha shook her head. "No, I mean something. I think we're dealing with another one of the Firsts. Like the tunnel.

Like Peter Black."

The words hit me like a thunderbolt. I blinked again, and felt a shiver rush down my spine dropping a sour feeling into my stomach. A First.

Samantha had been dancing around the name, but now it echoed in my head. Cybill. The monster Peter Black had tried to resurrect in the tunnels below Lovat. I tried to speak, but couldn't. Cybill had died as the tunnel collapsed on her, hadn't she?

"I should have recognized the signs immediately. The dreams…" her voice trailed off.

"The dreams?" I asked. "What about the dreams?"

"In the legends, the pre-Aligning manuscripts. There are stories that speak of the Firsts communicating through dreams. Remember when I talked about my research into the Nameless?"

I nodded.

"Well, I remember reading stories of sleeping Firsts communicating through dreams. Usually instructions… sometimes warnings. Instructions for people to mar their flesh. To go into woods and perform rituals."

"So, what do our dreams mean?"

"I'm not sure, but it's too similar not to mention. Keziah Mason herself says the founders impregnated her wits at chimera. In less crazy speak: the Firsts talked to her when she was sleeping."

Samantha looked at me, her large dark brown eyes searching. Her brow was furrowed, and her hands were clasped tightly together.

Firsts.

I didn't know what to say so I took her hand, tried my best to comfort her without revealing my own worries. Samantha was strong and likely the smartest among us. She had saved me once before. If she was worried, I knew I should be terrified.

"Damn it, I wish I had more of my books. Keziah is worthless beyond speculation. I'd take anything right now. Something to track down a lead on this thing. Maybe find out who or what it really is and kill it."

I released her hand and rubbed my face, feeling the dirt and grime that had collected on my skin. I opened my mouth to speak, but nothing came.

"I'm just worried about it, that's all. I needed to tell someone—I wanted to tell you."

She blinked at me. Our heads drifted closer together, almost touching. I could smell her. The sharp scent of ritual incense, fresh flowers coupled with the familiar smell of road dust. It lifted me. That old burning desire I felt when we first met flooded into me. Our eyes met. Her large dark brown eyes, my narrow ones the color of dust.

Flames... in the darkness. Cybill. A First.

The thought of another monster out there drove out everything warm. I stood upright.

"I..." I began, my words still a struggle.

I looked at Samantha, courage bubbling up. "Have you mentioned this to anyone else?"

She shook her head.

"For now let's keep it that way. We have enough to worry about without our people thinking a First is wandering the mountains."

"What about Wensem?"

"Even Wensem," I said. I felt guilty saying it.

She nodded warily and inhaled a deep breath. Her chest heaved up and my eyes were drawn to it. She caught me looking and smirked, the change lighting up her face and bringing a little warmth to the coldness of Methow.

We looked into each other's eyes for a long moment. Our faces close. My heart was hammering so loud I swore she could hear it. Everything told me to lean forward and plant my lips on hers. Damn the Reunified's rules...

Her forehead touched mine, and our lips were drawn slowly together.

Then—

"Hey, boss. You said you wanted to inspect the barri—aw, hell, sorry. I didn't see... sorry," Hannah said awkwardly, realizing what she stumbled into.

My heart sank. I caught a flash in Samantha's eyes, and then she looked away. Her lips turned down as the wind whipped her hair around her face. Was that disappointment or embarrassment?

"I'll see if Taft needs help," Samantha mumbled, rising, and quickly walked away, a hand on her cheek. The moment had stretched between us, and then snapped. I stared in the direction she had walked.

"Carter's cross. I'm sorry, boss," said Hannah.

The meal was successful and the townsfolk were grateful. The mood around the square had changed. Occasional laughter rippled through the crowd, and words were spoken not in hushed whispers but in raised voices. Smiles could be seen breaking through once icy facades. It's amazing what a full belly can do.

After the meal the men and women who volunteered as guards gathered around Wensem as he gave them their orders and times of watch. Between the citizens of Methow and my company we were able to scrape together two full watches, each taking a six-hour shift. It was a relief. A blanket of protection for a town that desperately needed it.

I drew first watch.

Later that night I stood on a small platform that ran the length of the western barricade. It was a shoddy thing. A stack of barrels. A hammered section of panel. Some rough-hewn timber holding it all together. It wobbled as I climbed it. A frightened ox could have knocked it asunder.

The torches burned in pools of amber light around the town, winking like summer fireflies. The lights popped and danced in the evening breeze and the Forest became a mass of shadows that seemed to writhe in the flickering.

A gray mist seemed to hang around the town, barely there but promising a morning fog. A few hours earlier the sun had dipped behind the western mountains and now thick clouds swept in from the north and loomed above the town. The late autumn heat disappeared along with the sun leaving the valley shadowed in cold darkness. The occasional flash of heat lightning could be seen among the peaks of the western mountains, silhouetting the jagged stones against the clouds. Like the sharp teeth of some immense beast.

I was grateful for the darkness. Six hours of staring out at a forest of corpses wouldn't do me any good. The torches already exposed too much.

It had been Range and Chance who volunteered to set up the torches. The job gave them another chance to look for Shaler, but just as before, they came up empty. I felt bad for the two boys. I wanted to find their quarrelsome cousin, too. I hated thinking of her dying in such a terrible manner, but I also didn't want to think about what it meant for us as a company.

Next to me on the platform sat Range. His keff was pulled tightly around his cheeks and jaw to lock in warmth. His brown eyes flicked around looking for something, anything. Jumping at each shadow and flicker of torchlight. His rifle was propped up on a small wall of paneling, his finger never far from the trigger.

"Maybe she's okay," Range said absently, his words coming out in a cloud of vapor in the cool air. The kid seemed calm but a hint of madness lingered somewhere beneath. I wondered if I had the same tone in my voice.

"Maybe," I said, not wanting to dwell on it. Somewhere far off the sound of thunder rumbled low.

Silence fell between us. Our watch would keep us up till one or two in the morning. The townsfolk brought us pots of thin black coffee and Taft had prepared skewers of salt pork to help keep us energized. It didn't seem to be working. My eyes felt blurry and I was growing tired. I tried to calculate the time. It couldn't have been much past ten or eleven.

As we sat in the darkness my thoughts wandered back to the moment with Samantha. Why had it taken me a year to get to this point? Why hadn't I just kissed her? In Lovat we weren't together as much, sure… but out here on the trail, and in Syringa, we saw each other almost daily. I knew the drifter in me wanted to wander. I also knew that Samantha wasn't the drifting type. She was the settling type. But was that really the reason?

I yawned and rubbed my eyes. Sleep was edging in. Everything was getting jumbled. The gray fog that seemed to hang around the town looked thicker. Everything seemed blurry, less sharp, like paraffin rubbed over a pair of goggles.

An hour or so later the noise returned. It started low and long like the horn of a ship and echoed into a loud hammering like a gas engine on its last leg.

The rickety barricade we sat upon vibrated. Something was different. The noise didn't sound quite as deafening, it was brash and offensive but also more subdued. It was less explosive and loud and more… organic, somehow.

It had changed.

Something had changed.

I shuddered. Machines couldn't alter their rhythm like that. Something affected that noise. Something alive.

The boats in the old fishing fleets were said to have unique sounds to their engines, such that folk from the fishing villages could recognize boats by the sound they made as they chugged across the water.

I didn't recognize this new noise. It wasn't an engine I knew.

It wasn't the same sound we heard along the road to Methow. It had changed, and it had done so intentionally.

"I hate that damned sound," said Range, pulling his coat tighter and taking a swill from a cold cup of coffee.

"You and me both," I agreed. My eyes were fixed on the sky. A worried expression sketched across my face.

We listened to it drone on and I wracked my brain trying to understand what it was and why it changed. My eyes continued to grow heavier. After a few moments I shifted, trying to wake myself up and asked, "Does it sound different tonight?"

Range let out a loud yawn and peered at the sky. "What do you mean?"

"Well, I'm not screaming these words at you. It's not as loud. Also the pattern is off. Way off, by the sound of it."

Range paused and I could see him breathe in the cold air, the side of his face lit by the torches. Eventually he nodded, his expression altering as he tilted his head to listen.

"Less moaning metal," I said.

"Yeah, it's—" his words cut off as his eyes flicked out somewhere across the Forest of the Dead. "You see that?"

"What?" I said dumbly. I looked up, feeling surprisingly calm.

Range stood on the shaky barricade and peered out.

My own gaze turned to the pools of light scattered around the village. The gray fog seemed even thicker now. It seemed to subdue some of the torches. I blinked, exhaustion creeping into my limbs.

"I don't see anything. You sure it wasn't a raccoon? A shambler maybe?" I hoped it wasn't one of the gargoyles.

Range pulled his rifle to his shoulder and for a while we

stood gazing out at the foggy area beyond the bank of lights. Blurry-eyed, I looked over at the kid. The feeling of exhaustion deepened. I wondered what time it was. Second watch should be coming around to relieve us soon.

"I don't see anything," I repeated.

"I'm telling you, something was out there."

"One of Hannah's gargoyles?" I asked, another yawn creeping into my question.

"Maybe," said Range, his own voice sounding heavy with sleep as he leaned forward and peered out into the blackness.

"She has never seen them close. Not this close, at least," I said. "Always from a distance."

"It was there," he pointed a finger towards the north. "Along the edge of that last pool of light," he sniffed the air sharply and then declared, "I'm beat."

I squinted.

The fire atop the torch danced.

There was nothing.

"Me too."

Pay attention, Wal! Something yelled from within.

The mist felt heavier now and I really needed sleep, but the kid thought he saw something…. I squatted back down and stifled another yawn. "Okay. Let's check it out. Rouse Wensem. We should at least send a party to investigate that area. See what it is you think you saw. I'll stay here until relief comes by."

Range nodded and hopped down off the wall, disappearing into the gloom of the town square.

Almost immediately, sleep overtook me.

EIGHTEEN

My eyes snapped open. It took a while for my brain to register that it was morning. My back and knee ached. My neck was stiff and sore. My head still felt foggy and my eyes struggled to adjust. That same feeling from the previous evening. The blurriness hung with me, making it difficult to focus on details.

How long was I asleep?

Asleep!

I had fallen asleep! On watch, no less! Cursing, I jerked upright.

Range was nowhere to be found. In the gray morning I could see the shapes of the corpses scattered beyond the town. Among them tendrils of smoke rose from snuffed torches mixing with the low fog that hung above Methow.

How long was I out? The exhaustion had come upon me so suddenly it was hard to remember. I went over everything.

We had seen something.

Range went to fetch Wensem so we could inspect the area.

Then… nothing. That must have been when sleep took me.

I blinked and stared at nothing for a moment. I struggled to process everything through the muddiness of sleepy consciousness.

My stomach growled and snapped me out of my daze. Where was Range?

I rolled from an awkward sitting position up into an even more awkward squat. My jacket and jeans felt damp with dew and my fingers and toes were frightfully cold. I flexed them, inhaling a deep breath of cool morning air. I had a brief sense of déjà vu.

I pulled myself off the barricade and hobbled between two buildings towards the square at the center of town.

A thin wisp of smoke mirrored the action of the snuffed torches from the center of the laager. Nothing else moved. Was the whole damn town asleep?

A body was lying halfway between my post on the barricade and the laager. As I approached, I realized who it was and my hobbled walk turned into a hurried rush.

Range!

The young man was lying face-down in the dust. His rifle was off to one side. His lips and nose were stained with dried blood. Had he been attacked?

"Range!" I blurted in a panic, dropping down and placing a hand on his back. Please don't be dead, kid, I thought.

His back rose with slow breaths. Unconscious. Alive. Relief washed over me. Range moaned.

"Range! What happened?"

"Time for the second watch?" he mumbled through a lethargic yawn, his eyes slowly blinking open.

"Far past due. It's morning."

Range seemed to come to his senses and he scrambled up-right. His eyes widened. He looked around, his breathing escalating as panic sat in.

"I fell asleep."

He looked around before repeating himself. "I fell asleep!" He rubbed his nose and bits of crusty blood came away on the back of his hand.

"Looks like you took a spill on your way down."

"I…" he paused. "I really don't remember it happening."

"Me neither. Lucky I was sitting down."

I didn't like where this was going. Range and I had fall-en asleep almost instantly and at the same time only a few feet from one another. Taft's story about Bowles' Folly flashed through my memory.

"Let's rouse Wensem."

I pushed off the ground with my good leg and hobbled over to the laager where the second watch dozed.

Wensem lay in his bedroll quietly snoring. His naked chest rose and fell with each breath. I nudged him with the toe of my boot.

"Huh? What?" Wensem said as his eyes opened. His hand jerked for his rifle until he realized it was me standing over him. "Is it time for … wait … is it morning? It's morning!"

I nodded.

"Carter's bloody cross! Wal, what happened?"

Wensem sat upright looking the laager over. I waited as he pulled a shirt over his pale chest and slipped his long legs into old brown trousers.

"I fell asleep," I said.

Wensem looked at Range who stood just past my left shoulder. "You let him?"

"He did as well," I explained. "We both did. Best as I can figure—at the same time. Neither of us really remember it happening."

Wensem grew serious, his lips drawing together tightly. He looked down at his bedroll. "Would explain why I didn't wake up."

"Check the laager," I ordered. "Account for everyone. I'll see if the others along the barricades also fell asleep."

"I'd wager we already know the answer to that."

"Maybe," I said over my shoulder. "Come on, Range."

I moved to one of the barricades along the north edge of town with Range trailing behind. I found two women volunteers—a dimanian and a maero—quietly dozing. We woke them, and listened to their embarrassed confusion for a while before continuing on to the next barricade.

Again, we found another one of Methow's citizens sleeping atop a barricade that consisted of piles of logs hammered together by heavy planks like a frontier wall. I roused him.

"You fell asleep," I said as he woke, blinking at me dreamily. "You here by yourself last night?"

"No..." He looked around confused. "How long was I out?"

"Most of the night," said Range. He was holding his rifle at the ready, his face a mask of worry.

"Who was with you?" I asked.

"The scout, Clay..." said the man, nodding towards Hannah's rifle which was propped up against a short wall. I picked it up. Dread filled my chest. "Last thing I remember, she went to get coffee and use the latrine. I don't remember much after that... just you waking me up." He rubbed his eyes.

Worry nested itself in my gut. I wanted to rush around and find my scout before checking the rest of the barricades but I forced myself to breathe. My rational side told me there was a million other places Hannah could be: she could be sprawled out between here and the chuckwain or collapsed on the privy.

I picked up her rifle and looked over my shoulder towards the laager. Signs of life could be seen as Wensem woke the members of the company and explained what had happened. She was probably there, among the group, having fallen asleep. Maybe a spilled cup of coffee laying next to her.

But nothing I said to myself could shake the feeling that something was wrong.

Thanking the man, I forced myself to walk to the other barricades to make sure everyone else was accounted for. As expected, all of the first shift had fallen asleep.

When Range and I finished we hurried back to the laager where the company was milling about. I wanted to see Hannah among them.

She'll be there, I told myself. Drinking black coffee and swearing up a storm.

Taft looked exhausted as she worked furiously at the grill off the rear of the chuckwain. Samantha stood, eyes open in that not-quite-awake expression, her hair a wild nest atop her head and tangled around the horns that grew from her temples. I passed into the center of the circle and did a mental count of the people gathered.

One. Two. Three. Four. Five. Six.

I counted again.

Taft. Wensem. Samantha. Chance. Range. Myself.

Six souls. Not seven. Hannah was missing.

Carter's cross, I swore to myself. My heart started to pound. "Wensem, have you seen Hannah?"

He shook his head, noticing her rifle in my hand. The familiar barrel, the heavy scope, the dusty cloth wrapped around the stock.

"Wasn't she on one of the north barricades?" he asked, his words rising in a worried octave as he realized why I asked.

Range answered. "The guy she was with said she went to get coffee and use the latrine. He fell asleep shortly after."

Wensem let out a long slow breath, his steel-colored eyes meeting mine. His expression tinged on hopelessness.

Hannah couldn't be missing. I refused to believe it. She was one of the core members of the company, a potential partner in Bell Caravans. She was a hardened scout, could handle herself. She knew how to survive in the wild with nothing but her wits; something I wasn't sure even I could do. There wasn't anyone else who knew the Territories better. For Hannah to disappear... I couldn't finish the thought.

What were we dealing with?

The dreams. The noise. The Forest. The kidnappings.

Samantha's words from the day before rose in my memory. "I think we're dealing with another one of the Firsts," she'd said. I remembered the worried look in her eyes.

It couldn't be true... could it? Cybill had been killed. Crushed in the tunnel. She was supposed to be the one who prepared the way for the others. Shouldn't her death have stopped the others from returning?

If I was a praying man, I'd be praying it wasn't true.

But I wasn't a praying man. Another member of my company missing and I was going to find her. I didn't have time to dwell on old legends and worry about Firsts.

"Circle around, everyone," I ordered, spinning an index finger in the air about me. It took a lot to force the words out. "It seems Hannah is missing."

Whispers, gasps, shakes of the head, and agape expressions met my words. I felt it as much as any of them. I continued. "I don't want to believe it's true. So let's fan out and search the town. Check each bulwark and barricade, search each building. Be respectful but be thorough. Ask if anyone has seen her. Gather back here after you're done. Let's hope she passed out in some doorway and she's all right."

The company disbanded in silence, canvassing the small town. It only took ten minutes.

Hannah was nowhere.

The mayor and the sheriff stumbled out from the Big House and met us gathering our crew for an expansive search. The two council members, Boden and Eustis, were also nowhere to be seen.

"Trouble?" drawled the sheriff. His eyes moved over my company as they readied themselves for the expanded search.

I looked at him silently for a moment before answering. "We're missing someone. We're going to find them."

"Who this time?"

"Our scout. Hannah Clay."

The sheriff shook his head. "That pretty little human?"

I nodded.

"Damn. I am sorry, so sorry. She seemed like a firebrand."

"We're going to find her."

He looked doubtful.

"We are," I repeated.

"I have been there," said the sheriff. He reached out and put a hand on each of my arms. His small dark eyes met mine. "Especially in the beginning, I had the same determination. Find my family, my friends. I marched all over the valley, searching. It's always the same." He shook his head. "Believe me."

"This time is different. We have to try!"

"Don't you get it? You've angered them! You took down the body of your roader yesterday. The dauger. They weren't happy about that. This is their payback. You remove a body, they take another. It's the way of things."

I started at him.

"You're not going to find her," he said again, his voice sad. "Stay behind these walls. Before someone else goes missing. Please."

I wanted to hit him. Make him eat his words. Wensem noticed and stepped between us, putting a hand on my chest and pushing me back gently. I took a deep breath and turned away and started walking towards the town's gate. As I marched I drew my weapon and checked the chambers before I returned it to its holster.

I had someone to find.

"Mister Bell," said the mayor sleepily. "Please don't. You'll only risk making them angrier." He reached out and grabbed the sleeve of my shirt as I passed.

I shook him off and spoke as I walked. "We don't leave our people behind and we don't just let them go."

"Whatever you see outside our barricades, Mister Bell, don't disturb it," the sheriff called. "You'll only bring more trouble. I'm trying to help you. Believe me."

I turned to my company. "Open the gates! We'll explore the Forest first and if we can't find Hannah there, we expand our search into the woods beyond. You find her, shoot into the air."

Everyone nodded, their faces uniformly determined.

"Let's go," I said, moving towards the gate we had passed through just yesterday. I cradled Hannah's rifle in the crook of my arm. I vowed to return it to its owner. Two Methow citizens scurried to open the gate and I gathered up what remained of my courage to face the forest of corpses once more.

The doors swung open.

Two loud shouts of anguish erupted from behind me.

I blinked at first, unsure of what I was seeing. Then realization set in.

Shaler. She hung dead, naked, and crucified on a simple pole. Her eyes were closed but her face was twisted in frozen anguish. Blood matted her blond hair and sat in dried clots around her nose and mouth. Bruises and ragged slashes covered her neck and arms. A large sign painted with blood-red letters covered her chest and hung down to just above her knees.

Red words on a black background.

"Wal…" Samantha gasped.

Over my shoulder I heard someone vomit and I could feel my hands shaking. The world swam below me. Dizziness overwhelmed me. I felt like I was going to faint. The words on the sign burned into my skull like a red hot brand:

GUARDIAN:
I HAVE GIVEN
YOU SIGNS
NOW YOU WILL
SEE WONDERS

NINETEEN

The words on the sign caused me to stop in my tracks and fall backwards on the hard packed dirt of the square. I stared at the words, not fully able to comprehend them. Guardian. The name triggered another flood of memories. The horrors I faced. The world before me became a swimming mass of gray.

The words from the sign trailed after me as we searched the forest and the valley looking for Hannah, haunting me like an old ghost. They rattled around in my head as I numbly assisted Chance and Range with taking down Shaler's body. Taking her down was an act of defiance that gave us only a day to prepare. I didn't care, this was a finger at whatever was doing this, whatever had decided to communicate with me directly.

The painted words rose up, swelling like a wave as I helped dig the grave. They played over and over in my head. Signs. Wonders. They would stutter to a stop at one word in particular, the name: Guardian.

Peter Black, the satyr and self-proclaimed demigod, had christened me Guardian a year earlier. A glorious title given for a repellant task. He had hired Bell Caravans to deliver a large crate from Syringa, tricking me into unknowingly guarding the mummified corpse of a First. This simple action, unbeknownst to me, awarded me the title.

Along with the title came instructions. According to some ritual laid down in tomes written by madmen from eons past, anyone connected to the Guardian—friends, family, acquaintances—was fair game for the sacrificial slaughter needed to bring Cybill to life.

It lead to the death of many of my friends and very nearly took the life of Samantha's brother Hagen, Wensem, and his newborn son.

Black had been stopped and I was the one to stop him. Peter Black—Pan—was dead. Very dead. I had seen him killed as an ancient tunneling machine smashed him into a tunnel wall. There was no way he could have come back from that. His ritual failed. Cybill, the writhing, twisting mound of eyes and fleshy tentacles had been lost beneath the city. Hadn't she?

I had seen the tunnel come down on her as it collapsed. I nearly drowned in the process. It had been the road priest who shook those memories loose, and now this sign cemented everything for me.

Guardian, a mocking title. Only a few people in the Territories would know that name. While Black couldn't be doing these atrocities, one of his followers could be. His cult—the Children—also knew me by that title. Many were killed when the tunnels collapsed but some had to have escaped. Were the gargoyles actually the Children of Pan?

Black hoods and robes weren't really their style, though. They fancied colors of blood red and forwent hoods. Their leader was dead. Were they in mourning? Or were they plotting?

Still, the Children were just people: humans, dimanians, kresh, maero. Simple, ordinary, a bit crazy, sure, but still just people. How could simple folk pump dreams into our brains? How could they create the devastating racket that plagued us from the sky?

The six remaining members of my company buried Shaler next to Ivari Tin. His grave was undisturbed. I was grateful for that. If Methow's tormenter was keen on taking back the bodies of the dead, at least it hadn't gotten around to my people yet.

The ceremony was simple. Reunified. Traditional. Led by Samantha. I didn't pay much attention. My mind was caught up racing through all we knew and worrying about Hannah. A numbness seemed to sink into me. A familiar feeling and one I didn't like much. I mechanically repeated the chants and followed along with the small service as best I could; out of respect for the dead more than any personal belief.

As Samantha finished the prayers and we each paid our respects I tarried over the fresh mound along the Broken Road. Margaret Shaler had been too young, much too young. Hannah was even younger. I looked at the forest, the real forest of scattered lodgepole pines and the occasional copse of hemlock. Hannah was out there, somewhere. I hoped she was okay.

The words from the sign flashed again in my memory. That single word burned: Guardian.

Service finished, we made our way back to the town. Range

walked next to me. His cheeks were stained by trails of fresh tears. His eyes red, mood sullen and despondent.

I dreaded sending word to her family. I tried not to think about the consequences.

I reached out and placed a hand on the back of Range's neck. It was something my uncles did to me when I was growing up. He turned and looked at me with angry eyes, but said nothing. I nodded, trying to intimate that I understood. That it was okay to get angry. We needed to get angry.

Up until now we had been tormented at every turn and our best defense was rolling over and exposing our belly. We sought out and took shelter in the very town these tormenters placed under siege for nearly a year.

I was tired. I was tired of the torment. I was tired of being the victim. That single word burned hot, only instead of inside my head, it burned inside my chest.

Guardian.

I'd make it true.

I'd step into the light and find out who was doing this.

And then I would kill them.

As the sheriff predicted, our first search turned up nothing. As did the second. When we returned to town I gathered my people and sent them out on a third search of the Forest of the Dead looking for Hannah. It also came up nil.

A third member of my crew was missing. Two were now

dead. Why us? Was this meant to scare us? Scare me? Was this a warning? We kept rolling even after our company split. Had I listened, maybe Hannah would be all right. Maybe Tin would have been released. Maybe Shaler would still be alive. Maybe Hannah and I would be sharing drinks in Syringa watching the monochrome and waiting for the Big Ninety to reopen.

You can't live in a world of maybes.

I hadn't listened. I hadn't seen the warning. I came to Methow anyway, and broke one of the tormenter's rules. I removed the body of Tin.

This… thing, in all its madness, followed some code. By pulling down Shaler we violated it yet again. If history was our guide, that left us only a few days to find Hannah before she would turn up as another corpse, crucified or impaled, another twisted tree in the Forest of the Dead.

I didn't intend to give it a few days.

The decision to remove and bury Shaler was intentional. It would force the tormenter to act again. They'd come back into town, tonight most likely. As the mayor and the sheriff told us, disturbing the forest brought reprisal.

We only had a little time.

After our fourth search Wensem, Samantha, Taft, and myself sat in the same room in the Big House where the previous day the mayor had spun the town's story. I was starting to realize whoever or whatever was doing this was also watching us. I had sent the Shaler boys on a fourth reconnaissance mission. Partly to get them out of their own heads, and partly to keep the kidnappers guessing.

Across from us sat the Methow leadership, their backs to the boarded up windows and minus the sheriff who was again absent. As we talked, a clock missing its glass face ticked away the time on the wall above.

We discussed the events of the day, the sudden rush of sleep that had befallen the first watch, our missing scout, the body of Shaler, and the plan going forward.

"We all fell asleep around the same time," Wensem said. "The guards along the barricades confirmed it, by the Firsts, Wal found Range face-down, sleeping in the center of the square."

"It moved fast," I nodded.

"What could be causing that?" asked Samantha, rubbing one of the small black spurs that jutted from her chin with a thumb and looking at me. A long sigh drifted out from between those perfect lips. "There were legends of an old demigod who could put people to sleep: Morpheus, the Lord of Dreams. He wasn't malevolent, though. But he had many brothers, and they all had various dream-like abilities."

"You think this is another demigod? Like Peter Black?" Wensem asked.

Samantha shrugged. "It'd make sense…"

"Who is Peter Black?" asked Boden.

"Long story. Troublesome bastard. He claimed to be a demigod, a husband of a First. He's dead now."

Boden hemmed and frowned but didn't press the matter further.

"Dreams, sounds, and now instantaneous sleep," Taft said loudly, lost in thought. She sipped from a flask. She started carrying it with her after we found Shaler. I noticed her hands quaver.

"Maybe poison put us all to sleep. Something similar to a chloroform? We have long thought the town's water was poisoned and that poison brought the nightmares. We even tried to filter it, but never could figure out if that was the cause," said Boden. I hadn't seen him since the previous day as he spent most of his time lurking around the Big House. He looked livelier than before, though he still wore his hood.

"Has anything like this ever happened before?" I asked.

He shook his head. "As the town drew in on itself we always had night guards. They, like anyone, eventually fell asleep, but none ever reported anything like this."

"Did you have a watch schedule?" I asked.

"No, just a few guards who would trade off," admitted Boden. "They'd check the barricades. The gate." He waved a gloved hand.

"I think it's magic," said Eustis earnestly.

I could see Boden's eyes roll in the shadows beneath his hood. If I wasn't looking directly at the councilwoman my own eyes would have rolled as well.

"What we're describing is supernatural. Think about it. All of us dreaming the same dream? Not similar dreams, mind you, but the same dream." She looked around at all of us. "That is impossible! Then the noise! Louder than the trumpets at judgement and so particular. Now this mass lethargy! Surely some spiritist or a group of them is conjuring all of this—feeding off our fear!"

"It's not magic," Taft said gruffly without looking up, taking another pull from her flask. She slowly pinched one of her cheeks with her thumb and stared at the table.

"I…" I began, then closed my mouth. I glanced over at Samantha, who was looking at me. I remembered what she had said the day before. She believed this to be a First. They did exist. This much I knew. And they seemed to operate outside the laws of our reality. Magic might not be the right word, but there was… something… happening.

Eustis, obviously outnumbered, huffed and folded her arms across her chest. A silence fell. Eventually it was Boden who broke it. "What did the message mean?"

"Guardian," said Eustis, and I shivered. "I have given you signs. Now you will see wonders," she repeated from memory. "See, more proof of my magic theory."

"Who is the Guardian?" asked Boden.

Samantha and Wensem looked at me. Their faces were drawn but I gave a small shake of the head. It wasn't the time. I didn't want to have to explain the situation in Lovat to the council. The less we told them about the past, the better.

When I looked at the council all three of them were watching me. Expressions placid. Waiting. I shrugged and lied. "Not sure, a reference to the sheriff maybe? He's the sworn town protector."

And what a great job he has done so far.

"Ahh… signs and wonders," said the mayor in his sleepy tone.

"That, I recognize," said Samantha.

"A threat?" I asked, trying to move the conversation past my unwanted title.

Boden was watching me carefully and it made me uneasy. Did he know?

"No, it's from The Second Law. One of our scriptures. It's tied to an old legend about God leading his people from a foreign land. Obviously it's being used with different meaning here."

"Gibberish is what it is!" Boden said. "Flowery words meant to scare us."

You have no idea, I thought. I had a pang of envy for the old man's ignorance.

Boden threw his hands in the air in exasperation. "More bodies, a sign with nothing but threats. We have no answers, just as before, and you removed the latest victim. That means they'll come again! They'll come again and take who they want."

Taft made a noise. I turned and looked at her. She was still staring at a blank spot on the table but she was shaking her head.

"Something on your mind?" I asked.

She looked up, snapping out of her trance. "Yeah, actually… you're wrong, Mr. Boden."

The old councilman huffed at her impertinence. Taft ignored him and continued. "I think we have an answer. I think it's been with us for a while now. I should've seen it sooner. It was right there. It was always right there. It just took us being backed into a corner for me to see it."

"Explain," said Wensem in that soft tone. His shoulders arched forward slightly as he leaned into his words. It was only obvious to me—after years of working the roads with him—that his usual relaxed posture was tightened.

"We're being gassed."

Wensem straightened further. I blinked. Gassed? Chemicals? I remembered Taft's story about Bowles' Folly. The tale told over the fire. The Syringan plan to gas the Victory soldiers as they slept in their bunks. If they succeeded in knocking them out they'd have been able to walk into Crowsnest without a fight. It was eerily similar to our own recent experience, only—unlike Victory—we didn't have masks to filter the air.

"Think about it," Taft leaned forward. Her massive chest pressed against the table. "It all makes sense. At least the physical portions. Whatever is doing this is gassing the populace. Until now Methow hasn't really had any sort of watch in place, and those they did have would fall asleep and that was that. Those asleep when the gas hit just fell into a deeper sleep. I bet if everyone really started talking they'd discover they all felt like two shades of shit when they woke up the next morning and all dozed off at a very particular time."

"Just like we have," said Samantha. "Ever since…"

Taft nodded, finishing the sentence. "…ever since the noises started."

"We just didn't realize," said Samantha, a bit of awe slipping into her voice. "We all turned in for the night and slept pretty deeply. All that was on our minds were the dreams."

We'll find you yet, Hannah.

"I have some experience with chemicals," Taft explained to the Methow leadership. "Spent years in the Syringan militia. Trust me when I say: this has all the signs. This town, our caravan, we're all being gassed. I'm sure."

An uncomfortable silence settled over the room. The mayor looked slowly at the council and smiled a languid smile. Boden chuckled, shaking his head. "Gassed? Heh. I don't know if I buy that. We're miners. We're loggers. We're farmers. We're not soldiers."

"Where is the sheriff?" I asked, intentionally changing the subject. Taft was on to something, and the sheriff's odd behavior was starting to incriminate him. He was also missing.

The mayor looked up, smiled, and then gave a big yawn. "Yes? The sheriff?"

"I appreciate Councilman Boden's concern but I am going to go with my chuck here. The sheriff should warn the town. Let the people know what we think is causing this. Do you have any protection? Masks?"

Being a mining town I was sure there would be some sort of chemical protection hidden away in one of the buildings.

Boden shook his head. "We did but they wouldn't be of any value now. When we thought the water supply was poisoned we disassembled them and used their filters to try and clean the water."

Dammit.

That heavy silence settled back over the table.

"It still doesn't explain the dreams or the noise," said the councilwoman, cutting through the silence. Her voice sounded frail.

"No, it doesn't, but that doesn't mean those couldn't come from different sources. The legend of the Firsts describes the old ones having various powers. Causing hallucinations. Even mass hallucinations," explained Samantha. "The gas very well could be a means to an end. Putting townsfolk into a deep sleep could put a crack in someone's mind. Allow something to slip inside…"

She shrugged.

"I still don't buy it," said Boden.

"Well, this is our best lead." I looked at the clock. "I want to get another search for Hannah in before we lose the light. Can someone notify me when the sheriff comes in? I need to talk with him about security."

Wensem shifted uncomfortably.

The mayor smiled and nodded and the meeting adjourned.

Councilman Boden and the mayor remained inside with Samantha and Wensem but Eustis followed Taft and me out of the Big House. I was starving, my mind rapidly flipping through our options. A bowl of Taft's chili would help me think.

"Are you sure this isn't magic?" Eustis asked again. Her hand played over the horns that extended from the back of her head.

"Ain't no such thing," said Taft as she fired up the small gas stovetop mounted to the back of the chuckwain and moved a cast iron pot atop its blue flame. The scent of warming chilies, garlic, onions, and beans began to waft from under the lid. I could see that there was something going on inside her head. She was mulling over another idea. I wanted to talk to her about it.

"I agree with my chuck," I said to the councilwoman. I figured it was better to hold my cards close to my chest. "It's best we deal with this on a rational level rather than try to assume it's something out of our ability to fight or control."

My voice sounded strong in my ears, but my chest felt hollow.

Eustis frowned and nodded nervously. Her old eyes flittered about.

"Now I need to ask you a question," I said.

"Yes?" she said.

"About the sheriff."

"Go on," she nodded, the lines in her face hardening a little.

"He seems to be absent and missing at pretty critical times. Like right now. Yet no one gives a damn. I haven't seen him since he actively tried to stop me looking for my scout. Is he involved in the kidnappings? The murders? Have you considered it?"

She blinked, taken aback. "Joul? Involved? Oh, no. No, no, no. He's not involved. He could never be."

"What makes you so sure?"

She looked nervously over her shoulders. "He—well…" She stopped and looked down at her feet and rubbed her hands together.

Taft watched her, stirring the chili with a wooden spoon.

"Go on," I urged, my voice almost a whisper. "It's okay."

With a jolt like a lightning strike her eyes flashed up at me. "No, it's not. It's never okay. Not anymore. Not in Methow."

"What's going on?" I asked, sternly this time.

She melted again, looking back towards the Big House. Samantha and Wensem were stepping out, talking with the mayor. I could see the form of Boden inside the doorway. Rail thin. Draped in his baggy hood.

"He, his wife. I … look … I … it's not my place to say," she stammered. "I'm sorry. Look, I'm so sorry."

I reached out to gingerly touch her shoulder. To try to ease her into talking but she scuttled away before I could say anything else.

Taft and I watched her go. Bubbles were beginning to rise to the surface of the chili.

"Well, that was weird," Taft said. Her thick hands rested on her ponderous hips, wooden spoon extending like a riding crop. She looked like a general watching her troops march to battle.

"I'm not sure I trust any of them," I said. "Boden lurks inside the Big House like a vampire. Half the time he's timid and flighty, other times—like today—he seems more grounded."

"The mayor is batshit insane," said Taft with a humorless laugh.

"Right. She…" I pointed with my chin towards the councilwoman. "She is adamant that this is some supernatural occurrence and since no one agrees she weakly sides with Boden, the mayor, or the sheriff. Whoever has the strongest voice at the time."

"What do you think she knows?"

"No idea," I said flatly, watching Eustis pass the group gathered near the Big House's entrance.

"And the sheriff?"

I breathed out a huff. "The sheriff. As far as I can tell he seems to actively work against us, and I think he's the strongest of that council. He also seems to be the most coherent… the one with an agenda. Though what that is I can't tell."

Taft nodded in agreement. "Yeah. Something's up with him.

I wouldn't be surprised if he is a part of what's going on here."

I agreed but something inside me was wary. It was difficult to see the man as a killer. Then again, I had been wrong about Peter Black, so what do I know?

Taft paused, tasting her chili and finally dished me a big steaming bowl. I could smell the heat in it. My mouth watered.

"That's why I didn't say anything inside the Big House," Taft began. "Wanted to wait until we were alone."

She looked around for prying ears. The nearest townsperson was across the square sweeping a dusty porch. Chance and Range were coming in through a crack in the gate moving towards the wellhouse along the western edge of the town. They saw me watching and each gave me a sad shake of his head, indicating they hadn't found Hannah.

"We're as alone as we'll get in this town," I said, taking a spoonful of chili. I spoke around my mouthful. "Say what you will."

"I know it's gas. I'm sure of it."

I nodded in agreement.

"Well," Taft continued a wide grin splitting her face and making her cheeks rise like round apples at bob. "We can get around it."

I raised my eyebrows, swallowing another spicy spoonful. "Yeah? We couldn't before."

"We didn't know it was gas then! We just thought we were all drinking too much and working too hard. Now that we know, we can thwart it." She stabbed a meaty finger at me.

"How do you figure?" I rocked back on my heels. Taft was inventive if she needed to be, I had seen it with her cooking. This, however, was something even beyond her normal resourcefulness. She was almost giddy with excitement.

"I have gas masks," she said in a hushed voice followed by a jovial chuckle. "Working gas masks. Two, actually!"

My heart instantly began to beat faster.

We could beat this thing.

TWENTY

In my own ears my breath sounded like a roaring gale. Quick inhalations whooshed past followed by the rush of an exhalation as I pushed air through the filter that hung off my mask like mandibles.

I found myself flexing and clenching my hands as gooseflesh danced up my arms. Somewhere beyond the roar of my breathing I could hear my heart thumping rapidly. Beyond that, the noise in the sky had returned, pushed to the background behind my breathing.

It would happen again tonight, I was sure of it. The signs were all there. I shivered with nervous anticipation.

My view of the world was reduced to small circles surrounded by darkness. Portholes of near-light through the rubber mask revealed a darkened Methow. A muddy orange light from our scattered torches silhouetted the town. I faced the town, my keff drawn up around my head like a hood, shadowing the mask. I watched the windows, doors, and barricades of Methow carefully.

Wump. I started, my breath seizing in my chest. That was the first of the watch, the first to fall victim to the gas.

I had shifted the watch around, telling everyone I was adjusting for Hannah's absence but also setting it up so Taft and I were alone. I put us on opposite sides of the town along barricades that gave both of us clear vantage points of the square.

Taft was on the north side, crouching in the shadows atop a barricade between the Big House and a smaller building to the west. I sat alone along the south side atop a barricade next to the gate. Being alone was important. That way neither of us had to deal with answering questions as to why we pulled on the rubber masks as darkness fell.

It had been Taft's idea to keep the gas masks secret from the rest of the company. "We should tell no one," she'd said, narrowing her eyes as she handed me a stained hopsack. "No one. Even Sam. Less folk who know about this, the better. It'll makes things cleaner. Easier."

Samantha would have been furious. I felt guilty not telling her. Anyone without protection was essentially bait. It wasn't the most welcoming thought but what else could we do? Our resources were limited and the more people who knew about the masks, the greater the danger that our adversary or adversaries would find out.

As in the previous night, we fed the town. Taft prepared a stew using the last of the dried meat, a handful of carrots, and onions in a thick dimanian-style broth that she poured atop reconstituted potatoes. With full bellies for a second night the town's spirits lightened again.

The sheriff eventually returned after the group meal was

finished. Mud covered his boots and jeans, and dried leaves were tangled in his hair. He clutched a rifle with a scope in his sizable hands. A look of determination was on his face but as I approached, he replaced it quickly with a wide forced smile.

"Gas?" The sheriff had said, his brow knitted. "It's a theory, I suppose."

"Boden said you destroyed most of your masks trying to filter the town's water," I said. "Is there anywhere you could think of that there might be more? It might help stop whoever is doing this."

The sheriff had rubbed his chin, thinking the question over. "Not in town. I assure you, we swept the place clean looking for filters. Might be more up in the Kadath—but ever since the landslide it's near impossible to get in there. Teenagers used to do it, and they say that if you know an entrance it's still accessible by the old mine tunnels but hell if I know."

"Maybe we try tomorrow," I suggested with a swallow. Last time I was underground I had nearly been killed and was almost buried alive.

The sheriff had looked at me warily, his plastered smile wavering. Finally, he shook his head. "Don't think that's a good idea. We haven't been up there in two... three years? With the winter snows that place is probably near collapse if it hasn't already."

I drew my lips tight as he resisted the idea. What was he hiding? I wondered if it wasn't him I'd be seeing through the lenses of my mask later that evening.

A silence hung between us. The big maero stared down at me with an awkward sheepish expression. I held his gaze.

He coughed and then rubbed the back of his neck before

flashing me a nervous smile. "Look… er… I'll see what I can do, tell the townsfolk. I'll try to keep 'em as calm as I can. Maybe some of the remaining miners can figure out how to rig something up."

"Anything would be helpful," I said flatly, trying to study him. He was difficult to read.

"Do you have a plan?" the sheriff inquired, scratching his chin.

"Not yet," I lied. "We're still planning on running watches tonight. You're replacing me for second watch. I'm at the south barricade, near the gate."

"Same side as the wellhouse?"

I shook my head. "Opposite."

The fake smile returned, and his tone grew a bit wry. "If what you say is true, let's hope we get to that second watch!"

We parted ways after that, the sheriff chuckling to himself as he disappeared into the Big House. I started issuing watch assignments to the volunteers. All the while, a rough-spun hopsack hung from my belt holding the mask.

A second sound jolted me from my recollections and I turned my head to watch another member of the watch topple from his post and land on the dirt fast asleep. He'd feel that in the morning.

It was beginning to happen. I felt my pulse quicken. I looked around warily, hoping the masks would work, my breath rushing past me.

A gray mist settled over the town, much like the marine layers that hung around Lovat on summer mornings. It filled crevices and seemed to drip from the roof like rainwater, always at the edge of my vision and fluttering away when I tried to focus on it. The mist had an almost sentient quality to it. A creature of crawling chaos pulling itself across the town.

Wump.

Wump.

Two more. I could feel eyes on me. That creeping tickle at the edge of perception.

I rose into a squat, my bad leg extended to the side, and played up a nervous looking around, hoping my acting skills were dramatic enough to not overplay my hand. Someone was studying the town. Watching. I knew it. I was certain no one would recognize the gas mask I wore, the light of the torches silhouetting me against the sky, my mask invisible. I waited for a few heavy breaths before dropping to one side with my own heavy wump.

By all accounts, Waldo Bell should look like he was fast asleep.

I fell on my shoulder, so I had a fair view of the square and the laager at the center. My pantomimed fall was harder than I expected and I had bit my tongue. Warm blood trickled into my mouth and I wanted to spit.

My lungs inhaled, drawing breath up through the filter in that rushing sound. I wasn't tired. The mist was all around us. The first watch was fast asleep and I was still wide awake. It was working! Adrenaline surged through me. Nervous heartbeats fluttered in my chest.

A light, sudden and brief, flashed from the north. A mirror reflecting moonlight. Taft acknowledging my mock fall. I heard a heavy sound as she followed suit but I couldn't see her fall.

I counted the noises I heard. That was all of us. If the ritual was being repeated, the citizens of Methow and the remainder of my company were lost in a deep, deep sleep.

Now what?

I waited.

I'm not sure how long I laid there. Time fueled by adrenaline moves in loping gaits. Night drew in and grew darker. Heavy clouds rolled in from the northwest blocking most of the light from the moon. The mist settled, growing thicker and heavier and the torches around the town began to wink out. Slowly their orange light faded and the silhouettes of the buildings merged with the darkness. Eventually even the noise in the sky faded away, growing softer and eventually disappearing altogether.

Night was at its darkest when the thing emerged from the Big House. I blinked rapidly, unsure of what I was seeing, trying to sort shape from shadow. My breath caught in my throat. A silent scream formed on my lips and I had to bite my lower lip to keep it from escaping.

First a hand. Then a shoulder—or what I thought was a shoulder—pulled itself from inside the door frame. Something was coming out from inside. A face appeared. It was totally unlike any face for as the thing moved it melted and slopped, merging with another mass of inky blackness. Then something bigger, something heavy and wet followed.

Carter's cross!

I struggled to comprehend what I was witnessing. It was everything I could do not to look away. The thing was both repulsive and familiar to me. There was something in the way it moved, a writhing, oily black mass that seemed to half-pull, half-slink its way out of the doorway... It reminded me of Cybill. It dragged itself across the open ground and towards the laager. Towards where my friends slept. Towards where Samantha slept.

Samantha!

Thinking of her asleep on her bedroll inside our small camp sent a surge of panic through me. My hand moved to the grip of the Judge. All I wanted was to rush from my position, intercept the creature.

I didn't.

I didn't move.

Faces seemed to rise and fall within the form, difficult to make out in the darkness. Arms topped with hands of various shapes and sizes seemed to emerge, gripping the dirt and hauling the living morass forward with a weird sloshing motion. Tentacles that wriggled in the air were pulled into the body and reemerged as a leg, or a face, or something unrecognizable.

It was growing faster. My eyes were wide. I forced myself to breathe as I watched the bizarre unearthly locomotion of this ... thing. The form kept to the darkest shadows as much as possible, circling the laager like a buzzard to carrion. A bizarre half-form of something ancient and long forgotten.

Taft's words played out in my head. "We follow it. Whatever happens, don't expose us. The trail will lead us to Hannah."

Sam! Don't take Sam! I thought. Right then, I was willing to sacrifice the rest of my caravan as long as she remained in her bedroll.

I squeezed my eyes shut as the thing crawled into the laager. Most of its bulk was hidden beneath the tarpaulins. A heavy wet slurping sound echoed in the square followed by a light moan, and then it was on the move again: retreating backwards, towards the Big House.

It was larger now. A tan arm flopped out limply, a knee covered by faded blue trousers rose from the blackness. Someone was inside it! It had taken one of my people!

I shuddered involuntarily and bit down on my cheek to keep myself in the moment. Keep myself from going into that gray zone of mindless action.

Please, not Sam!

Not again.

I thought of Hannah, of Tin, and of Shaler. And of older faces, faces that still haunted me, lurking on the edge of memory.

I bit down harder on my cheek. The pain flared brighter, but I remained focused.

We follow it. Whatever happens, don't expose us.

My breath came out in a huff and I watched as the creature pulled itself backwards, awkwardly entering the Big House and disappearing into the gloom. There was no way it was keeping my people in there. We had searched that building high and low earlier that morning, left no room unturned. There was no sign of Hannah or that creature. Where did it go when it was inside?

I waited a moment. Two. Move! Something inside screamed at me. It has one of your people! Are you going to lay there and let it take them?

I was.

I remained motionless.

We wait. Moving immediately would reveal everything. It

was agonizing, but waiting would give Taft and me enough space to follow at a distance. If it entered through the Big House that meant it left by some other means.

Finally, I could wait no longer. I rolled down from my barricade and landed in a crouching position, the Judge in my hand. A sharp pain flared in my knee, reminding me I was still hobbled. It didn't matter. Nothing mattered except my people.

I moved towards the laager as fast as I could. All I wanted to do was check on them, make sure they were all right.

I burst past the tarpaulin near Taft's chuckwain.

Samantha lay in her bedroll. I exhaled and slumped backward against a barrel. She was safe. I felt at once relieved and guilty. If she was still here, someone else was missing.

Wensem had taken first watch on the east side of the square. Range and Chance were second shift. Chance was curled up tightly next to Shaler's prairiewain. The bedroll next to his was empty.

Range.

Taft materialized at my side. Her voice was muffled by the mask but the emotion in her voice was evident. "Did you see that thing?"

I nodded, and swallowed the lump in my throat.

"Who did it take?"

"Range," I said. My voice cold.

A familiar numbness took over. My panicked breathing eased slightly. An emotionless void that dwelled deep inside me rose up. It filled my chest and calmed my nerves. I felt it before. First in a police station in Lovat, then in the tunnels below the city, and most recently outside Methow. Now it emerged again.

Air rushed through the mask as I inhaled deeply and checked the chambers of the Judge.

The Big House loomed large in the dark night. Somewhere inside was the town's tormentor. Somewhere inside was that thing.

I motioned with the barrel, pointing it at the wide open doors of the house.

Taft's eyes narrowed behind the mask.

It was time to move in.

TWENTY-ONE

The inside of the big house was even darker than the town square. We moved in slowly, creeping along carefully, hoping the old flooring wouldn't squeak. The ticking of a clock echoed from somewhere inside. My heart pounded, my breath a roar as I sucked air through the mask. I held the Judge out before me, partly for defense and partly because I was worried I'd smack into a wall.

The interior oil lamps had been extinguished for the evening and it was hard to navigate the hallway. The first few rooms in the south end of the building were meeting rooms. Narrow slivers of light cut in from outside, revealing enough to make it clear that both were empty.

"Think it's still in here?" whispered Taft through the mask, her voice cracking.

"Where else could it go?"

Taft moved next to me, the snub-nosed shotgun looking tiny in her hands. We crept along, making our way deeper into the old building.

A loud scrape followed by a thundering boom caused both of us to jump.

"What was that?" Taft hissed.

I shook my head. "It sounded like it came from deeper inside the house. Towards the back…"

I hadn't spent too much time in the Big House. I wished Wensem was with us. He and Range had searched it twice looking for Hannah, and he would know the interior layout.

Something else haunted me. About a third of the town slept here. That left us with a lot of potential suspects, and top of my list was the shady sheriff.

Sweat ran down into my eyes and I wished I could remove the mask and wipe it away but I was too worried about the gas. Who knew how long it hung in the air?

"We can't go banging around in here," I said. "We need a light."

"One second, boss," said Taft and she disappeared back the way we came. She returned with a small lantern cranked to about half its brightness. In the gloom of the interior the light was meager but it let us see where we were going.

I lead the way, moving down a hallway that lead to the windowless interior rooms. The walls were a stained gray and were lined with black and white photographs in modest frames. The gray gas hung around the floor, so thick that it obscured our feet.

The Big House was comprised of a central staircase with a single hallway that encircled it on each floor. Clustered in the center of the building were small rooms, now used as bedrooms for families. Along the north and south ends were larger rooms with windows that faced outward. I knew the council occupied the rooms at the back, though I wasn't sure about the rooms on the floors above. Storage? More bedrooms?

In the interior rooms we found citizens of Methow fast asleep in their beds, chests rising and falling beneath their covers. Eyes shut but moving behind their lids as they dreamt the awful dreams that came with the night. Occasionally one would move or moan and Taft and I would start, our hearts hammering.

We moved to the exterior rooms along the house's north side. This was where the sheriff, mayor, and the two council members slept. Each had individual rooms.

We opened the door marked "Mayor" and found the old man in bed making mewling noises. His knuckles were pale as he clutched the threadbare blankets. Across from his bed was a dresser with a cracked mirror. A few chairs sat next to a small table along the windows that ran the length of the living space. Piles of yellowing papers covered every available surface, collecting dust, curling in the corners. The strong smell of urine penetrated even our gas masks.

I moved quietly inside and tried to rouse the man but he didn't wake.

"This stuff is stronger than I expected," said Taft.

We proceeded to the next room. A small plaque on the door read "Sheriff."

Taft pushed it open. The room was laid out much like the mayor's: the bed, the dresser with a mirror. But the bed hadn't been slept in. The big maero wasn't here.

"He's gone!" I nearly shouted.

Anger filled me.

The sheriff was involved. He could even be the thing that took Range.

We began to hurriedly toss the room, looking for an exit, a trapdoor, anything that writhing mass could have escaped through. The windows of the room were boarded shut and heavily reinforced. No light leaked in from outside. I rolled up the ancient carpet but found only solid floor beneath. We moved furniture, checked under chairs, looking for something, anything.

We found nothing. If the monster used the sheriff's room as an escape point, it had done so through means we wouldn't be able to follow.

"Not here," I said, a harshness creeping into my voice. "Come on."

Councilwoman Eustis's room was next to the sheriff's but it was also silent and undisturbed. The small dimanian woman didn't wake when we tried to rouse her. Still, we checked for exits and found none.

"Maybe it went upstairs?" suggested Taft, her voice louder now. I hoped not. With all our banging around the creature would certainly have heard us by now.

"One more room and then we head up there," I said, pushing open the door to Councilman Boden's room.

His bed was empty.

I turned and looked at Taft, my eyes wide. Her expression mirrored my own.

"Boden!" I hissed.

The frail old man in the hood with the gloved hand who lurked in the shadows of the Big House.

His room was much like the others. The large bed dominated one wall. A dresser the opposite. Unlike the others, though, the windows were blackened and in the space normally occupied by a table squatted a black ornate trunk with golden slats and gold pictograms painted in patterns on its surface. Scratch marks marred the floor around it.

I pointed at the trunk and Taft and I struggled to push it to the side. It was heavy. Finally it gave and slid across the ancient wooden floor with a loud scraping sound.

A neat hole about two feet by two feet was cut into the floor below. A tunnel dropped straight down, disappearing in a shroud of black. It was clear the passage was used frequently. The edges of the wood were worn smooth.

"Too small for me," said Taft. "Here."

She handed me the lamp and I tried to shine it down. There was a floor down there, barely visible. I guessed it was about a ten foot drop. I wasn't sure which direction it went from there.

"How far you think it goes?" Taft asked.

"No idea." I wasn't relishing the thought of moving underground again, nor of dropping the ten feet. My knee wouldn't appreciate it.

"Here, lower me down," I said, attaching the lamp to my belt and sitting on the edge of the hole. I glanced down into the dark and then extended my arms toward Taft.

She gripped my forearms, lowering me, and I dropped the last few feet to the floor. Taft's bulk blocked the hole above me. Her masked face peered down, the glass lenses reflecting my lamp light. They looked like a pair of dim orange suns.

I looked around. I was in a small chamber about six feet by six feet, a tunnel branching off northeast towards the mountains. I explained what I was seeing up to Taft.

"Has to come out somewhere. I'll circle around and meet you wherever you come out."

"How will you find me?" I asked.

"You have a bright lamp."

I grinned and nodded, watched Taft's face disappear from the opening. It'd take her a while to circle the town and find the end of the tunnel, so I leaned against the wall of the vertical shaft and caught my breath before heading down the tunnel.

Certainly a part of me knew how idiotic this was. I had seen the writhing mass take my people. Its movements were part physical and part liquid. My movements, on the other hand, were hobbled. How would I be able to stop it? I doubted that even a heavy caliber revolver like my Judge would do much to the creature.

My hands were shaking. The numbness that welled up previously was fading. I looked down at my hands and willed them to be still but they ignored me.

I took a few deep breaths. Hannah was out there and now Range as well. I had to help them. That was my duty. I wouldn't let it take any more people. It ended tonight. Here.

After a few moments, I began to hobble forward. The ceiling was low, and I moved with my back bent. The lamp did little to light the way ahead and sometimes I jostled myself to one side to avoid hitting a gnarled root or the occasional stone.

The tunnel stretched on for what felt like miles. A few times

I had to rest and catch my breath. After what seemed like two hours of my awkward scrambling it began to slope upwards. Soon after, I found myself outside. I was at the base of a huge fir tree, standing in a waist-deep hole.

Drag marks were etched into the ground running from the hole and leading north. They disappeared a few feet beyond the exit where the underbrush began. I wished I had Hannah's help. Her tracking skills.

I looked around, trying to get my bearings.

I was on a steep hillside, in a forest. Thick bushes and narrow trees rose up around me. To the south I could see the last of the torches burning around the town. The gray fog seemed to have disappeared. I cranked the light of the little lamp and moved around the tree hoping Taft would be able to spot it among the bushes. I waited, grateful for the rest.

Taft found me about half an hour later.

Sweat soaked her shirt, darkening the fabric around her neck, down her back. Her chest heaved in heavy breaths.

"Lucky I found you!" she panted, leaning up against the tree. "You okay?"

I set the lamp on the ground and stretched, feeling my spine pop. I tried my best to brush off the dirt that found its way into my shirt and trousers.

"Can't... remember the last time... I ran like that," Taft said, her voice a muffle behind the gas mask. "Especially uphill. And in this damned mask."

I smirked and motioned with the Judge. "There are drag marks leading north."

"Isn't that where the old mine used to be?" She tried to peer above the trees.

"Yeah. According to the sheriff, it's somewhere up here."

We moved uphill between lodgepole pines, picking our way through bramble thickets that had lodged themselves between the skinny trees. Looking over my shoulder, I realized the dense growth blocked any view of Methow.

"Think it's safe to remove our masks?" Taft asked.

I shrugged.

"It's getting hard to breathe in this thing. If I keel over, just let me lie," she said pulling the mask free and inhaling deeply. We waited for a moment. When she didn't topple, her face broke into a grin. "By the Firsts, real air feels good."

I pulled off my mask as well and inhaled my first breath of clean air in what felt like days. I also realized that the stink of the Forest hadn't traveled this far up the mountainside. It tasted crisp and sweet. Like home. The scent of the road. The fresh smell of pine and the rich earthy scent of moss.

"How far do you think we are from Methow?" I asked.

Taft shrugged and looked over her shoulder to the town. "Three or so miles, I guess."

It was hard to believe I was in the tunnel that long.

We continued to move north up the side of the valley. We didn't see any other sign of the creature on the forest floor. No broken branches. No trails cut into the pine needles that scattered below our feet. Nothing.

"This thing is tough to track," I admitted. Taft said nothing.

It was probably another mile before the forest began to thin and we came upon a clearing. A small church with a crooked steeple occupied most of the space. It leered away from us like a brawler with a puffed up chest. Its roof was bent and twisted awkwardly.

The little building was thirty or so feet square and butted up against the steep slope behind it. The northwest corner of the building was buried up to its roof in what looked to be landslide. Thorny raspberry bushes and saplings grew out of the piled dirt.

"It's a wonder that it's still standing," I said.

We moved closer and took stock of the church, hunkering behind an abandoned, decaying wain. Long rows of stacked firewood covered in a gray lichen lay between the trees, slowly rotting away.

The steeple leaned over the roof, stooping like an old man with a bent back. A faded sign of hand-painted red letters above the entrance read "Kadath Chape", the "L" missing. No other adornment marked the building.

"Part of the mine," Taft said.

I nodded. If the mayor or sheriff were to be believed, somewhere behind that landslide was the Kadath Mine and that massive headframe we saw from Methow. I tried to spy the tower, but it was hard to see over the steep slope and through the trees.

"Come on," I whispered, dimming the lamp. "Let's check it out."

We moved at a hunched walk past the wain and towards the little church.

The soft pine needles silenced our approach. The building faced the southeast. Its front entrance was a yawning, toothless mouth. I spied the double doors lying about thirty yards away near the clearing's edge.

"I don't like approaching it from this direction," I said and led Taft around to the side unaffected by the landslide. Three windows missing their glass peered out above us from the clapboard siding. We huddled below them. Sounds of movement came from somewhere inside.

My heart seized.

There was no lamp lit but we could hear more movement now. A shuffle. A quiet clatter. Whoever was in there was working in darkness.

"There is someone inside," Taft hissed.

I nodded and tapped a finger to my lips and crouched even lower.

I turned the lamp down to a mere ember.

Better to remain unnoticed for now.

A light rain began to fall, pattering on the metal roof of the small church. It would give our movements some cover.

More clanks. The sound of metal scraping on something. A grunt.

Boden was probably in the church, probably the sheriff as well. At least one of them was that thing. We might surprise them, but I didn't relish the idea of charging through the front door. Maybe I could come in from one side and then have Taft go around the other.

It was dangerous.

Whoever was in the church began humming Father Armstrong's "Life is So Peculiar."

I took one last deep breath, steadying myself.

Ready or not, here I come.

I placed my hands together, making a hoisting motion to Taft. The windows were a few feet above me and I needed a leg up. If Taft could hoist me, I could spring in through the window and surprise whoever was inside. I tucked the Judge into my waistband and readied myself to be lifted. Taft knotted her fingers and I placed a boot into her meaty hands.

She grunted quietly, bending with her knees.

I rose upward, pulling myself up when I could and stepping onto the window's frame. In one fluid motion, I stood, cranked the lantern, and held it out, lighting the interior of the church in a blaze of orange light.

TWENTY-TWO

It all happened so fast.

The meager light from my lamp penetrated the gloom inside the old church revealing Hannah lying unconscious and naked on a table made of rough hewn timber. Her chest rose and fell with small breaths.

Alive, I thought. My heart sang. She's alive. Hannah is alive!

Cuts and bruises covered her body, red and raw against her bronze skin. She was apparently being prepped for crucifixion. She was bound to a T-shaped cross. Ropes held her arms tightly to the horizontal beam and legs to the vertical stipe. No spikes had been used. At least not yet.

I wanted to rush to her, cut the ropes, and carry her out of the church. I held back, wary.

It was hard to wrap my head around the interior. The windows opposite me were blocked by the remains of the landslide. Tables lined most walls, covered in strange instruments. Contraptions with sharp edges, pointy bits, and jagged glass. The old wooden floor was stained dark. Sharpened stakes waited in a nearby corner, their tips white and brilliant in the lantern's light. Pictograms, written in something dark, covered the walls. The scrawls reminded me of the graffiti that covered the sublevels of Lovat.

On the opposite side of the room, where an altar would have been, was Councilman Enoch Boden. The heavy hood that he always wore was drawn back revealing a bald pate. His back was bent and he was heaving a body up onto another table. He started and turned as I lifted the lantern, dropping Range onto the wooden table with a heavy thump. His jaundiced eyes blinked rapidly against the bright light.

Only a second passed.

A heartbeat.

Boden's eyes met mine.

"NOOOOO!" he screamed, his mouth a gaping hole, his eyes enormous. The old man rushed towards me with alarming speed and struck the lantern from my hand before backpedaling away and crashing into a table. The lantern tumbled, striking the windowsill at my feet before falling outside. Surprised, I slipped, barely catching myself on the window frame with both hands and twisting my knee violently as I struggled to regain purchase. Boden was yelling. He seemed to be… burning. His skin bubbled. Peeled.

The small bits of glass that remained in the edges of the window dug into my palm.

The lantern was gone, the room once again swallowed by darkness. I heard it shatter somewhere outside and below me. A mumbled "Oh shi—" drifted up from Taft.

"NO!" Boden screamed again, recoiling almost as quickly as he lurched forward.

A rushing woosh sounded from behind me and my jacket billowed with a flutter of air. An orange flickering light rose up, re-lighting the interior of the church. I could feel the warmth on my back and hear the crackle of the flames. I glanced over my shoulder. The lantern had set fire to the dry pine needles that covered the open area around the church!

Boden wasn't pleased. His face was turned down in disgust. He spat and slid down to the floor, backing beneath a table. He sank into the shadows. He shook his head and wiggled his fingers before him, his movements jerky and unnatural.

Outside, the noise exploded in the sky, returning like a thunderclap. The ripping metal warble filled my ears. Boden glared at me and gritted his teeth. His eyes bored holes into me. The noise grew louder.

Pulling myself inside, I drew the Judge and fired at the old man, striking him in the chest. He coughed. Spat black blood and grinned. As I stepped down to the church's floor I made sure to place myself between him and Hannah. He would not take her.

BAM. The grip of the Judge punched my hand. A second shot.

Boden twitched and grinned as the slugs impacted. They didn't seem to slow him. A thick viscous liquid dripped from the entry wounds. He scrambled across the floor, running beneath the tables towards Range, still unconscious, leaving a trail of goop in his wake.

Flaring my nostrils, I fired into the floor in front of him, sending an explosion of wood splinters into his face.

That got his attention.

He started and spun to face me, peering from under a table.

"You ruined it!" he growled, his voice somehow discernible over the noise in the sky, the hammering rain, and the crackle and pop from the fire.

I squeezed the trigger a fourth time. The Judge boomed again, belching white smoke from its barrel. Boden jerked and then rolled into a sitting position beneath two tables. He began to shake his head in long pendulous motions, craning his neck to one side and then to the other.

"It's over, Boden," I said, feeling more confident.

Taft stepped through the front doors of the church, her sawed-off shotgun held in front of her. She leveled it at the councilman.

Boden glared at her and then at me.

His head began to shake again. He waved around violently.

Then he began to change.

Taft and I glanced at each other. What was this?

His movements became less jerky and more supple and smooth. He rose, transforming as he did so, lifting the tables and sending the tools that covered them clattering to the floor.

His clothes seemed to lengthen and shift in hue. It was only when he stood that I realized what I was seeing. The man from our dreams.

He was tall and slender with a straight back and a handsome swarthy face with sharp features. He was draped in billowing red robes that moved slightly in the heat from the fire. A prince standing in his ravaged kingdom.

Suddenly, there seemed to be a shift. We were in the church, and yet... we were somewhere else.

I looked around, confused. I could still feel the heat from

the fire, hear the small sound of the flames, but gone was the macabre interior of the abandoned chapel. Taft was nowhere to be seen. It was just me and the Red Man, standing amidst ruins. These familiar ruins. A scorched flat plain stretched off in every direction uninterrupted. No hills, no mountains, just endless wastes. In the distance a broken sun was setting, and it lengthened our shadows across the flat expanse.

Boden smiled at me, a wicked grin that seemed to waver in the heat. A pair of coyotes circled him, licking at his hands.

I shuddered. My head ached as I tried to comprehend what I was seeing. How could I be in two places at once? I must be somewhere in the Territories... The mountains and rolling hills I was used to had been flattened. Replaced, reshaped into a flat expanse. This was no world I knew.

In the distance were the smoldering ruins of an enormous city. Lovat—it had to be. Though how I could recognize it, I wasn't sure. The great city was broken, its towers shattered, its levels pancaked atop one another. I could smell death on the wind. Beyond its silhouette something immense and unknowable moved along the horizon.

I took a step forward. I heard my foot fall on the wooden floor of the chapel but felt it slap against the scorched hardpan of the wastes.

"Stop this!" I said.

Boden just smiled.

So I shot him.

The Judge roared and Boden jerked, then blinked.

A gust of wind rose, bringing with it dust and sand. I closed my eyes and moved to shield them. When I opened them again, the scene had faded and we were standing in the burning chapel yet again. Boden looked less like the robed prince of a shattered land and more like a small elderly councilman again.

I heard Taft mumble a curse, and glanced at her as she took a step back. Her face was locked with an expression of terrified panic.

Boden chuckled, grinning maniacally. A glop of black slopped from one of the bullet holes in his chest. He quaked and his skin darkened, turning a deeper tan and then fading into a midnight, oily, black.

His arms and legs seemed to simultaneously thicken and melt into his body. A massive black tentacle burst from his chest and then uncoiled before him. I stepped backward in horror. He stopped shaking his head, and looked up at me. A horrific grin split his face, long globs of black falling across it. He seemed to occupy a dual space, looking both like the old man from Methow and like something else. Something older. A creature beyond.

His yellow eyes glowed as his face split , becoming wider and wider. Two new eyes appeared below his mouth, then a nose. With a slurping sound, it broke and became a pair of faces. I shuddered, staring.

The twin faces elongated, stretched, and broke apart. Now there were four. Eight eyes blinked at me. Four wide smiles grinned, wet laughs burbling from somewhere within, trickling out over drool-covered lips.

"You never should have come," it said. The mouths kept laughing. The words seemed to come from within my head.

"I had plans," it said.

The thing rose, pulling itself up with arms that disappeared inside its mass until it hung against the window frame behind it. There it paused, sagging like a wasp's nest.

Just then, Taft's shotgun belched a throaty boom as both barrels fired. The shot spluttered against the wet mass causing small ripples to cascade across its oily form. If the blast had any effect the creature didn't show it.

An arm elongated from the mass, lashing out across the room and striking Taft, sending her crashing backwards.

"You can't kill me, Guardian. You won't." The voice was in my head.

I stepped forward and pulled the trigger. The Judge clicked empty. I flipped open the cylinder and reloaded as I braced for a lashing of my own.

None came.

The Boden-monster began to seep backwards out the windows like rainwater being sucked up by parched ground. It disappeared in between cracks in the rocks and dirt, the four faces staring at me, mouths lolling open. Bemused.

I blew them apart, but the face reformed, cackling as it disappeared into the cracks.

Boden was gone.

"Taft!" I rushed to her side but the big woman was already rising. She pushed herself up off the floor.

"Bastard," she said, spitting blood and wiping her mouth. She raised an arm and looked down at a gash that opened beneath her left breast through her jacket and her coveralls.

"You okay?"

She grunted. "I'm fine. It just looks nasty."

The fire had latched on to the old church and was hungrily consuming the wall through which I had come. It was working its way to the roof. Black smoke belched upward and the sound of raindrops sizzling could be heard.

"Come on," I said. "Let's get the others and get out of here. This place is going."

I quickly moved over to Hannah. She was still unconscious despite the gunfire. Her lips were cut and bruised and a swollen purple mark crawled along the right side of her face holding one of her bright green eyes shut. She was filthy, and smelled like a musty cellar. Shallow cuts crossed her stomach and chest, and I could see more angry bruising along the insides of her arms and legs. I pulled my knife to free her from the ropes that held her tightly to the wooden cross.

It was then that I realized.

Her left hand was missing at the wrist. A rag was tied over it, stained red with blood.

The bastard had taken her hand!

I stepped back, blinking. Staring.

"What is it?" asked Taft, rushing over. Her words caught in her throat. "By the Firsts—"

I shuddered violently, my hands tightening into balls. I looked to the windows through which Boden had escaped. There was no sign of him.

"I will kill you, Boden," I promised.

The noise in the sky went silent.

TWENTY-THREE

Samantha shifted to her other knee as she examined the pictograms on the side of Boden's heavy trunk. Shortly after our return we went through his small room, searching it high and low looking for anything that might give us more insight. His room was much like the others. The same four-post bed. The same dusty mattress. The same dresser. The only thing that stood out as any different was the trunk.

It was large, about four feet across and three feet deep, and about waist high. It was made of a black wood, lacquered to a finish that rivaled granite. The man—if you could call him a man—liked his gold. Gold metal slats squeezed it together and ran its length, fastened with heavy, gilded clamps and thick gold bolts.

Between the slats queer little pictograms were painted in neat rows in flaking gold paint.

The windows had been blackened with tar so we brought in several lamps to illuminate our work. The pictograms caught the light oddly. In the flicker from the lamps they gave off a sickening yellow sheen, not the brightness you'd associate with gold.

"This is a language," Samantha finally said, breaking the silence that had settled for the last twenty minutes.

"Aklo?" I asked. I didn't know of many languages. I knew Strutten, obviously, and Cephan was spoken by some species along the coast. Aklo was the only other language I knew of. I learned about it last year when Samantha used it to translate some ancient tomes that led us to Peter Black. It was older than Strutten, older even than Cephan. It was said to be the language of the Firsts.

Samantha shook her head. "No, but it's nearly as old."

"It have a name?"

"Not in Strutten, no," Samantha said, her voice lacking its usual warmth. She looked tired. She ran her hand over the markings that were etched into the golden slats. "It was once on here too, though it's not as noticeable. Age has worn the characters soft. Gold doesn't hold carving well, especially with a lot of handling."

"Can you read any of it?" I squatted down next to her and squinted at the little symbols. A bird. A couple of wavy lines. Next to those was what looked like scales, and below that a cross with an oblong shape near its top. Nothing I could decipher.

My stomach rumbled, loud enough I feared Samantha could hear it.

If she did she didn't react. "Maybe..." she said, her voice drifting off as she squinted at the shapes.

Footsteps could be heard coming from the hallway and soon enough Wensem entered the small bedroom. He leaned silently against the doorframe and watched Samantha work, his arms folded across his narrow chest.

I looked over my shoulder. "How's Hannah?"

He grimaced and shook his head. "Rough. Real rough. She won't talk, just stares at that stump. Taft washed her up good and bandaged her with some fresh linens, still nothing. She's trying to put food in her belly right now."

"She taking it?"

"Not much, but Taft is persistent. She's getting something down, though it's not more than a watery gruel. What did that son-of-a-bitch do to her hand? Did you see it anywhere?"

I shook my head. "No, but I wasn't looking, either. Between Boden's transformation and the fire, we didn't linger. Taft slung Range over her shoulder and I carried Hannah. We high-tailed it back here."

Wensem rubbed his chin with a finger. "A lot of the bodies outside are missing parts as well. Parts of legs. A foot. An arm. Even a few heads."

Parts. I cringed. Peter Black had collected body parts, too. Specific ones: lips, eyes, ears, and so on. Each had a sacred significance in the ritual to awaken Cybill. Was this something similar?

"And it was then," Samantha said suddenly, reading the pictograms, "that... hum, I can't read this word. It's special, though."

"Then what?" I asked, turning my attention back to Samantha and trying not to dwell on the missing body parts.

"Then... whoever this is," she tapped a symbol that looked like squiggly helixes drawn atop one another surrounded by a wavy starburst. "...came out of Kemet."

"What's a Kemet?" asked Wensem.

Samantha waved a hand. "An ancient civilization. Very ancient. Existed well before the Aligning. Before the Territories. Before Lovat. They still teach about it during Reunified services. It's a part of our scriptures. Haven't either of you attended?" she chided, not looking up.

I wondered if this Kemet really existed or if it was just a myth like the fictional nations of Columbia or Le Vieux.

Samantha continued to run her hands over the pictograms, mumbling as she did. I leaned forward, squinting for a better look. It placed me awfully close to her. I could smell her, feel the heat radiating from her. My mother always said, "Dimanians run hot."

Hot indeed. Samantha had been livid when Taft and I returned.

We arrived late the following morning to a chaotic scene. Townsfolk were running everywhere, guards from the barricades were shouting at one another and Wensem was in the thick of it, trying to regain some semblance of control. When Methow woke, and a bunch of us were missing, the town panicked.

We were initially greeted with shouts of relief. Samantha rushed up to me and wrapped me in a big hug and kissed my cheek. After things settled down and Taft and I explained ourselves her mood changed.

"What was that? Why didn't you tell anyone?" she said, her dark eyes flashing.

"I'm sorry. Taft had the idea and we figured it'd be better to move on our own," I explained.

"Why? You didn't think you could trust Wensem? You didn't think you could trust me?"

"Look, it's not like there were a lot of options! We had the chance and we took it." I had shrugged, trying to play off our decision like it was not a big deal.

"You know, when Hagen first brought you to Saint Mark's I didn't like it. We argued. Then, after you returned from confronting Black something changed. I could see how much you cared. How much you wanted to stop the killers. Something inside of me changed. I somehow overlooked how reckless the whole thing had been."

I had looked away, not wanting to meet the fire I knew was in her eyes.

"Just like this was. Reckless. Reckless and selfish and stupid. What if you were taken? What if it was you who'd lost a limb? What if you had been set up, ambushed by those gargoyles?"

"Look..." I said, reaching out to place my hand on her shoulder. She pulled away roughly.

"Don't touch me."

"Sam..." I said softly.

Her dark hair shifted as she shook her head no. "No, Wal. No. Not again. The last time you just reacted you ended up nearly getting yourself killed. Remember? This isn't Wal versus the world! You have a company here, a company that relies on their caravan master. A company that needs communication between one another, that needs leadership. Between this, between you almost blowing the damn doors off the town... I don't know, Wal..."

I winced and she let her voice trail off. I stared down at my boots but I felt her eyes staring at me. Those dark beautiful eyes filled with disappointment.

Reckless. It was definitely a more fitting title than Guardian.

"I'm sorry," was all I could say but it sounded weak in my ears. She was right. At the very least I should have let my partner know. We were damn lucky no one was killed. It was a mess.

My father always said that in the end a man's failures revealed his strengths. How we handle them, how we deal with the fallout. It had been my call. I accepted full responsibility. As a result, a distance grew between Samantha and me. It was clear in her sepia stare over the fire last night and in her dispassionate tone that morning as we stood waiting in the chuck line.

Wensem had also been displeased that I hadn't mentioned Taft's plan to him. Yet one more step in a long line of missteps. He had the temperament of a glacier. Was the slowest of slow burns. Until now I ignored him, forced my way. Hell, I made decisions that he was supposed to help make. He was responsible for security and I had pushed him aside. I left him out of the plan and put the company in danger.

"This isn't much of a partnership, Wal," he had said, his blue-gray eyes tinged with sadness. "I had a right to know."

I apologized. I meant it but he only looked at me for a long moment before walking away quietly, shaking his head. I wondered if this wasn't a permanent crack in the foundation of our company. If the bonds of trust had been broken.

Sitting in a corner, pounding my head, and chanting "stupid, stupid, stupid," over and over sounded good at that moment.

Samantha turned and looked at me, eyes wide.

"What is it?" I had seen that look before. She'd found something.

"It's..." Her mouth hung open.

"Yes?"

"Wal, we're dealing with another First. Another monster. Like Cybill."

The words slapped into me like slugs fired from a pistol. I blinked.

"You think Boden's trying to bring another one back? Resurrect it? Like Black?" The words stumbled out of me.

She shook her head. "No. I think Boden is a First. I think he's one of them."

Something flipped in my stomach. I didn't go much for the old stories, the tales of monsters from beyond returning to earth. The prophecies of the re-Aligning. It all seemed like religious gobbledygook. But then I had seen Cybill. Seen whatever she was. Some bizarre alien madness given form. Thrashing around in the Humes tunnel below Lovat. Her eyes focused on me. Watching as I killed Black. Watching as I brought the tunnel down around us. Was Boden another version of her? He had transformed before my very eyes...

"We need to open that trunk," said Wensem. His crooked mouth was drawn tight.

I agreed.

"Hold on. I need time," said Samantha. "I need to finish translating the exterior. Know what we're messing with inside. Make sure whatever is in there isn't dangerous."

I rose, my right knee popping as I put weight on it.

"Sounds good to me. I'm going to go check on Hannah. If you discover anything come find one of us."

Wensem and I walked outside from the shadows of the Big House and emerged into the bright overcast day. Last night was uneventful. Uneventful! The very idea made me smile. I couldn't remember the last time an evening had been uneventful. I looked up at my partner and slapped him on the shoulder, surveying the town. He gave me a cool reluctant look.

"I'm sorry," I said again, spreading my hands in penance.

Wensem looked away and frowned but didn't say anything.

"Really," I said. "I am. It wasn't right. You're right. I was too wrapped up in my head. This whole time I have been rushing around and pushing you off to the side."

"We used to make decisions together," said Wensem.

I nodded.

Wensem continued. "Something has changed in you, Wal."

I swallowed.

"Before the thing in the tunnel with Black, you used to rely on me. Talk with me. Now…" He studied me with his blue-gray eyes. "I'm not so sure what you're doing."

"I…" My mouth closed. I didn't have an explanation. I was making decisions without him. Choosing the Broken Road, forcing the Lytle twins on him despite his protests. This whole trip had been a bumbling disaster brought to you by yours truly.

We walked slowly, taking in the perimeter of the barricades

and nodding to passing citizens. We made our way absently to the laager where Taft was trying to feed Hannah.

"Look, I am sorry I wasn't there when you were in trouble. Maybe this is some subconscious thing where you feel you need to be totally independent." Wensem stopped speaking and looked down at me, meeting my dusty gaze. "Just because August betrayed you doesn't mean I will, Wal."

I blinked. A flash of anger bubbled up, but I batted it away. What remained was a pang of loneliness. Regret. August. My friend. He had been killed before I could get answers, but it seems he had betrayed me. Betrayed me to Black. Put me in the position to become this... Guardian.

Was Wensem right? Were my actions based on some fear of betrayal? I was speechless. I had nothing to say in response. Just a mix of confusion and worry.

Wensem sighed. "It worked out. You saved Hannah's life and stopped Boden from taking Range."

"I should have told you."

"You should have."

"I am sorry."

"I know," Wensem sighed again, and then a crooked smile flashed on his lips. "You're a pain in my ass, Wal. It does the company no good for us to be at one another and we both know I can't remain mad, but this worries me. Without trust this caravan will evaporate. Look at what's happened on this trip already. You led. I followed. We didn't discuss. We had no strategy. We had no backup."

"I—"

"No, I'm not finished," Wensem said. I closed my mouth. "I'm your partner. You're my best friend. Hell, my son bears your first name as his own. Remember that next time you have a plan. If you can't trust me, Wal, there's probably no one else you can.

"I like Taft, I do, but she's been with us for two runs. Two." He held up two of his long fingers. "You and I have been together for hundreds of runs. That has to count for something."

"It does," I said, and then repeated myself. "It does. I'm really sorry."

My brain was spinning. I wasn't sure what I believed now. Wensem was right, I was putting myself in position where I didn't rely on anyone. I made the decisions. I acted, or didn't act, alone. I thought of Samantha.

"It worked out this time. Staying mad at you for being an ass won't help. We're now one night free of a kidnapping and that damnable noise. I'd really like to get out of this town, off this road, and see Kit and my boy."

"We can't leave these people here," I said. Boden was still out there, and the sheriff was still missing. We might have ruined whatever he planned for the time being and rescued our own people but if we left, nothing would be here to stop him. He could go right back to terrorizing Methow.

"I know."

"I'm sorry," I repeated. "Really."

"I know," Wensem said, looking over his shoulder at the Big House and then back at me. "I was the easy one. Wait till you have this conversation with Sam."

Hannah sat on a stool near the campfire and stared at the stump where her left hand had been. Taft had cleaned her up. Dressed her in her only other change of clothes. Her finer things, the stuff she wore when we walked into a town. Khaki trousers. A white shirt. Her bandages were redressed.

I squatted in front of her, searching her face for the Hannah I knew. She just stared down at her stump.

Gone were the wisecracks. The wry grin. The bright flashes from her pretty pale green eyes.

Now she was bruised and broken. I wondered if this incident had finished her. Would she ever roam the roads again? She was a good scout. The best. The roads would be the lesser if Hannah Clay didn't walk them.

I sat down next to her and draped my arm around her. She felt so small. Together we stared: Hannah at the stump, I at the smoldering fire at the center of the laager.

For a long while she didn't react, she just kept staring in silence. Her breath came slow and steady, her shoulders rising and falling like the bellows on a forge.

Finally she leaned into me a little, and turned her eyes away from her missing hand, resting her head on my shoulder. I gave her a gentle squeeze.

"He hates you," Hannah mumbled. "He h-hates you so much."

"Who?" I said, surprised to hear Hannah speak.

"Curwen. He calls himself Curwen."

"Curwen? You mean Boden?"

She ignored my question. "I never saw him. He always worked in the dark. Beating me. T-t-torturing me. He made me w-watch. Made me watch as he crucified Shaler."

She paused and drew in a breath.

"I didn't see much. It was dark. But I could hear. Oh, I could hear. She was still alive Wal. Still breathing. She kept screaming. Nothing tangible. Just horrible… horrible screams."

Hannah leaned into me and buried her face in my shoulder. She began to shake, and after a moment I could feel moisture soak into my shirt as she cried.

You don't move in times like these, so I sat. Running my hand gently over her hair. Telling her she was safe. That it would be okay. I hoped it was true.

Taft came over and settled near the fire. Mouthing a "she talkin'?" to me, pointing with a wooden spoon.

I nodded.

Taft smiled and tucked the cooking utensil into the pocket of her apron.

When Hannah's tears let up she pulled away, wiping her eyes with the back of her remaining hand.

"He said this was all an experiment. The grandest experiment. Methow is the first, a control group. He said life was a hideous thing and humanity is the most hideous of all and he's going to prove it. He wants to show that people can be broken. That left to their own devices they revert to evil. He wants to see how long it would take to break us."

Hannah paused and took another breath before continuing.

"This whole thing: the deaths, the dreams, the sounds. He's doing it all. Manufacturing it all for some sick experiment."

She erupted into more tears and leaned back into me.

Samantha walked up, Wensem in tow.

She glanced quickly at Hannah, and then me, before speaking. "I got it. I think we can open it."

"You want to be there when we do?" asked Wensem.

"Give me a moment."

Hannah, pushing herself away from me, sniffled and wiped her eyes again. "No, boss. Go."

"You sure?"

She nodded.

I gave her shoulder a squeeze and rose, following Samantha and Wensem back into the Big House.

The mayor and Councilwoman Eustis were in Boden's room when Samantha, Wensem, Taft, and I returned. The small room was now quite crowded.

"Where's the sheriff?"

"I am sure he'll be back," said Eustis.

"Do we need to go looking for him?"

The mayor shook his head no.

"You realize we think he's involved," said Wensem.

"He's missing and Boden is missing."

The mayor chuckled. "Joul? Involved in this? No, he's not involved. He'd never be involved in this."

I raised an eyebrow and the mayor smiled a vapid little smile before turning back to the chest. "We can discuss it later, but for now let's talk about Boden's chest."

Wensem gave me a sideways glance and I let the matter rest. The sheriff had to be involved in this somehow. He had tried to stop us from the beginning. I was sure it was no coincidence he disappeared the night Boden took Range.

Samantha laid a hand on the chest and smiled. "This box is thousands of years old. Maybe ten thousand, maybe older than that. It's hard to date specifically."

"What's it say?"

"Well, it tells a story. About a prince who comes up out of Kemet to show the world wonders. It's not very specific on the details. He is called…"

"Curwen," I said absently, thinking about Hannah's words.

Samatha tilted her head to one side. "How'd you…"

"Hannah. She said Boden was calling himself Curwen. Is this the same Curwen the Curwenites follow?"

Samantha nodded. "If these pictograms are right it's one and the same."

Curwen was said to be chaos incarnate. His followers wore blue jumpsuits and would collect icons and idols from various faiths and weld them together creating unholy abominations that changed and shifted. Each idol was said to be one of Curwen's faces, and as often as their idols changed so did their beliefs. Violent fights would break out between sects who disagreed with one another, and still they all found it enrapturing. The perfect way to worship chaos. It was strange to think we could be facing their god.

"Curwen," Taft repeated as if tasting the name.

"Wait, so Curwen is Enoch Boden?" the mayor asked, his mouth set in a scowl and his eyebrows drawn tight.

"Seems that way," Samantha continued. "According to this story Curwen arrives at a small town and the residents dismiss him, so he begins to punish them with nightmares and howling laughter from the sky. He brings them visions of dead worlds and eventually deposits them on the footsteps of a vortex."

Samantha stopped and looked at each of us.

"Is that it?" I said.

"Is that it? That's the oldest legend in Curwenite doctrine! This matches their holiest scriptures. Do you realize how important this is?"

"Does it say anything about the killings?" asked Wensem.

"It doesn't say anything about the killings," said Samantha, exasperation in her voice.

"So is opening that thing safe?" asked Taft.

"Well," Samantha smiled, her eyes lighting up. "This isn't just a trunk."

"Sure looks like a trunk to me," said Wensem.

"Well, it has four sides, a top, hinges, and the like, but this is a specific type of trunk. These symbols near the latch refer to it as the "Prince's Travel Trunk." Not a direct translation mind you, but close. These are his personal effects for traveling between worlds."

"What if... whatever is inside is dangerous?" asked Eustis.

"Well, then you'd better stand outside," Samantha said. She looked at Wensem and me. "We need to open this thing up."

Wensem nodded and handed me a crowbar and we went to work.

The chest popped open easily. It revealed an interior devoid of dust and well worn. Resting just below the lid was an insert that ran the length and width of the chest. It was filled with paper clippings about the northern Territories describing the small towns there and the rumors of the Broken Road. A map with a few locations circled. Alongside those items were a few recent newspapers from Lovat with headlines reading: "COLLECTOR KILLER DEAD. BELL EXONERATED," "BELL WALKS ON LPD's FAILURE," and finally, "TUNNEL COLLAPSE CAUSES DAMAGE UP TO LEVEL FOUR. PEOPLE MISSING."

The old man had been doing his research.

Atop this collection lay a small leather-bound journal. It was tied with a bit of leather that was tipped with gold charms that looked like tiny cat heads. A small icon of a tree branch with five limbs was embossed into the leather.

Samantha plucked it up and, undoing the leather tie, began leafing through the yellowed pages.

Her eyes instantly went wide and she looked up at me.

"Aklo?" I guessed.

"Aklo."

The dead language of the Firsts. To be able to read and write Aklo Boden either had to be a scholar of great renown, someone Samantha would know personally, or a native speaker. I drew in a long, deep breath.

Wensem and I lifted the insert out. "Let's see what else he has in here."

A second insert lay below the first, split into two trays as opposed to one long tray. In these were folded robes of luxurious fabric, a pair of crisp white shirts, some silk slippers, but nothing more.

"Enoch had these?" gasped the councilwoman.

Below those was a final insert with small drawers. They were filled with all manner of nicknacks. Gold jewelry. A small scepter. A few pocketbooks written in the pictogram language that lined the outside.

Wensem lifted this last set of inserts out and set them on the floor. I could feel bodies press around me as everyone leaned in to get a good look at what lay below, inside the trunk.

Gasps went up around the room.

A small human body lay in the space. Mummified and withered, the skin tightened against the bone, lacking its original color and looking more like leather gone to patina. Through a hole in the skull flashed a bizarre-looking crystal, as if the brain had hardened into a mineral.

My mouth went suddenly dry as I recognized this man's face. It was withered and shrunken, yes, but the resemblance was still there. The noble nose. The trim jaw.

"I think we found the real Enoch Boden."

TWENTY-FOUR

I...I can't...I can't believe it," mumbled Councilwoman Eustis.
She blinked rapidly, shuffled across the room, and collapsed onto
the edge of Boden's bed where she wept quietly into her hands.

The mayor didn't react. He stared dumbfounded down into
the trunk, his eyes wide, his mouth hanging open.

"How long you think he's been here?" asked Wensem peering
into the trunk. The corpse was crammed into the small space,
neck bent forward, knees almost touching his jaw. The arms were
twisted and looked as if they had been broken trying to stuff him
into an awkward fetal position.

Samantha peered down and touched the skin very carefully.
I stifled a shudder.

"It doesn't make sense," said Samantha absently.

"What do you mean?" I asked.

"Well, he shouldn't be in such good condition. The body
is preserved, mummified. This valley isn't as dry as the plains
or the central plateau. It'd have to be carefully prepared to get
like this. Based on the condition of his skin, the coloring of

the bones, it looks like he's been dead for hundreds... maybe thousands of years."

"Maybe it happened because of the lack of air in the trunk," I suggested.

"Or something else could be at work," said Wensem.

I looked up at him from across the open trunk. Wensem's cool presence always made it easy to forget how deeply religious he was. He followed the direction of his warren's lama and attended services regularly when we were back in the city. Perhaps he held to a more deep-seated faith than I realized.

"Boden, er..." Samantha looked down at the mummified corpse again. "...the thing masquerading as Boden, Curwen, did originally hail from Kemet."

"What do you mean?" I asked.

"Mummification was common there. According to the tales, they removed internal organs and stored bodies in huge underground tombs chiseled out of cliff faces. The dry desert air assisted in the preservation of the corpse."

"So you think this Boden-monster did all that, without anyone noticing here in this room?" It sounded implausible.

"Wal, we're dealing with something..." Samantha paused and let her voice drift off. "...preternatural. Something that operates outside of our environment. It changes shape, taking on any form it desires. It can give us dreams and force us all to fall asleep. It's not much of a stretch to believe it has the ability to mummify."

"So Curwen has been playing the role of Enoch Boden for who-knows-how-long," said Taft.

"At least a year," said Samantha.

"Right, at least a year. This explains why no one noticed his sudden appearance," I added.

"Since the killings Enoch rarely came out of his room," said Councilwoman Eustis from the bed. "We haven't held regular council meetings for months. At least not until you folk showed up. When they were held, half of us never attended."

"Maybe the sheriff helped," said Wensem. "It'd explain why he hightailed it when you and Taft followed Boden the other night."

"I told you," the mayor stated, his eyes still on the corpse. "Joul has always done this. He disappears. Calls them his sojourns. He'll go away for a day, maybe two. Says they help him clear his head."

Wensem's lips turned down into a frown and his gaze met my own.

"You have mentioned as much, but we need to know more," I said. "We need to know all of it. Why is the sheriff able to go on these sojourns and is never taken? Why did he disappear the same night we caught Boden?"

"It's not my business to share more."

"The sheriff is missing and the thing that masqueraded as one of your council members for a year is the root cause of these problems. Whether you like it or not this has now become our business."

The mayor huffed and stared into the trunk for a while, his glassy eyes seeming to focus for a moment before he pushed away and paced the small space between the bed and the trunk. It was obvious that clear, direct questioning made him uncomfortable and this whole ordeal bothered him.

"Mister Mayor," said Samantha, her tone softer than my own. "It would really help us."

The mayor stopped and turned, smiling a sad smile that looked sadder below his bleak colorless eyes. "This isn't my story to tell. This is Joul's story. His loss."

"What do you mean his loss?" asked Samantha. "What did he lose?"

The mayor shook his head sadly. "Two of the first to go were Joul's wife and child. Lovely woman. They hadn't been married long. Few years. Sarah, his wife, was the first woman to be taken and impaled. His daughter, Larissa, wasn't more than a year old. She was the first of the children to be taken."

"That's horrible," said Samantha.

I could see Wensem swallow. His son—Waldo dal Wensem—was just over a year old. I knew he was thinking of him in that moment.

"Joul never forgave himself for that. It was his idea to take down the bodies the first time. His idea to bury them and defy the tormentor."

Sobs were now coming from Councilwoman Eustis but she said nothing.

Mayor Feeney continued, his old wavery voice cracking. "Joul never acted after that. He always made excuses. Always tried to calm down the protests. He blamed himself for the deaths. Always has. He wanted to die, but couldn't do it himself. So he wanders. Tries to goad the tormenter into taking him. When Sarah showed up dead he was heartbroken, but when Larissa…"

The mayor left the sentence unfinished and stared at his old boots. He stopped pacing. The dull growls from the oil lanterns filled the silence.

What do you say after something like that?

The sheriff had been acting out of his own loss. He was worried more would die. Had probably seen many die. When you are placed in a position of protection and you fail there isn't anything more heartbreaking. I knew. No wonder he always tried to stop us. In his mind that was the right thing to do.

"He would disappear," said the mayor, his voice sounding loud and imposing as it broke the silence. "He'd wander the hills."

"I wonder why Boden, er... Curwen never took him."

"The experiment," offered Taft. "Maybe Curwen was trying to break him. Watch him go mad. Maybe that's why he hasn't been taken, perhaps he's close to the edge. Ready to kill."

"He's big enough, if he wanted he could have hurt a lot of people," said Wensem. "He'd be the perfect candidate."

I tried not to think of an armed and crazed maero running around in the hills. I had faced off with one before and I didn't want to revisit the experience.

"Joul never liked Enoch," said Eustis between sobs. "They never got along. Even before Methow became... what it is today."

"You think he'll be back?"

The mayor shrugged.

"It's been almost two days. We might want to operate under the assumption that Curwen changed its mind and the sheriff might be a victim," said Samantha.

"If the sheriff was taken, then we're also assuming this Curwen is still active despite our action against him," said Taft.

She settled on the bed and was cradling the sobbing Eustis against her chest.

"We didn't kill him," I said. "At most we scared him away. Probably temporarily."

We told the mayor and the councilwoman our story shortly after returning with Hannah and Range, so it wasn't surprising when Mayor Feeney asked, "Any more information from the scout?"

Taft ignored him. "During the night he would drag her and Maggie Shaler out of an old cellar under the chapel. Bring them up into the building where he would go to work on them," she visibly shuddered. "He put them back into the cellar before dawn broke."

The mayor frowned. "That mine is cursed. Always has been. Many men were killed in its depths before the tormenter arrived. Fires, explosions, and then the earth-slide. It is a dangerous place."

"Dangerous, yes, but it's our best bet to find Curwen," I said. I wasn't relishing the idea of going back into tunnels, but it seemed the only way.

Feeney shook his head sadly. "I would advise you not to go to the Kadath. Methow has been abandoned by God. He has given that mine to the devils."

TWENTY-FIVE

Orange sparks lifted skyward carrying the remnants of the fear that had bound us so tightly in the beginning of our journey. Smoke clung to our clothing and filled the air between us: the Shaler boys, Taft, Samantha, and Wensem. Six of our seven. Only Hannah didn't sit around the laager's central fire. Instead she slept in a bed we made up in Shaler's prairiewain. She still wasn't herself. She was talking, but the fire was missing from my scout. A creeping despair seemed to fill the shell that remained.

There is something about having looked at the enemy clear in the face. It becomes known. Lesser than it was. The frightening thing becomes measurable. Curwen had become measurable.

We had finished a meal of biscuits and the last of our dried beef earlier that evening, and were now taking advantage of the silence in the lull before watch. The sun had just dipped below the western mountains and turned the clouds the color of iron.

I worked the soft wool cloth in my hand, cleaning the chambers, the rod, and barrel of the Judge. Peering through the cylinders, looking for a stray bit of dust I might have missed. I did it mindlessly, my hands accustomed to the process as I prepared the gun.

This night, like the nights before, brought with it no sounds. No nightmares. Only silence. The deep silence of the vast wilds. I wondered what that monster, the creature called Curwen, was thinking. Was he expecting me to come after him or did he expect me to pack up after our last encounter? Did he think I would leave the valley of Methow to him?

"He seems to have an aversion to light," I said, remembering how he recoiled from the fire, the light from the lamp. How he had lurked in the shadows of the Big House. "He dug a pretty extensive tunnel under the Big House. I followed it and it emerged in the forest up the hillside. If he played his cards right even on a sunny day he could get around fine."

"Can we use that somehow?" asked Range. The boy was livid when he'd woken up, bumping along on Taft's shoulder. When she set him down and explained the situation to him he was stunned, but grateful. That shock changed over the last few days, hardened into a seething hatred. He'd seen what Curwen did to Shaler. Realized how close he had come to a similar fate.

"We'll try. Odds are, he's set up in one of the old mine tunnels. It'd be dark there and reasonably safe from detection. When he fled the chapel he was moving in that direction."

A memory of his slopping movements flashed in my mind and I shuddered.

"That would provide him with a clear view of the valley. If so, he's protected by nearly impassable terrain."

"If it's nearly impassable how're we going to get to him?" asked Range. Chance nodded in agreement with his brother. I noted how closely they sat together. Chance was what—sixteen? These kids have lost a lot, I thought. And early.

"Good question," Taft said, looking at me from across the fire.

"I want to check that cellar, see if there aren't any clues there. If we find nothing, we'll climb that landslide."

"Making this up as you go along?" asked Samantha.

I shrugged and admitted, "It's what I do."

Samantha's expression was stony, her eyes glinting in the fire light. My wry comment didn't draw the smile I'd hoped for, at least not from her. Nervous but warm chuckles echoed from the others. It was good to see the company in better spirits.

"One more thing," I said, looking in the direction of the Big House. "The sheriff is still missing. The mayor said he disappears often but it's been two days. He's never gone that long."

"Think Curwen has him?" asked Chance.

"Maybe."

"Where?" asked Range. "It was just me and Hannah at the chapel, right?"

"At the time, yes... who knows now."

"There's still the potential that he's working with Boden," added Wensem.

"You think?" I asked. "Even after the story of his wife and kid?"

"If he's a believer, if he knows who Curwen is... who knows?" said Samantha. "Faith makes people do crazy things. If he's working with Curwen he might try and stop us."

I didn't relish the idea of facing down the big maero, but

Samantha was right. Besides, I still wasn't sure how much I could trust the mayor's story.

"So… we're raiding the Kadath," said Taft with a wicked smirk.

"So we are," I agreed, flipping the chamber of the Judge back into place with a metallic clunk. The gun felt heavy in my hand, and threatened to weigh me down with memories I wished to forget. History felt like it was repeating itself. Another… thing. Another tunnel.

A voice rang out from outside of our ring. Hannah appeared at the edge, her stump held to her chest. Lit from below she looked a rough sight. Her bruises had darkened, the bandages that covered her cuts, gashes, scrapes, and scratches were showing hints of red. A long rifle was slung over her shoulder and she wore a full bandolier.

Six sets of eyes turned to look at her.

"If you're going after him, I'm coming with you."

TWENTY-SIX

When Bell Caravans arrived at the site of the old chapel we discovered the fire had eaten its fill and the building was burned to its foundation. The tables and utensils that once lined the interior were blackened, twisted abominations of their former selves, fitting reflections of the monster that once wielded them.

Of the seven of us, no one remained behind at laager. We all marched from the small town and moved north together, towards that bleak mine tower that poked up from its ragged cavity in the mountain.

Though the sun was breaking over the eastern plains we carried torches, not sure what to expect once we stepped underground. The flames snapped and popped in a freezing wind that threatened to extinguish our lights. It blew down from the north dragging with it dark clouds that promised cold autumn rains or maybe an early snow before the day ended.

We stood below the trees, their bark bearing scorch marks from the chapel fire. We examined the ruins before us. I was struck with a sense of déjà vu as my stomach gurgled in hunger, an appeal that felt as familiar as it was absurd.

"Well, you didn't leave much in your wake," said Samantha as she edged closer to the old church. I wished she had been able to see the scrawls Curwen left on the chapel's interior. They might have revealed more clues.

"We were a little busy," said Taft.

Wensem grunted but said nothing and followed Samantha, his rifle held at his waist. He was coiled like a spring: shoulders tight, back straight.

I signaled to the Shaler boys to circle the clearing, make sure there wasn't anyone lurking on the edge of the forest. I didn't want to risk the possibility of an ambush.

Hannah said nothing. She just stood, arms holding her coat tight around her as it whipped in the wind. Her face looked gaunt in the dim light under the tree canopy and her auburn hair whisked about her face. Her green eyes, circled with bruises, were as cold as the northern air that encircled us. She stared at the chapel ruins.

Edging closer, I spoke just loud enough to be heard over the rustling of branches. "You all right?"

"Haven't got much of a choice, do I?" she said.

"You can go back, it'd be okay."

She paused. Then turned and looked at me for a long moment. "I really can't."

She shifted the rifle on her shoulder and trudged away from me, following Samantha and Wensem.

Taft gave a low whistle, and stepped up next to me. "She's tougher than I'd ever imagined."

"There's a reason I hired her. No other scout I'd trust more."

"Think she'll pull out of this?"

"That's up to her," I said, appraising Hannah as she talked with Wensem and Samantha by the edge of the chapel. "Come on, let's go find that cellar."

The entry to the cellar was partially covered by the landslide. A huge stone boulder had lodged itself over one of the double swinging doors that opened on a set of rough stairs leading down into a chamber below. It didn't leave much of an opening. I squatted on my haunches and held out the torch trying to peer down into the darkness.

"I'm really sick of tunnels," I said slowly, absently. The light of my torch didn't penetrate far into the gloom, and it was difficult to make out what lurked beneath.

"That's a tight squeeze," Taft said gauging the entrance.

I knew what she meant and she was right. She wouldn't fit. We'd miss her skill with her shotgun but there wasn't much to be done about it. "You mind standing guard? Make sure nobody comes in behind us."

Taft looked around, snorted, and shrugged in agreement. She leaned against the boulder and drew a tin of sardines and a small packet of crackers from a jacket pocket. "You all be safe. You all come back. You hear me?"

Everyone nodded and mumbled agreement.

"Well," I said, summoning my courage. The cellar's maw lay

open before us. "I guess we better get to it."

Gingerly I stepped down into the gloom and pulled my sidearm. I held the Judge in one hand while I thrust the torch out with the other trying to light the path. Waving the flame before me, I attempted to get a better sense of the underground space but the descent was steep and narrow. We were well underground before we emerged into any semblance of a chamber.

Packed earth surrounded me both below and above and I stooped slightly to avoid smacking my head on the roof. Wensem appeared behind me, nearly doubled over. Together, the pool of light cast by our torches was meager.

"Carter's cross, it's dark," he grunted.

"Yeah, stick close. I'm having a hard enough time seeing down here with both our torches."

In a few moments six of the seven members of Bell Caravans were huddled near the exit of the cellar. Combined, our lights were enough to make out one side of the chamber, the rest dissolving into a shadowy murk.

The cellar was larger than you'd expect. Larger than the chapel. The ceiling was low and partly lined with rough wooden beams walling off small sections of the space into what appeared to be tiny cells. Chains ran everywhere—attached to poles, embedded in the packed earth walls, running between the wooden bars, and fastened to a large stone in the far corner.

Hannah was visibly shaking. I wondered what was playing through her mind at that moment. This was where she had been kept during the day. Had to be. Deep enough underground so that no light could get in and no sound could get out. Even now with our torches and the cellar door thrown wide open very little light penetrated the darkness.

Leading the way with Wensem close behind the six of us pushed down a passageway that seemed to run the length of the chamber. Our pool of light followed us like a spotlight. The smell in the chamber was awful—a mix of excrement, sweat, and the lower scents of blood and rot. Someone gagged and I pulled my keff over my face, wrapping it around my nose and mouth and pushed onward.

One after another, we checked the cells. Each cell was empty. In the vacant silence, the scratches on the packed earth walls told stories. Buckets swarmed with white wriggling worms, and rusty chains littered the floor like dead snakes.

"No sheriff," I noted quietly.

"I'm not sure if that bodes well for him or not," said Samantha from somewhere in the darkness behind me.

I nodded invisibly in the darkness.

The chamber ended in a larger cell at the far end from the entrance. A few pews that looked like relics from the chapel had been dragged down and sat vigil along the walls. It gave the space the feeling of a sinister waiting room.

The openings of two narrow tunnels gaped at us and led away from the waiting room, one leading right, the other to the left. No sound came from either and both seemed to smell equally horrid.

"He would wait over here sometimes..." Hannah's voice drifted into the gloom. "Speaking with someone. I couldn't understand the language... It wasn't Strutten, Cephan, or that weird language the bufo'anur speak."

Samantha moved next to me and I met her eyes: dark pools in the flickering torchlight. She held up Curwen's worn journal.

Aklo, we agreed silently. The language of the Firsts.

"We should stick together," said Wensem pulling on one of the two operating gas masks. My own hung at my side in its sack.

It had been Wensem's decision about who carried the masks. It should have been his decision from the start. He'd selected me and himself. We had more experience killing. We could shoot if it came to that.

Everyone agreed.

"Left or right?" I asked, looking over my shoulder to where Hannah stood.

"Left," said Hannah. "Wait—no. Right. Yes, right."

I turned and looked at her, that same deadpan expression on her face. "You sure?"

She nodded.

"Wal, one of us should take the lead and the other should follow up the rear," said Wensem.

I looked down the tunnel. "Which do you want?"

"How about you and Sam lead, Shalers in the middle, Hannah and I can follow?"

"All right," I said, squeezing into the narrow tunnel.

My shoulders rubbed the sides and I ended up walking sideways, torch outstretched, head lowered to avoid the protruding roots and rocks.

No one talked. The only noise was the crackle of the torches and the scraping of boots on the dirt. When I first heard the hiss of whispered voices I thought it was a breath of air passing through the network of shafts and tunnels. But it didn't dissipate and disappear. It grew louder.

The voices were muffled initially, but soon we could hear their inflection. The rising and falling of voices, what sounded like a discussion. We paused and crouched down, trying to block the light from our torches as much as possible.

I leaned back. "Samantha. Come up here." I hoped she'd be able to understand the words and perhaps provide translation.

"Too muffled," she said with a shake of her dark hair.

We pressed on.

The packed earth eventually gave way to stone and the tunnels widened slightly, the low ceiling rising so that even Wensem could finally stand upright.

The floors and walls were smoothed out now as if chiseled by machine and cut through the ground by some raw power. We were in the mine.

"The Kadath," I hissed over my shoulder to Wensem. In the dim light I could just make out a nod.

Our pace slowed. Some to quiet the sounds of our footfalls, some to make sure we didn't trip. It seemed a number of loose stones had fallen from the ceiling.

The voices grew louder and Samantha could make some of it out.

"They're speaking Aklo, but… gibberish. I don't understand it.

The words are all jumbled. The sentence structure is unfamiliar… happenstance… and… kill, no… create… green… but, your Guardian." She shook her head and looked confused. "I honestly don't know."

My heart was pounding against my ribcage and I paused to wipe my palms on my trousers. We were close now. I could feel it.

I double checked the chambers of my gun. It felt heavy and cold in my hand. The five shells stared up at me from the cylinder, twinkling in the torchlight. Ready. Waiting. I heard sounds of metal and leather behind me and knew the others were drawing their guns, too.

As if in answer more mumbles came from somewhere ahead. Echoing off the stones in a gibbering rush.

"Come on," I said, not wanting to take another step further.

Time underground is funny. I don't know how long we moved along those mine shafts, the voices ahead guiding us forward.

We spilled from the mouth of the tunnel into a vast chamber, other tunnels pockmarking the wall like the aftermath of the blast of an enormous shotgun. Meager light oozed downward from a hole in the ceiling and an elevator descended like a stalactite into the gloom. It was thick, square, and rusted to ruin. It was clearly not functional. The ropes that would have lifted its cage upward had long since rotted away. A spiral staircase wound alongside it, missing a few of its steps.

Four figures were gathered near the base of the elevator and they started as we emerged. Heads snapped in our direction.

The faces.

There was something wrong with their faces. They lacked, well, everything: no eyes, no nose or mouth. Heads covered by a dark fabric. A cold sweat broke across my shoulders and ran down my spine.

My arm snapped upward, Judge in hand.

These figures were familiar. I knew these figures, though I had never seen them up close: tall pointed hoods and billowing ink-black robes that soaked up the light. These were Hannah's gargoyles, the ones who watched us from the ridges as we moved toward Methow.

I could see now that they were completely covered in the dark fabric: faces, arms, legs, hands, even individual fingers were wrapped in a shroud of black. It seemed to hang off them like heavy folds of skin, moving about them like the branches of a willow.

At once the four of them turned towards us and began to howl, a high-pitched sound that filled our ears.

Hannah responded with a scream of her own that sounded like a battle cry. She dropped her torch and lifted her rifle in one fluid motion. Resting the forestock atop her wounded arm, she began to fire one-handed. The strangers didn't return attack, instead their howl choked into mewling cries of panic and they scattered, rushing to opposite corners of the cavern.

The sound of the gunshots crashed against the stone and echoed throughout the space. I fired at another figure, the Judge erupting in my hand as I drove the thing into the shadows.

Hannah advanced on the gargoyles, shooting as she went. She was livid. Her teeth were bared and raw hate burned in her green eyes.

The closest gargoyle wasn't quick enough. It stumbled, then went down, bleating a wet cry before evaporating into a cloud of black smoke that quickly dissipated. Other figures were diving for cover as my crew continued to drive them down.

"He's making a break for another tunnel!" shouted Chance, running to intercept an escaping figure, rifle to his shoulder. Seeing his route cut off, the stranger dropped down, pinned by Range's gunfire.

We were now in a standoff. The three figures were hiding behind stones and we had them surrounded.

"Waaait!" called a voice, echoing off the stone. It sounded oddly like rushing water. A pair of wrapped hands shot up behind a big rock, barely visible in the light of our torches.

"Noooo," hissed another voice. "Noooooo."

Hannah's rifle clicked—empty.

"Hannah, Range, stand down," I said, advancing next to Hannah's position. The Judge bled smoke in my hand.

"Come out!" I demanded. "Now."

"You will kill us."

They had me there.

"It's possible," I admitted.

Eventually one of the figures rolled out from behind the stone. Bits of moss and dirt were stuck to the black fabric. The figure huddled on the floor pathetically, the blank covered face seeming to look up at me. Its arms were raised in surrender.

"Peace! Peace. Guardian, we are not your opponents."

"Then who are you?" I asked. "Were you watching us on our way to Methow?"

The thing backed up a few steps and raised its head in a motion that seemed to indicate it was studying me.

"Why are you here?" it asked. "This is not your place, Guardian. This is not the great tottering city on the sea."

"I asked first," I growled, drawing the words out menacingly.

A second figure rose from its hiding spot and spoke, tilting its tall pointed hood to the side like the hand of a clock. "We are messengers. We are watchers. We observe in silence and carry word across the stage."

"Get up, you," said Range, moving to the third figure. The creature rose and Range pushed it towards the others with a shove of his boot. It went sprawling across the floor of the cavern, coming to rest near its companions. My crew circled, guns trained on the three of them.

"What stage?" Samantha asked, and then repeated the question in Aklo.

One of the figures looked at her but didn't respond. Another made a whimpering sound. The fallen gargoyle clambered to its feet.

"If we trade question for question now it is your turn to answer," one said.

"I came to stop Boden," I stated.

They disregarded this, but closed in together like a flock of birds. Moving and twitching as they slowly rotated in place, each taking an opportunity to study us. It was impossible to differentiate between them and in the wavering light it was difficult to completely distinguish their forms.

"Boden is dead," one of them said flatly.

"Fine, whatever that things calls itself—Curwen, whatever. I am here to stop it. That thing that took my people. It slaughtered half that town."

"You speak of Curwen... but he is Chaos. Mirza of a thousand forms. He cannot be stopped."

Hannah, who had been slapping more shells into her rifle, now brought the gun up in a rush.

"Hold!" I ordered.

"Let me kill 'em, boss. It's clear they work for the bastard." She licked her lips nervously.

"No. Wait. Not yet," I said. I didn't know what awaited us deeper in the mine but I knew these creatures could have answers. "What is the stage?"

They erupted in loud whoops of laugher, sending a wave of chills through my body. I was grateful none of my crew were startled enough to begin firing. When their laughs calmed down one of them finally spoke in a sing-song, saccharine tone. "You are a fool, Guardian, to ask such a stupid question: all the world is a stage!" More laughter. "Do you intend to bury Curwen? Like you did his niece?"

"I intend to stop him," I said.

More laughter.

"Let me kill 'em, boss," Hannah pleaded through gritted teeth. A sheen of sweat glistened along her brow and her hair stuck to it.

I ignored her and asked, "Where is he? Curwen. Is he in the tunnels?"

"He is where he deems he should be."

One of the figures turned to Samantha and asked, "Who taught you the old words?"

"Th-the words?" Samantha stammered and blinked in surprise, shocked the creatures were speaking directly to her.

"Yes. Yes, impertinent priestess," it said, impatient. "The royal language. Who taught you?"

"Nobody! I taught myself. From books."

"You speak it poorly. It is profane on your tongue. You do not understand the meanings," it said, and then turned to me. "You do not stop the Mirza. You cannot hope to stop him. You just delayed him."

"I stopped Cybill," I said.

"Humm… did you?" asked one of the figures.

I blinked.

"We grow tired of this chatter. We abhor this gutter speech… these raw words. The questions are over."

As one, they took a step towards the elevator.

"You're not going anywhere," I said, stepping in their path.

"You do not order us around. We serve one greater than you. One greater than the Mirza. You are not in a position to make demands, Guardian."

"Oh?" I said, looking at the six of my caravan that surrounded them, weapons still raised. "I could probably say the same about you. Don't move. We're tying you up.

"Range, see if you can find some rope, chains. Check by the elevator."

The three figures all began to howl and pushed forward, one struck me in the chest and sent me sprawling backwards. The touch felt like ice. It burned into me. I gasped for air.

Wensem immediately opened fire. Blasts of light lit the faces of my company and the robes of the gargoyles. The smell of gun smoke filled the chamber and stung my nose. I struggled to my feet, lifting my Judge from the ground and stepping towards the last of the strangers left standing.

It was hunched over and seemed to be wheezing though its shoulders and back didn't rise and fall. I placed the barrel of the Judge against its face and immediately felt a cold surge down the gun and chill my hand. It seemed to ooze off the thing.

It stood motionless. My finger tightened around the trigger and it gave one final, agonized whoop. The Judge barked, and the thing was thrown backwards.

Slowly, we all lowered our guns.

I edged closer and nudged the figure I shot with the edge of my boot. Ragged bits of fabric lay scattered across the ground. Unlike the first stranger Hannah killed, these creatures didn't evaporate and drift off into smoke. They just lay there in a pile of fabric.

"By the Firsts. What the hell are these things?" I asked the room.

"I have never come across anything like them in my research," said Samantha. She edged closer. "Their robes, the hoods. They seem... I don't know."

Hannah spat on the pile. "Damn them."

The Shalers mumbled in agreement.

"Let's find out who they are," Wensem said, squatting down and drawing a big bowie knife from his boot. He reached a hand out toward the pile. "They seem to radiate coldness… OH!"

There was a burst of motion and a sound of wings as the bodies erupted into the air with extraordinary speed. They moved up the stairwell, and disappeared above. Wensem jerked back, falling onto his ass, his knife clattering to the ground.

"After them!" I shouted.

TWENTY-SEVEN

We rushed up the rickety staircase. My knee howled in pain. From somewhere I could hear the noise start up, the bending metal moan, only this time it was closer.

The elevator shaft and stairs landed inside a wooden structure about thirty by thirty feet and continued upwards. Mining gear filled the building: ropes, spools of cable, and stacks of rough-cut lumber. The strangers were nowhere to be seen.

I looked up, my gaze following the stairs as they ended at the ceiling twenty feet above my head. A small trapdoor was nestled at the terminus.

We were in the headframe. Inside the mining tower that watched over the valley from its mountainside throne.

Slivers of light seemed to be leaking between the slats of the old building so I swung my torch around looking for the exit. A door was set into one wall and it swung on its hinges as if it had been recently used.

Outside, I thought. They went outside.

I shouldered through, emerging into a heavy rain and a sky

darkened by gray clouds. I was in the Kadath mining camp.

I spun, looking for the gargoyles but I didn't see them anywhere.

No signs hinted at their passing. No footprints. No rocks rolling down the steep hillside that pressed in around the camp.

They were gone.

The strangers had disappeared.

"Where'd they go?" asked Range, coming up behind me. His chest heaved as he caught his breath.

"Gone," I said. "When I came out at the top the door was swinging."

"Could they have gone up higher?"

I looked up at the building we just exited. "I doubt it. They'd have been more trapped up there than they would be out here."

"So, where'd they go?"

Spinning, I took in our surroundings. How could they do that? I had seen them take round after round. I had seen them collapse. How could they just escape like that?

The landslide had taken out about half the camp, and an old road that cut through the middle of the Kadath at one time had disappeared beneath a pile of boulders to the south.

Other buildings withered away within the depression sprouting next to the steep hillsides like mushrooms. A brown and withering machine shop. A brick dynamite house with a moss-covered roof. A few graying management structures gathered near a huge crater at the far north end of the camp. Heavy timbers covered its opening and a faded sign hung off the wood reading: "Keep Out. Mine Closed."

The structure nearest the mining tower looked to be the

remains of a bunkhouse. I surmised the other half was buried somewhere beneath the slide. Saplings were growing in the open spaces, rising up from tall wild rye that covered the ground.

Wensem and Chance burst from the mine's tower and skidded to a stop when they saw Range and me standing there. Samantha and Hannah weren't far behind.

"You see them? Where did they go?" Wensem asked.

I shook my head and holstered the Judge. "They're gone."

"Shit!" shouted Hannah, kicking at the dirt. "Shit. Shit. Shit. Shit. Shit!"

"They could still be in one of the buildings," I said.

Wensem nodded. "Hannah, you stand guard here. I'll take the Shalers and start on the western side. Wal, you and Sam work the eastern buildings."

I nodded and Wensem and the Shalers moved towards the management buildings on the west side of the mine camp.

Samantha was already heading towards the dynamite house. Curwen was here. Somewhere. I could feel it. It was like a buzzing in the back of my skull.

The rain soaked my head and the shoulders of my jacket. The horns that sprouted from Samantha's cheeks glistened.

My torch was nearly used up. The flame hunkered close to the oil soaked rag, beaten down by the wind and the rain.

An old oil lamp hung from the wall near the entrance to the dynamite house and I was pleased to find a splash of oil still in the font. It took a few tries but eventually I got it to light. The steady glow was welcome compared to the flicker of the torch.

Samantha and I moved close to the building and carefully

peeked inside. A few nervous rats scattered and it was clear the roof had sprung a leak. Crates labeled "Durbin Dynamite Co." were resting among rotting straw or had fallen apart, spilling their contents over the floor of the building.

Big red stenciled letters spelled out the contents: dynamite, flares, fuses, timers. I couldn't tell how long the explosives had sat there but I knew it was dangerous. Age wasn't kind to explosives. The whole building was probably unstable. One wrong move, a stray lightning strike, and boom—this whole mining camp could be leveled. On the plus side, it'd probably clear that landslide.

We stepped back outside and Samantha's torch winked out.

"Damnit," Samantha swore. A peal of thunder boomed overhead mixing with the noise.

"Take my lamp. I have an idea." I ducked inside and carefully picked my way to a small pile of boxes labeled "Flares" and "Danger No Smoking." I gingerly lifted a crate of flares off a stack and quickly slipped back outside being careful not to bump any of the dynamite crates or step on any of the escaped explosives.

"What's that?" asked Samantha holding the lamp up high.

"Flares," I said. "They'll burn longer than our torches."

I pulled one of the faded yellow sticks from the box. A big black arrow with the words, "Light this end" was printed on the stick. Following the directions I pulled the cap free and struck the button to the coarse end of the cap.

Nothing.

I tried again.

Nothing.

The third time was not a charm, and the flare stayed unlit.

Damn.

Undaunted, I drew another flare from the box and tried again. The flare popped to life, casting a bright red glow on our surroundings. I used the hot flare to light the dud and was pleased when it fired. They were significantly brighter than the torches. I stuck a few extra flares in my back pocket.

"I'm going to go give Hannah a few. Shame to let our torches go out. Especially if this rain holds."

"Meet you at the machine shop," said Samantha.

The machine shop was devoid of equipment and seemed to only be home to another family of rats who squeaked their displeasure at being disturbed.

It didn't take long for the five of us to scout the camp. We met up with Wensem, Chance, and Range as they huddled beneath the overhang of the closed mining tunnel.

The Shalers looked ashen and Wensem seemed relieved. His brow was knitted and his crooked jaw was set unnaturally. Something was amiss.

"What's going on?" I asked, my hand instinctively going to the grip of my pistol.

"Nothing good," Wensem said flatly. "Didn't want Hannah to see. Glad it's just the two of you."

My stomach dropped. Wensem's tone was dark.

"What do you mean?" I asked tentatively.

"We found the sheriff," he said and guided us into a small

gray house marked "Foreman's Office."

Bile rose in my throat. I rushed back outside and around the corner of the building. But I could still smell it. I could smell the thing that was inside.

What little that remained in my stomach lurched upward. I could feel my limbs quiver. What was that thing?

It was wrong.

I squeezed my eyes shut as another bout of gags lurched forward inside me.

There are clues inside, my brain said to me. I took a few deep breaths. Tried to calm my nerves. You have to go back in there.

My throat burned.

I took a deep breath and wiped the back of my mouth with my keff as I pulled it up over my face and pushed away from the building. Samantha and Wensem stood outside and waited for me to approach.

"You okay?" Samantha asked.

I shrugged.

"I've been better. Come on."

We reentered the foreman's office.

The inside was a single room and a gallery of horror. The room smelled vile, the scent stronger than the reek we encountered in the cellar. Tables lined the walls, covered with an array of body parts and organs from all sorts of species. Intricate drawings stained with gore were pasted to the walls and showed some mechanism built atop the mining tower and labeled in Aklo. Next to those were drawings of anatomy, also labeled. If the chapel had been Curwen's torture chamber, this was his workshop.

The sight that had sent me outside quivered in the corner. Half alive, a construct roughly the height of a man made of parts taken from the victims of the Forest of the Dead. Arms and legs sewn together. Skin stretched across ribs to form rib cages that inhaled and exhaled breaths from mouths unseen, bloodshot and cataract covered eyes blinked out at us. A few tentacles jutted from the mass but were curled tightly like fiddleheads. As it seemed to register us, they uncurled, revealing twin rows of black suckers. Atop it all, watching us, was the head of Sheriff Joul dal Habith.

The maero's dark eyes looked at us, blinking slowly. His lower jaw was stitched to a forearm from another victim so when he moved to open his mouth the top of his head lolled backwards. A left hand somehow attached to the mass below gingerly touched the sheriff's cheek.

"What... is... it?" I asked, holding my hand to my mouth and pressing the keff to my nose.

Samantha faced the thing like a soldier, feet planted to either side and arms at her sides. "It's an abomination. A construct."

"It looks like one of those Curwenite altars," observed Wensem. "Only—alive."

"I think it is, of a sort..." Samantha said. "I have a feeling Curwen made it."

As if in response, the construct gurgled. It was a pitiful sound, not far off from the mewling the gargoyles made when they first saw us. It sent a shiver down my spine.

"We need to kill it," she said.

"Sam," I said, unsure why I wanted to stop her. If the sheriff was alive he was obviously in pain, and whatever this... thing was, Samantha was right, it was an abomination. Nothing good could come from that.

Samantha Dubois, Priestess of the Reunified Church, grabbed the Judge from its holster and moved across the small hut. She planted the barrel against the part of the mass that contained the sheriff's forehead. His black maero eyes stared at her and a long low moan leaked out from somewhere within it.

With a wince, Samantha turned her head and squeezed the trigger. The gun boomed loudly, and gore spattered the wall. A high-pitched squeal leaked out of its mouths and then slowly fell silent.

As if in answer, the noise in the sky that had hounded us across the prairie and into the mountains exploded directly above us.

TWENTY-EIGHT

I burst from the office at a dead run. A gray mist had descended along with the rain and was spreading across the ground wrapping around the buildings of the mining camp. I sprinted towards the booming sound. My knee shrieked but I didn't have time to listen. Wensem and Samantha were right behind me, Samantha still holding the Judge. It smoked and hissed as the rain hit its hot barrel.

Hannah backed away from the tower and was huddled near the landslide, staring up in utter horror. Her mouth hung open in a silent scream.

He's at the top of the headframe, I realized. That's where the sound is coming from!

The Shalers moved near her. For some reason they were in the process of lighting more and more of the flares and scattering them all around. They cast panicked glances upward. So many flares were now burning that the area around the base of the headframe was bathed in a hellish red light.

"He's inside!" Hannah shouted, tears streaming down her

face. She pointed with her right hand at the big building. "Wal! He's at the top! He's at the top!"

Samantha tossed me the Judge and I caught it mid-run and returned it to the holster.

I nodded and moved towards the door, not breaking stride. The whole building quaked with the sound, swaying like an old man. Bits of loose dust puffed outward after decades between cracks of wood only to be beaten down by the heavy rain.

Thunder boomed overhead.

"Wal!" shouted Samantha, her voice nearly lost to the sound coming from the tower. "Your mask! Don't forget your mask!"

Blinking, I realized the gas mask still hung at my side, flopping wildly against my thigh. I looked around me.

The gray mist wasn't fog!

Hannah's scream drifted away and she slumped forward against the ankle deep grass that covered the grounds. The Shalers followed, Range giving one last hurl of a flare before dropping backward sound asleep.

Quickly, I drew the mask from its bag and pulled it tightly over my face. I inhaled a lungful of filtered air, hoping I wasn't too late. Wensem appeared at my side and gripped my shoulders giving me a curt nod.

I was woozy. Sleepy, but I hoped the clean air would keep me awake. I took another deep breath and turned to look at Samantha. I felt slightly better and clearer of head. Her eyes met mine and time seemed to hang there between us for a moment. She mouthed a "good luck" before letting the mist take her and settling onto the ground.

I looked up at the quaking headframe and then back at Sam, asleep in the grass. So much between us had slipped away. I hoped I'd be able to make things right.

Wensem and I pressed through the tower's door and into the darkness within. It made perfect sense that this was where Curwen dwelled. It was the best seat in the house to view the valley. From there, he could watch the citizens of Methow struggle with the horrors he inflicted upon them. Like a malevolent child studying the ant he tortured under the burning gaze of a magnifying glass.

We moved to the stairs. I could feel the sound from above reverberate through the floors of the place. My heart pounded in my chest. My mouth was dry, and I found it difficult to talk.

"Wensem," I finally said, pausing on the first step and turning to look at my partner. "If things go sour, if it gets bad, you get out."

Wensem's blue-gray eyes stared at me silently through the lenses of his mask but he didn't respond. I placed my hand on his boney shoulder and looked him straight in the eye.

"I'm serious. You leave the headframe and get the people of Methow out. Get back to Kit."

I could feel him sigh.

"Is that an order?" he asked finally.

"It's an appeal."

Wensem finally nodded.

We had work to do.

TWENTY-NINE

As if in anticipation, the noise went silent as we ascended the stairs. The roar of the hammering rain and the whistles of wind slipped through the cracks of the rickety walls of the headframe.

The lantern light felt meager and the darkness around us ponderous, but we climbed on. My knee protested the entire way, throbbing with pain. At the top, we stopped and crouched near the trapdoor fixed into the ceiling..

"Together?" Wensem asked.

"Fools rush in where the wise fear to travel," I said with a nervous smile, forgetting Wensem wouldn't be able to see it under the mask. I hoped my old man's words would be good luck.

"On three."

I pulled my knees under me, and felt the old wound fight against the motion. The ache made my stomach hurt. Wensem crouched next to me.

"One."

My heart hammered in my chest. My breathing rasped out through the filter.

"Two."

More thunder boomed in the sky. I checked that the Judge was secure in its holster.

"Three."

We pushed upward, lifting and throwing the trapdoor aside as we moved into the chamber at the top of the headframe.

Curwen, the Lord of Chaos, was ready for us.

I barely got a look in before something heavy caught me across chest and I was thrown backwards. Everything seemed to move in slow motion. I immediately lost my grip on the lantern and watched it tumble end over end through the air before it clattered and then shattered between two pieces of machinery. The uppermost floor of the headframe was swallowed by darkness.

With a crack, my head collided with something solid. Sharp pain erupted behind my eyes and I could feel warm blood immediately make its way down my face from my forehead. I collapsed to the floor. The world was swimming. Even staying conscious seemed like an immense effort.

How had he reacted so fast?

I struggled to rise. My head muddled. Shakily I stood, spinning, looking around, expecting to see something else coming. Another slam drove me forward and behind it came a sharp tear that traced a burning sensation across my back. Something cut a deep gash through my jacket, shirt, undershirt and into my flesh.

I crumpled to the floor, writhing in pain and scrambling in the dark for cover. Everything was pain and swimming. Dark and swimming and pain and thunder.

"Waldo!" Wensem called out. "Wal, where are you?"

I could hear more movement and then a grunt of pain and a reverberating gong that shook the floor. Wensem was thrown and collided with something heavy. I breathed. Tried to clear my head and focus on the fight. I felt like I was forgetting something.

Somewhere in the darkness Wensem cursed and there was the noise of scuffling. Wensem struggled to his feet only to be thrown down a second and then a third time.

"Wal, stay back!" I heard him shout. There was a crash and a gut-churning thump.

"You're a tenacious little bastard," said a velvety voice.

I tried to lean around the object I was slumped behind but couldn't see anything. It was so dark. I had seen him... or at least thought I had. In that brief flash of light before I was thrown, before the lantern was torn away.

The blow to my head must have been harder than I thought. Everything swam around me. Memories. It had been something horrible, I knew that much. Gone was Boden, the man I saw in Methow. Gone was the writhing black morass, too. Curwen had become something else... monstrous, something terrible.

His true form.

"I wondered when you would come," it said.

Wensem grunted from somewhere in the dark. The beast moved with a heavy dragging sound and then a bright flash illuminated the space for the briefest of seconds followed immediately by a rocking boom.

I saw him. In that brief flash, I saw him. Curwen. And he was rushing towards Wensem. My partner was dirty and dusty, and blood covered his chest but he was standing. He raised his gun and fired at the thing.

A great yellow eye, lidless and leering, occupied most of its head. Its alien hourglass-shaped iris stared at Wensem as the rifle went off. Tentacles seemed to drape the creature, writhing under the shadows of great leathery wings that stretched and moved and carried its form forward. Then it and Wensem were gone. Lost to the darkness. A loud slam and a sickening crack accompanied the dying of the light.

"Wensem!" I called out, my own voice sending waves of pain. Thick blood ran over my cheeks. I struggled to rise but couldn't maintain my balance and I collapsed back down.

No answer.

"Wensem! Wensem!" I called again.

A chuckle rumbled through the air. "I'll deal with you in a moment, Guardian."

Small bits of light, like stars in a summer sky, slipped into the headframe through the slats of the exterior wall. It was hard to focus but my eyes slowly adjusted to the shadowy forms. After a few more seconds I could begin making out shapes.

The outlines of great gears and cogs were set into the floor. By the feel of the metal I leaned on I could only guess that everything up here had long gone to rust and wouldn't have been able to move the hoist.

I slumped lower. A great form moved in the space across from me. Small bits of light winked out as it passed in front of them.

I breathed. Breathed and tried to remember. There was something. Something else I could do. The floor felt like it was spinning. I looked over my shoulder. An immense shadow moved slowly back and forth opposite me. Was he looking for me? Or doing something horrible to Wensem?

A chill traveled down my spine. He was so big. Did Wensem's shot even hurt him?

I felt for the handle of my pistol and pulled it from its holster. Suddenly the noise returned, flaring up in the sky above the headframe before it slipped away, becoming a quaking laugh. The sound shook the headframe, and bits of dust and debris rained down from the rafters overhead. I covered my ears and tried to block it out, but it was so loud! So vast!

"What are you going to do with that, Guardian? Didn't you already try to shoot me?"

I crouched lower. Could he see me? His eyesight had to be better than mine, but could he really see that I pulled the Judge or had he simply heard the movement? Neither idea was comforting.

"You think that tiny machine can harm me? I am an element. A force of nature! I was old when your world was young."

I wanted to respond but it was hard enough just to get my sense of balance.

"Why you were chosen to be the Guardian I will never understand. You are just like that stupid sheriff. You are a impetuous fool." His silky voice changed, lightened a bit. "Ah, maybe that is why you were chosen. After all you are shockingly similar to all who have come before you."

I rose, wavering, feeling sharp pain shoot through my head. I tried to gauge where Curwen was in the gloom. Tried to make out his form against the cracks in the wall. It seemed impossible. Shapes blocked what meager light penetrated the headframe and any one of them could have been the monster.

"I sent you running before," my voice cracked as I said it. So much for strength in the face of your enemy.

"Is that what you believe?"

The quaking laugh started up again, heaving like thunder. It seemed to come from my left, but also from outside, like the sky itself was laughing.

There was a flash from outside as lightning broke the sky. Beams of bright white light lit the interior of the tower, bringing with it a cold burning metallic smell that filled the upper chamber.

Lightning! The clouds had brought a storm!

Curwen's laugh caught and turned into a long wail.

In the brief, bright flash my vision burned and I could see Curwen writhing against one side. One gnarled claw gripped the body of Wensem—tiny and weak-looking compared to the immensity of the creature—while another dug grooves into the floor.

I raised my gun and aimed it in the direction of the thing. He knew I wouldn't shoot with Wensem in the way. The chance to hit him would be too great.

"Drop him!" I shouted over the sound of hammering rain. "You hear me? Drop him!"

My back felt warm. Sticky. My brain was frazzled. Everything seemed to double on itself. Somewhere in the back of my mind something was fighting with me... something was nagging. Remember, it said.

"What is one maero to you, caravan master? What is one maero to the Guardian?"

"I'm not here to barter. Let him go."

"There is no tunnel above us to drop on my head! Your small weapon will do nothing. So why have you come?" Curwen said, his voice almost normal.

"Someone has to."

He roared. "Hah!"

It rushed at me again, slamming into my chest. I sailed backward, crashing against one of the outer walls and collapsing into a pile of rusted buckets. The wall cracked in protest. My head smacked against a thick wooden beam, causing the world to spin faster, and I fell to the floor, landing hard on something and causing the gash in my back to scream at me.

"I knew you were in Syringa. The Ngranek told me as much. I believed that distance meant our paths would never cross. At least not for a while. I could finish my work here before I'd need to find you. I watched. Watched as you met your friends... I hoped they would convince you away from this place. But you left that fort to the east.

"This town... I am so close to breaking them. Their hope is lost. Madness will settle into this town... Swallowing it whole."

My whole body ached. My back burned. My head was swimming. My hand was light. The heavy weight of the Judge was gone. I was weaponless. Despair beckoned.

I fought it and pulled myself from the crates, dragging myself along the floor. Not sure if I was moving towards or away from Curwen.

"I have dealt with Guardians before. So I took one of your people..." His voice seethed with anger. "I should have realized you'd be just like the ones before you. You treat your subordinates like they're an extension of yourself. I cannot comprehend it... I realize I made a mistake. I should have focused on you from the beginning!"

He lunged to where I had fallen, but misjudged my movements. I could hear him slam into the outer wall. Feel the headframe shake with the vibration. Light leaked in, giving me a brief glimpse before it disappeared into the shadows.

"When you rolled through the barricade I realized I had to change my plans. I could exact revenge... do to you what I did to Carter eons ago. You see, Waldo Bell? This will end in your death."

I tried to swear, but my words came out as gibberish. I felt warm and cold all at once.

"Can't you see that? Yet you still came! Pitiful as you are, you still came. I suppose you think that makes you brave."

I struggled to rise. A bite of cool air whipped across my face and I realized one of the eye pieces in the gas mask had cracked. Air from outside was leaking in. Had that happened when I was thrown the first or second time?

"It makes you a fool," Curwen said.

I pulled the gas mask free and the cold smell of the burning metal was clearer and more evident. I thought about the metal and about the storm. I wondered...

My answer came suddenly.

Another crack of lightning sent Curwen spilling and screaming and whirling.

It jolted my memory.

Light!

I could beat this son of a bitch.

Wensem's body was still clutched in his four hands. No, two. Four? In my swimming vision two Curwens held two Wensems. I shook my head trying to clear it. I squinted and tried to bring my vision together. Everything was difficult to make out. The dark shapes were blurry and the floor before me seemed to wobble and veer away.

I shakily rose to my feet and rubbed at my eyes. I was tired. So tired. I somehow knew this was Curwen's mist working on me, but my body didn't care. I wanted to sleep.

Darkness settled back inside the headframe and Curwen boomed another laugh.

"Did I break your little mask? I must admit I didn't expect that. The citizens of Methow had no idea how I could waltz around, plucking their friends and family."

I didn't respond. It took all my will to focus on what I was about to do.

"Are you getting sleepy?" the monster asked. "It would be little fun for me to end this while you were asleep. I want you to feel what I am going to do to you!"

Wensem's body came crashing towards me, his limp arm slapping me in the face and driving me down to my knees. Please be alive. I reached a hand out and felt his chest, but it was difficult to tell if he was breathing or not. My hand came away warm and sticky.

Blood.

Curwen laughed and another flash of lightning and peal of thunder split the sky overhead. Beams of bright white light shot in between the slats and filled the chamber.

My body wanted to remain on the floor, but I fought it and with all the effort I could muster I rose. My eyes focused on the direction of the monster. Anger. Rage and hate filling my chest.

I would end this.

Curwen curled his claws over his single eye in an effort to protect it from the flashes of lightning. As darkness filled the space once more, the hulking form turned towards me. Claws curled menacingly, arms hanging at its side.

Time froze for a long moment as monster and man focused on one another. I grinned and hoped Curwen could see it.

THIRTY

The flare cracked to life in my hand.

Curwen's single giant pupil shrank as a brilliant red glow filled the upper floor growing brighter and brighter as the flare burned hotter and hotter.

The thing had no face but the emotion in that reaction was clear enough. It shuddered and recoiled in horror. I dropped the burning flare, and pulled the second from my back pocket.

When it popped, I tossed it across the room, away from the other, making it more difficult for Curwen to snuff out the light quickly.

He howled in pain, and the noise in the sky seemed to burst into my head. It drove the fog out and snapped me into reality. My head pounded. My skull ached, but I had remembered. The blows, the jolts. I had forgotten about the flares crammed into my back pocket.

The Judge was lying near Wensem and I hobbled quickly to retrieve it, picking it up and spinning in time to see Curwen throw himself at one of the flares, scratching at the stick with his gnarled claws. His claws dug grooves into the wooden floor.

"No! No! No!" he screamed.

The flares burned bright and hot and the dry floor of the old headframe began to catch, smoldering at first and then beginning to burn, bringing more light into the room. Curwen hollered and shouted. He seemed to be gagging as the light pushed away the darkness.

"No!" he screamed. "No! No! No!"

In the bright light I could clearly make out the creature for the first time. The single yellow eye dominated a massive skull with no apparent nose or mouth. Its torso was man-like, and two spindly clawed arms hung from its body like the branches of a dead tree. Its lower torso was a mass of writhing tentacles that seemed to move and twist like some terrifying dress. Its huge leathery wings slammed about awkwardly, crashing into walls and the floor as Curwen struggled against the burning light. Small scorch marks were appearing all over the sooty black flesh on his arms and legs, glowing orange at the edges like the coals of a hot fire.

So this was his true form. The body of a First.

I considered emptying the Judge at the creature but I realized it would do nothing so I tucked it away.

Light was another story.

I backed up to where Wensem lay and awkwardly struggled to haul him up over my shoulders. He was heavy and not moving. His gas mask was torn, and gashes were cut across his chest, and arms, and legs. Hot maero blood made him slippery. If he was still alive and if I could get him out of here, he'd recover. Maero are hard to kill.

"This isn't over! This isn't over, Guardian! Argh!" Curwen screamed, slamming himself against a wall with a satisfying crack. He moved towards me, stumbling, a claw reaching out. One of his wings hung limp. The yellow eye, once so bright, was turning a lurid brown.

I watched.

He slammed himself against the wall again, and then half-rushed and half-fell towards me. Old dust swirled in his wake.

I kicked out with my bad leg, my boot connecting with the massive eye. The motion was awkward and jerky but the strike was true. Between the light, the fire, and my blow Curwen recoiled. Falling backward, he slammed against the burning floor.

The flares erupted into an inferno. I could hear the old tower moaning and sputtering as the fire began to chew at the structure itself. I am apparently hell on old buildings.

We had to get out. I hobbled to open the trapdoor set into the floor and, panting, struggled down through the small hole and onto the curling stairs. Curwen returned to smashing himself against the side of the headframe, sending quakes down the whole structure. He is trying to break through, I realized. He is trying to escape.

"No, no, no!" he screamed.

The space below the upper floor of the tower was darker than the room at the top but fire was already creeping down the walls and bringing with it more light.

I moved down the stairs as quick as my knee and the weight of the full grown maero would let me. When I landed on the main floor my boots made an echoing heavy thud. My knee burned.

I pushed out the door and struggled into the mining camp. Wensem's hand slapped awkwardly against the gash on my back and I gritted my teeth, tasting blood in my mouth. We stumbled across the grounds toward where the others lay. The gray mist was dissipating. Eaten away by the rain or removed as Curwen burned, I wasn't sure.

I collapsed as I sat Wensem down among my sleeping friends. A nasty knot had formed above his left eye but his chest heaved in a breath and he coughed fitfully. He was still alive. The others were beginning to stir.

Curwen was still howling above and when I turned and looked up, the entire top of the headframe was wreathed in flames. They were shooting out from holes and roaring from portions of the roof that had already collapsed. The sounds of screeching metal and Curwen's roar echoed from atop the burning headframe.

He was dying.

Thunder boomed low and loud and lightning struck the top of the tower. In that instant, Curwen burst forth, exploding outward and howling as fire licked at his leathery wings and ran down the length of his tentacles. Time seemed to slow as his wings tried to catch and beat at the air. He tumbled, outward and then down.

The massive eye, charred almost as black as the creature's skin, looked down as it fell. A wave of recoil seemed to roll down its body. The bright flares Hannah and the Shaler boys had scattered reflected against his blackened skin. The harsh golden light burned him.

I stood, broken and bloodied, and stared upward, watching

as the fire and the light took Curwen apart. I smiled to myself as his body burned away and joined the rain, falling as flakes of blackened soot.

THIRTY-ONE

I t was gone.

Dead? Who can say? Some believe that Firsts never die. That if they fall on our world they are just banished from our reality to some cold darkness where they dwell and plot their return. Others hold to the belief that they might be destroyed but they rise again, after eons, pulling themselves back together with some unseen magnetic force in some endless cycle of destruction and rebirth.

I sat there, catching my breath, staring upward as the ashes of the creature that plagued the small town of Methow for over a year rained down around me. Slowly, my friends began to awaken, blinking and rubbing their eyes. They stared upwards as the headframe burned and fell apart.

The dark clouds bled out and were replaced with lighter ones, the rain lessened, and the sky finally cleared up. The oranges and purples of a sunset soon appeared behind the mountain to the west.

In silence we all watched the headframe burn and then

collapse in on itself, falling down into the large chamber it was built upon, forming a burning pit of smoldering timber and the remains of the hoist.

"There goes our way out," Samantha said, looking down into the hole.

"I wasn't keen on going back underground," Hannah said. She turned and looked at me. "You're sure he's gone?"

"I'm sure," I said, realizing I truly meant it.

Wensem woke in pain, and quickly realized his leg was broken and a few of his ribs were cracked. He wasn't in any condition to climb the steep slope that surrounded the mining camp so we fashioned a litter out of some old canvas and some boards to move him.

It took us the rest of the day to crawl up over the landslide, and a few more hours to safely descend back to the ground. Taft met us on the other side, her eyes big as pie pans as she heard us recount what had happened.

Together the company struggled back to the small town, pushing our way through the gate and falling into our bedrolls smelling of fire and smoke and sleeping better than we had in months.

The following morning we rose and told our tale to the citizens of Methow. Finishing triumphantly with the fiery end. A great cheer rose from the survivors. It was over.

We went to work immediately to remove the bodies that hung around the remnants of Methow and buried them in neat rows away from the valley, among a stand of pale aspen whose leaves were just beginning to turn and would eventually cover the dead in a blanket of gold. It took us over a week. When we were finished we cut down the stakes and crosses and burned them in a great bonfire away from the town. We watched the flames hungrily eat the pile of wood. A fitting ceremony to end the terrible reign of Curwen.

I looked at my people, and saw their eyes flash, reflecting the flames. Wensem's leg had been splinted and bandages were wrapped around his head and chest. He leaned heavily on a crutch that one of the refugees had made for him. He flashed a crooked smile at me when he saw me looking.

Samantha was next to him. The horns that sprouted from her temples and chin were longer than I had seen before. Even with layers of road dust, torn clothes, her hair tangled and ragged, I still thought her beautiful. Her dark flashing eyes didn't turn away from the fire. They didn't look up and see me standing there.

After we returned to Methow she had given me a long silent hug, those small horns on her chin pressed against my shoulder. We held one another for a long moment, neither of us wanting to let go. It was either a hopeful sign that things between us could be mended or a final hug goodbye.

Hannah and Taft were standing among a group of the Methow survivors. Hannah's eyes were empty, her stare stalwart but somber. She held the stump of her left hand to her chest protectively, her other hand jammed deep into her jacket pocket. The fire and life that burned inside her had been replaced by something else. Something colder.

Taft loomed above her like a protective older sister. A massive grin split her face and her cheeks jutted out like small mountains. She laughed deep heavy laughs, and drank from a thick flask, hugging the survivors around her jovially.

Away from the group stood the Shaler boys. From them there came no smiles. No hugs. No grateful thanks. The caravan that had been their family's livelihood had been broken. They came into this as boys but were emerging as men, gun weary and battle hardened.

I would offer them a job. They had proven they were more than adequate members of the caravan, though I was unsure if they would take it. I led them into misery. Who would stay with a leader like that?

What kind of leader had I become? I had faced another First—my second now—and somehow emerged alive. Mostly intact. The gashes would become scars, more memories scratched into my skin. When I looked in the mirror, I would now see Curwen alongside Peter Black and Cybill. Leering in the background.

"What happens now?" asked the mayor in his quavery voice. The old man stood next to me as we watched the fire, a shawl wrapped around his frail shoulders.

"Now we pack up and head out, I suppose. You and yours are welcome to join us."

"That is very kind of you."

"It's the least we could do."

"There is nothing for any of us in Methow," said the mayor. "Just bad memories."

"There's always Lovat, and if the big city life doesn't suit you there are handfuls of communities living up and down along the islands."

"Thank you for your help," the old man said. "For all of this. For everything, yes, we will go with you."

It was decided.

We had entered Methow as seven. We left as eighty-two. Our ranks swelled with the surviving men, women, and children of the dead town of Methow. Refugees bound for a new life on the other side of the mountains.

The journey was uneventful. We encountered early snows at the summit of the pass but were out and descending before it had too much of a chance to slow us down. We emerged on the other side as much colder weather blew in from the north, promising to close the pass for the winter.

Little was said among the caravan on the remainder of our journey. Each of us had our own demons to struggle against.

Guardian.

The title seemed to hang off me like a noose. You could call it a coincidence the first time I faced off against one of the ancient creatures. Now, with two notches in my gun belt, I had a feeling more Firsts would show up in my life. More monsters. More death.

What could one man do against the titanic forces of long dead monsters? The idea seemed ludicrous.

I stood along the last stretch and watched my column pass. Jagged peaks of the mountains rose from behind us. To the north the Kulshan volcano dominated the skyline, smoke rising from its crater.

Samantha pulled aside the gearwain and descended to stand next to me and watch the refugees from Methow move past. Smiles now occupied faces that had stared out hopelessly on our initial arrival.

"You've been quiet," she said.

I smiled. "I've been thinking."

"About?" Samantha asked.

"Curwen calling me 'Guardian' and what that means—what that really means. When Black gave me the title it had seemed a curse. Dictated by his screwed up ritual. Those around me were destined to become victims. I think Curwen was using it in the same way."

"But you aren't," Samantha said, her voice sharp and pleasing in the cool morning air. "In both cases you brought about the destruction of the creatures who tried to use you. You were willing to sacrifice yourself to stop them."

"I don't know any other way..." I admitted.

"That's clear. You rush into things. You don't listen to others. You're lucky you escaped with only a few more scars this time."

I frowned.

"It scares me, Wal. It scares me so much, my only option is pull away. I can't see you waltzing into danger every chance it presents itself."

She looked me in the eye. "I know... how you feel. How you

have always felt. But you need to know that I can't respond in kind. I've been down that path. I won't do it again."

"I..."

...had nothing.

I closed my mouth. Samantha was right. She gave me a sad smile and rubbed my upper arm.

My stomach interrupted, growling loudly and Samantha laughed. The tension eased. I smiled a sad smile.

"I was wondering when the famous ravenous hunger of Waldo Emerson Bell would rear its head."

Smiling, I said, "I need to inspect some of the Methow refugees' wains. Save a spot for me at the laager? Taft says she's making something special for our last night on the trail."

"You got it," said Samantha, standing on her toes to give me a friendly peck on the cheek. A promise—I hoped—that things between us could get back to normal.

But her words haunted me.

I watched her climb back atop the gearwain and glide on with the narrow column. Her dark hair shone in the sunlight and swayed with the roll of the road as the gearwain clattered along.

When she disappeared among the crowd I turned back to my vigil. Could I promise things would be okay? That if the opportunity presented itself I wouldn't rush in—heedless of the advice of friends—to stop what I felt needed to be stopped?

Along the hillside, a gargoyle stood observing the column. A scratch of black among the verdant greens of the trees and the slate grays of granite. I had been seeing them for a few days now, their tall hoods appearing among the hills and ridges as the column passed, silently observing us as they carried their messages.

If they were still active that meant more Firsts had returned. More of those creatures, so hungry for destruction. Moving along the surface of the world. The stage.

Wensem, Hannah and I had decided to say nothing to the rest of the caravan about the gargoyles. We were two days from Lovat, its spires clear and bright to the south. Besides, the messengers were helpless, impotent, weren't they? It was their masters we needed to be worried about.

As I watched the gargoyle something else stirred inside of my chest. The Broken Road was coming to its end. Tonight would be our last laager, the refugees would disperse and Bell Caravans would return to its caravansara in Lovat.

For me, battle lines were beginning to be laid down. Unseen forces were maneuvering into place and it was very clear which side of the line I stood on.

There, on the last few miles of the old Broken Road, I realized, I had a long way to go before the end.

ACKNOWLEDGEMENTS

Writing, much like caravan travel, is a journey. You don't set out alone. Just like Wal, there is a whole company of folks I need to thank.

First, my partner in all this, my wife, Kari-Lise. She is there to read every draft of every chapter immediately after I finish, to give great feedback, and to push me to be better every damn day. I could not do this without you, and these books would suffer without your input, encouragement, and advice.

Next, I'd like to thank my long-suffering editor Lola Landekic who has made this book what it is. Your patience, perseverance, and sheer will in dealing with my shoddy drafts should earn you a medal, or many medals. All the medals.

A huge thanks to Jon Contino, yet again. Without your skills, the cover of Old Broken Road would feature some freeware chalkboard font, and no one wants that. Your attention to detail, care, and professionalism shows through. I'm glad to work with you.

One more time, special thanks in particular to my friend Josh Montreuil who listens to my raving. I couldn't have written book one without you, and the same goes for book two.

Obviously, I need to thank my caravan, my crew of beta-roaders who offer insight, feedback, and opinions as I work though those first—and very rough—drafts: Ben Vanik, Brittany Bintliff, J. Rushing, Kelcey Rushing, Lauren Sapala, Sky Bintliff, and Sarah Steininger. I can't thank you enough. Thanks for giving me your time and energy.

And of course, a big thank you to my readers. I do this for you. All you amazing folks who read The Stars Were Right and now Old Broken Road. I hope it lived up to your expectations. Thanks for your support. Thanks for taking a chance on an indie author. Thanks for loving these stories as much as I do. You make it worth it.

Finally, B3S. *Magna voce ridere æterna.* We do this together.

K. M. ALEXANDER is a Pacific Northwest native and novelist living and working in Seattle, Washington with his wife and two dogs. *Old Broken Road* is his second novel. You can follow his exploits at: blog.kmalexander.com.

The Guardian returns in:

THE BELL FORGING CYCLE, BOOK III
Red Litten World
REDLITTENWORLD.COM

Available Now!

CPSIA information can be obtained
at www.ICGtesting.com
Printed in the USA
LVHW111734011019
632855LV00003B/505/P